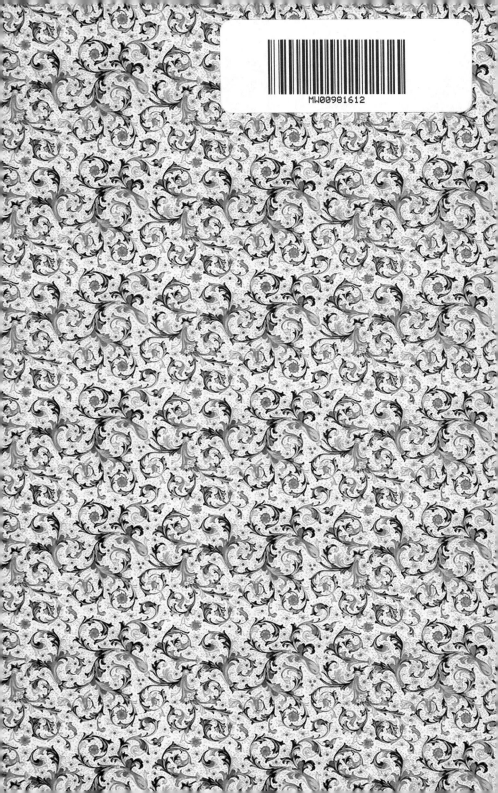

MW00981612

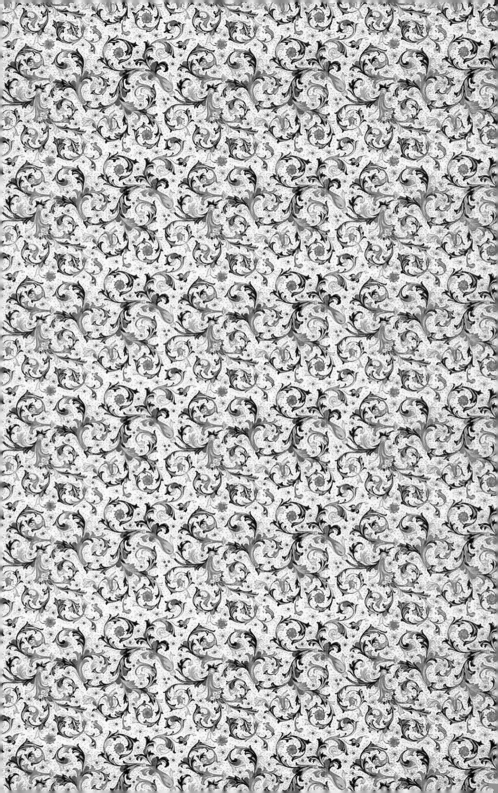

adoration
loving Botticelli

silent

K

PUBLISHING

Copyright © 2014 Veronica Knox
All rights reserved. No part of this publication may be reproduced or
transmitted in any form or by any means, electronic or mechanical,
including photocopying, recording, or by any information storage and
retrieval system, without permission in writing from the author.

Library and Archives Canada Cataloguing in Publication

Knox, V., 1949-, author
Adoration : loving Botticelli / V Knox.

ISBN 978-0-9937380-0-5 (pbk.)
1. Botticelli, Sandro, 1444 or 5-1510--Fiction. I. Title.

PS8621.N695A63 2014   C813'.6   C2014-901898-3

Editor: Linda Clement
Cover design: Veronica Knox
Typeset in *Granjon* with *Bickham* display at SpicaBookDesign

First Edition
Printed in Canada

Silent K Publishing:
Victoria, British Columbia

www.veronicaknox.com
www.silentkbooks.com

e-mail: veronica@veronicaknox.com

for

sarah & david

Adoration 1475 ~ Sandro Botticelli's self-portrait
added in 1480, age 35

sandro botticelli

What can we actually know about Sandro Botticelli? What can we possibly know? These are two different questions, and we can only answer the latter — the educated guess being no more valid than an emotional one.

Botticelli's face proves how much more he was than a generic woodcut printed in the frontispiece of Dante's *Divine Comedy*, a book he illustrated.

A self-portrait, more than any other, is an accurate representation of a physical person. Behold, a haughty moment captured from a prolonged gaze in a mirror. Introspection fused to a real reflection.

Vanity? Perhaps. Here is a man turned out for deliberate remembrance critiqued to the full extent of his professional examination. Clean-shaven and well-dressed, titian hair aglow. Eyes blazing life. Fire under the skin. Smouldering. Here is a whole person. Here is Tuscan sunshine glinting off the gold threads of an apricot cloak.

An image of oneself usually survives vanity only after it is found favorable. Is it flattery? Most definitely. Why else would a professional portrait painter abuse his best mode of self-promotion?

But the first question haunts us. What do we

absolutely know? We know Botticelli once lived and there were days when he breathed under an apricot cloak. We know this cloak is now dust – lost in the refuse of daily things. We know Sandro has been a child and a teenager and an old man. We know that the days during which Botticelli painted his portrait, he walked away from his mirror to eat and drink. He laughed or despaired, concentrating between sips of wine, and then he painted. We know that at one precise moment he set aside his brushes, deciding his work was done, which is a significant moment for an artist.

We know Botticelli's *Adoration* of 1475 was left to dry in the musty air of an artist's studio, wet and vulnerable in a corner, while other work continued around it. It is clear that no serious accidents befell it when it passed from hand-to-hand. And, we know Sandro's portrait remains alive as testament to his chance for creative immortality.

But, back to my subjective view as an author: Botticelli is having an intimate tease with us. Do you not feel it? He is there. He has survived five-hundred years of dust to meet us face to face. To stare into our eyes, soul-to-soul. Botticelli is ours now, to marvel at his silenced thoughts transmitted from eye-to-eye. I believe he was well satisfied with his portrait.

"Here I am," it says. "While you're trying to read me, I'm trying to guess who you are. Have we met? Could we? Yes, we're meeting now. My name is Sandro, and you are ...?"

contents

The Adoration of the Magi ~ 1475 ~ Sandro Botticelli

other books
by V Knox

'SECOND LISA' trilogy

'WOO WOO – the posthumous
love story of Miss Emily Carr'

'TWINTER – the first portal'

THE
DIVINE COMEDY

"The day that man
allows true love to appear,
those things which are well made
will fall into confusion
and will overturn everything
we believe to be right and true"

~ Dante Alighieri

Venus & Mars ~ Sandro Botticelli

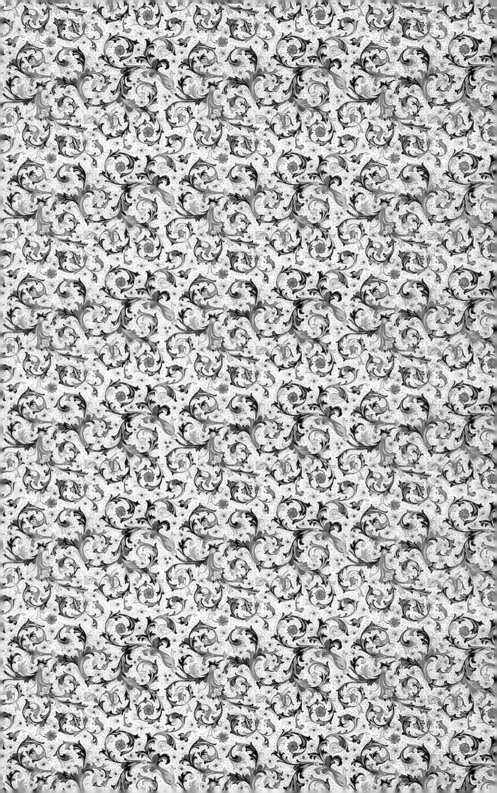

the inferno

the last circle of hell

~ THE FUTURE IS NOW ~

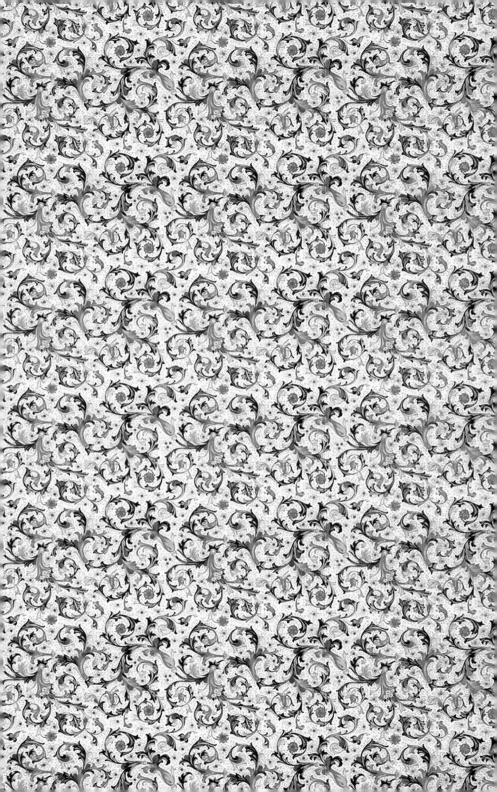

THE LOVE-SONG
of J. ALFRED PRUFROCK

"And would it have been worth it, after all?
After the cups, the marmalade, the tea,
Among the porcelain,
Among some talk of you and me,
Would it have been worthwhile,
To have bitten off the matter with a smile,
To have squeezed the universe into a ball?"

~ T.S. Eliot

retiring for the night

St. Mary's rectory, Little Cobiton, Cambridgeshire, England

DIARY OF LINTON ROSS-HOWARD
THE WINTER SOLSTICE, DECEMBER 21, 2013

It was twenty-nine years ago when an angel kissed me so hard on the mouth I almost believed in heaven, and so I've spent my life lusting after a man I could never have, pretending to believe in divine intervention, but then ... I saw his wings. ~ RH

All I can hear is the silent echo behind Professor Lennox's drumbeat words: Linton, the Uffizi ... *are you going?* ... New Year's Eve Gala ... *are you going?* ... that's your birthday isn't it? ... *are you going?* ... you should treat yourself ... *are you going?*... now that you're free ... *are you going?*"

So, here I am at sixty-four, approaching everlasting freedom on the longest night of the year, deep in my own midwinter when it's most fitting I pay heed to the ghosts of my regrets.

St. Mary's rectory, December 23 ~ 2013

Gentle snow was falling in the framed print of Botticelli's *Venus and Mars* as if it were a window. It hung over my bedroom fireplace, appropriately listing to the right since its original figures had shifted. The new empty space in the left side of the composition drew my attention by virtue of Venus's absence.

Other things were different too: the fauns were gone, although they'd left hoof marks in the snow; spring had turned to winter, and snowflakes dusted the bare branches of myrtle and the lone figure of Mars. He languished as before, filling the elongated rectangle with his reclining form, but now he lay fully-outfitted in his gleaming body-armour, helmet at his side, and his lance sported the orange favour of a lady. More importantly, he was now awake. His hair, white with frost, gave the impression of an old man but his face remained young.

Mars's defiant blue eyes followed me as I walked past him to the decanter of sherry on my dressing table and poured myself a much-deserved drink after an emotional day.

I eased my aching back into an overstuffed armchair by the fire, tucked my legs beneath me, and raised my glass to Mars in a toast. "Here's to war," I said.

Mars shook his head, and the crystals of frost in his hair scattered into an aura around his head, revealing his mane of dark curls, making him appear both virile and saintly. "I am thinking, love and beauty," he replied.

I was not to be patronized. "To hell with love and beauty; they fade, but the war against old-age remains constant."

He winked as he shook the last vestiges of white from his hair. "To victory then," he said.

I was too listless to care, distanced by pressing challenges. Tonight I was distraught.

I had no appetite for conversation or food. Supper was easy to forfeit after the formal tea at the faculty club. My going away celebration, decorated for the Christmas season, offered a banquet of cakes and scones and clotted cream, and mountains of dainty sandwiches.

I sat bewildered for a long time with my two cats for company, my black retirement dress shimmering on a hanger, waving like a sequined ghost. Sophie stared sightlessly through me from her own chair, and Simkin, her husband, looked like a fur boa stretched at the foot of my bed.

The curtains were open to the late afternoon and I huddled inside my robe as I moved towards the real window that pulled me like a magnet. I meant to muffle the chill that radiated from the glass where the December weather was framed as another white landscape.

It was still snowing and the weightless flakes hypnotized me, tumbling in a thick silent drop. I watched them fly, tiny white stars catching in the corners of the latticework. They drifted into each pane like crushed diamonds and settled in the elbows and bony fingers of the oak trees.

I imagined them clinging to the outstretched stone feathers of the angel statue in St. Mary's churchyard below as they draped over the countryside in a lazy blanket.

After the painting had stirred to life I couldn't shake the supernatural buzz that remained in the room. I felt moved by a strong premonition that something tremendous was imminent, and while my psychic connection lasted, I called out to a powerful animal totem both familiar and significant to me.

I held my breath, asking for a sign until, with relief, I saw the grey shape of a 'wrong-time bear' emerge from a line of rowan trees that marked the edge of my property. It lumbered through the snow, shuffling a path to the doors of St. Mary's church and disappeared.

Spotting a black bear out of season is a powerful visitation, a message to pay closer attention while momentous events conspire to settle a score with synchronicity. I was sure the trail the bear left represented my lifeline, but I knew trying to analyse it would only result in confusion. I'd been there before and failed.

This time, I would have to remain aware in order to make a vital decision. Paths were rarely straight lines, so the church was likely the first lily pad in a string of many. The only thing I was sure of was the wrong-time bear had gifted me a last chance to follow.

For a while, I rested my forehead on the window-frame, thinking of wrong-time bears, lulled by the rise and fall of recorded Gregorian chant, feeling comforted within its respite of peace.

Chanting monks have always seemed appropriate in my house. I inherited the old rectory of St. Mary's forty years ago, and am accustomed to my back yard being an abandoned cemetery. Indeed, I relish its solace and gentle reminder of time passing, and the stone angel nestled within his own fenced enclosure has become my perfect therapist. He watches over the 15th Century church and its garden of souls and I lay my wreaths of troubles at his feet.

Tonight, the inscription on the brass plate of his plinth should have inspired me: *'Vita nuova – here begins a new life' ~ Dante Alighieri.*

But this night, under the soothing chanting, I let my mind drift on the tailwind of Vera Lennox's words, following her intriguing proposal into an old labyrinth I thought was empty. As I stood at the window, the fog my breath made on the glass wafted through my body into the room and enveloped everything in a soft mist, transforming the familiar shapes into a pleasant phantasm. Sophie leapt from her chair and meowed at my feet.

For a moment, my formal dress hanging from the wardrobe door became a white gown embroidered with dainty orange blossoms, and I remembered the way it once hugged my legs, and how it had clung from the damp heat of recent lovemaking, crushed in foreplay.

My eyes ached from the bright flash of sunlight off Mars' silver armour, causing an aura to spin like a golden plate just out of reach to my left, the sinister side which always announced the approach of my nemesis.

The realization of an impending migraine pushed me to act. The bed came back into focus, and I pulled open the drawer of my bedside table in search of the cure. I downed two turquoise capsules with a swallow of sherry. All I needed to do was close my eyes a few minutes and let the demon pass.

Sophie sat with me while I silenced the persistent urgings of my fervent colleague, and floated with the monks and snowflakes until my vision was restored. When it cleared I realized I was alone in the room with two cats and a compelling invitation.

The nightstand was the repository of a new copy of *The Divine Comedy* presented to me as part of a retirement gift along with the crystal decanter of dark Amontillado sherry and a fine set of Edwardian sherry glasses.

My old diary with only a few blank pages left, weighed down Dante's pristine leather binding, and I faced that first to chronicle my thoughts on the last day of my career.

I splashed a drop more sherry into my glass and settled under the covers to write, patting the surface of the bedspread in the hope Sophie would join me. She was blind but she could hear just fine, and I made that kissing noise with my lips as one does to draw the attention of a cat. "Come on, old girl," I coaxed. Nothing. She'd done her bit and was back on her chair.

Simkin raised a sleepy head for an instant to assess if food was in the offing and deciding it wasn't, dropped back to sleep. Sophie licked her tail and paid me no mind, but the feline independent streak suited me.

All things considered, Dante's journey through hell was not such an inappropriate choice to read on this particularly-fractious night, and taken with a tipple of sherry, it reminded me of a hellish trip many years ago when I was thirty-five and still a hopeless romantic.

Power surges from the snowstorm made the light from the bedside lamp appear to sputter like a candle. It flickered through the amber liquor beside me as the monks finished intoning their prayers.

DIARY ENTRY ~ DECEMBER 23, 2013

Tonight is the last day of a singular purpose which has occupied my energy for forty-five years, and ironically, to borrow a hideous cliché, 'tomorrow is the first day of the rest of my life.'

A lifetime effusing over great art will soon turn into the living hell I pretended would never come, and I remember an apt quote from the actress, Bette Davis, regarding old age, altering it slightly to: 'retirement is no place for sissies.' All I can do is stare blankly at the wall and silently despair, NOW WHAT?

Perhaps old Dante will show me the way. He journeyed through hell and found peace, and Sophie, my blind guide, is here to lead the way as she has done for almost fourteen years.

In a few days it will be my birthday with its obligatory retirement milestone of sixty-five – a cruel number which represents the death of being valued. Tonight I was given a party of farewell meant to inspire a wonderful release from the daily grind. I gave a hesitant speech to the flutter of bright colours facing me – the dresses of red and green and gold for the Christmas party to follow. I wore black. Go figure.

Two days ago, a woman I've never been crazy about, shattered my dubious festivities of detachment with an announcement that left me momentarily dizzy: there is to be a New Year's Eve Gala at the Uffizi. Vera Lennox gushed the news at me. Did I know? It was perfect, she said, a double celebration to compliment my new life.

New life. That's how she put it.

I couldn't wait to get home to a hot water bottle and into my bed, to put my feet up and contemplate the past – the past that begged the confrontation with Mars, tonight. It's too absurd to think of going on such a long trip at such short notice.

I'm not the spontaneous sort, which is odd considering the whole premise of my art history syllabus was based on venturing off into the unknown without a net.

My fellows gave me a 1948 edition of 'The Divine Comedy.' It's odd to think that when this book was being printed I was waiting to be born. Tonight feels the same. Waiting to be born.

My old tattered copy suits me, careworn as an old map which I suppose it is.

The sherry and decanter beside me are offerings too, so I am surrounded by genuine best wishes for a tipsy evening and a new life.

I sit here in my warm bed with a good read, a sweet nightcap, and Sophie, my best friend, confidante, and spirit guide. There should have been something more. I once knew what it was but I've forgotten.

Tomorrow I face a blank page, all dressed up and nowhere to go.

Now that I'm free, what's it to be? Heaven or hell? ~ RH

I glanced over at Mars, still dressed for battle. He smiled and watched me as I lifted out of my body to hover over the bed. The ceiling above me was a glorious curtain of moving crystals, and as I stretched out my arms like wings, the pattern of small cornflowers on my nightgown slid off the fabric as I slowly rotated in the bedroom's sky. They swirled around me in a delightful blizzard of fragrant blue petals, and through them I glimpsed a peripheral flash of orange disappearing from the doorway.

From down the hall echoed a loving voice softly chiding, *now that you're free ... you're free ... you're free.*

Sophie's rough tongue licking the back of my hand startled me awake.

My bedroom sanctuary surrounded me in a protective bubble like the shroud of snow outside while Sophie pranced her front feet on my blanket.

"What's got into you?" I said.

She continued to purr her lion's share of space on the bed, churning it into a nest.

"To bring in the new year with Botticelli would be an amazing birthday gift to myself," I said to her. "The Renaissance is a perfect metaphor for a new life ... Sophe? ... Don't you think?" She ignored me, yawned in my face, and crept off to wash Simkin's ears. So much for being a feline poet.

I checked the painting. All was serene. Once more, Mars rested in perpetual springtime, sleeping naked, and Venus stared blankly with a sorrowful expression of abandonment that I understood. She'd had the poor judgement and bad timing to fall in love with a man she couldn't have.

LOVE AMONG THE RUINS
"When I do come, she will speak not,
She will stand, either hand on my shoulder,
Give her eyes the first embrace of my face,
Ere we rush, ere we extinguish sight and speech
Each on each."
~ Robert Browning

the straight way

I snuggled down, and opened the new Dante to my favourite passage: *'In the middle of the journey of my life, I found myself within a dark wood where the straight way was lost.'*

Sleep fell over me like the snowflakes covering the ancient headstones in the cemetery, but the straight way was *not* lost. Bear tracks in the powdery snow led through a windbreak of oak to the angel whose wings were now folded around his shoulders like a cloak.

Little Cobiton, Christmas Eve ~ 2013

The snow melted by noon and was replaced by lazy winter rain. From the comfort of the sofa I studied my framed print of Botticelli's 1475 *Adoration of the Magi* hanging above the mantelpiece and the dozen miniature reproductions of his Madonnas, displayed in a grid of shining iridescent squares. Women after the same convention of soft, docile goddesses.

All the while my mind sought an answer to the conflicted Uffizi decision. Going was expensive and tiring, mostly dismissed for its confrontational aspect that would open a can of worms sealed years before. The love worms that had been buried but could still be heard from time to time squirming their way to the sun. Going or staying, too expensive, too far, but too perfect to ignore.

As I continued along these lines in a pleasant stupor, listening to the rain recede into a drowsy curtain, I saw the distinct ripple of draperies in the *Adoration* move under the glass in the frame.

My first thought warned it was the precursor to another migraine but it was different, localized in the figure of Botticelli, and unsettling enough to make me shout *hello* out loud. Sophie tilted her head to listen.

I concentrated on the apricot cloak and although it had stopped moving, I felt drawn to it. I surrendered to the feeling of floating towards the figure in the lower right-hand corner where Botticelli made eye-contact using the convention of his day, inviting viewers into his painting with a compelling self-portrait. I knew him well.

The sound of rain and the warmth of the fire seduced

me into closing my eyes and immediately my head swam with a new vision.

Sophie leapt off her chair and scratched at the front door, meowing piteously until I opened it. I stood there, wrapped only in a blanket, facing a menacing downpour, gazing after her as she disappeared into the cemetery.

I splashed after her under an umbrella. Heavy rain pounded its canopy and cascaded from each spoke as I passed the stone angel with wings outstretched as usual, in a welcoming embrace. He stood, perfectly dry, shielded from the rain by an invisible umbrella of his own, yet raindrops trickled down his face. Water flooded his enclosure in a pool that reached up to his feet, making him look as if he was standing on water, an island unto himself. "No man is an island," I quoted to him.

"Heaven knows you've tried hard enough," he replied.

Sophie led me on through the crumbling headstones towards the dying echoes of chanting which became the sound of beating wings, and we entered the open door of the church. I froze in the porch.

At the far end of the nave, three candles burned on the altar which had been replaced with a block of dressed marble. Sophie jumped on its top and shook droplets of water from her fur that looked like beads of quicksilver. She ignored the magnificent sight of the live angel levitating over her, his orange robes rippling in a gust of supernatural wind.

A gentle spray of raindrops fell from his wings as he fanned them dry, showering Sophie in sparks of light.

The rest landed as pearls and rolled towards me like a broken necklace.

"Is it really you? Why did you go? Where have you been?" I shouted.

"Even angels have to sleep," he called as he started to fade.

I ran the length of the red carpet in slow motion, ankle deep through a river of pearls, sending my words ahead of me. "Please stay. I need you," but he was gone by the time I reached Sophie.

The altar turned out to be the check-in desk of an airline, and the gothic interior began to blur behind a cascade of water, washing down the ornate columns and the stained-glass windows to reveal the plain walls of an airport terminal. Behind the desk hung a travel poster of Brunelleshi's dome on the Santa Maria del Fiore in Florence, framed like a painting.

Sophie stared lovingly at me with eyes that could now see. She turned and sprang onto the moving conveyor belt behind her, looking back once before disappearing down the luggage chute.

Over the years, I've come to rely on my waking and sleeping dreams in which Sophie appears as a tour guide. They always reflect a subliminal truth or two and inevitably a solution to a choice I've been hesitant to make. In this case, she'd sent a message to call the last travel agent open for late business on Christmas Eve.

The next morning as I watched Sophie, dazzled inside the warmth of a sunbeam, chasing her tail, she took hold of it in her teeth and I was reminded of the pose of the mythical snake grasping eternity. She was, like many animal spirit guides, also a trickster. I smiled at the ironic symbolism that in the dreamtime I am emotionally blind, and Sophie acts as my far-sighted seeing-eye dog, and tapped out a white lie to my niece as if it were urgent Morse Code:

DECEMBER 25, 2013

Dear Budge ~

Merry Christmas darling. Short notice I'm afraid.

I've been called upon to research a recently discovered portrait of Botticelli's. It's all last minute and hush-hush. I wasn't offered the assignment until the retirement party and it was too good to pass up.

I said yes, so if you're unavailable, the cats will have to go into a cattery. Staying with you would upset Sophie. You know how feeling around a new place disorients her. She's better off in a cage than negotiating an unfamiliar space.

I know I will see you tomorrow but I need to get this request sent as soon as possible as it's rather time-sensitive and your phone is turned off. Love to your mum. I simply couldn't face one of her perfect Christmases this year.

I know you will understand when I tell you that I feel myself slipping towards Florence rather than flying, floating towards some new place where a phantom of art waits for me like Peter Pan's shadow. As such, I expect this trip to be a 'first star to the right and straight on till morning' kind of project.

Meaning, it's anyone's guess where it will end up, Florence or Neverland.

I've been on emotional standby for far too long. Say no more. I need this. Art calls and you know how much that means to me.

So, here's my request. I wonder if you could house-sit and look after the cats for ten days starting December 29th. I remembered you said you were retreating into chocolate and books for New Years to get over that last dreadful boyfriend of yours, so, mi casa su casa. I'll wait for your call before I book the cattery, but I should do that tomorrow. They're busy for the holidays, so it's all fairly urgent.

Looking forward to Boxing Day with you.
~ love Queenie

I pressed send, knowing my niece could be found at her portable computer pad most any hour of the day. And in a few minutes her reply came.

Dear Highness ~

A timely and perfect invitation. I am delighted to accept. A change of scene will probably save me from moping. You know me too well. I shan't want for anything but peace and quiet, Simkin and Sophie for company, and your shelves of old novels. Is tonight too soon? Just kidding. I am headed to Mum's in a few minutes.

I can stay overnight tomorrow, so we can catch up, and we're overdue for a game. Wow, Botticelli no less, and when art calls you must go. If you're prepared to put Sophie in a cattery it must be important. How exciting – a whole new career for you. You deserve it. See you tomorrow. We can pretend your birthday is a week late. ~ love B

Budge was referring to our ongoing tease of Scrabble, where new letters could be bought for chocolate buttons.

The best nieces, the creative ones, sometimes give their aunts nicknames. Mine was Queenie from the fact that I signed my letters RH in a flamboyant script with a surrounding flourish, which, to Budge, mirrored the title royal highness. Being a precocious child, Budge not only dubbed me Queenie but renamed herself as well. So from the age of six, and to me only, my sister's daughter, Iris Bird, became Budge.

Budge was my Little Orphan Annie in blue jeans. A tomboy with a reserve of steel impervious to her mother's continuous lure of bright-coloured dresses meant to hook her like a fish. When she first decided I was a queen, I mused to myself that I reigned as the 'virgin Queenie,' a spinster of the parish, and content to be so. I held court over my churchyard and it's angel, and my only persistent fear was that I would deteriorate into a less-than-regal caricature of decrepitude like Elizabeth I. A lopsided point of view as unbalanced as my Martian painting.

At the end of the journey of my life I found myself within a dark quandary where the straight way led directly to Florence.

VITA NUOVA

"In that book which is my memory,
On the first page of the chapter
That is the day when I first met you,
Appear the words: here begins a new life"

~ Dante Alighieri

the descent

December 29 ~ 2013

Budge handed me an early birthday gift of a diary at the airport.

"I figured this would make a great travelogue," she said. "Write down everything. I want to know all the details. This is so exciting. It's so like the old you."

"I *am* old," I said.

"Queenie, that's not what I meant."

I gave her the look of 'have it your own way, then.'

She kissed both my cheeks in the Italian way. "You should write your memoirs," she said.

"They aren't that memorable."

Budge continued to smile. "There's still time," she replied without skipping a beat.

When my phone rang from the innards of my handbag I ignored it.

Budge raised her eyebrows. "Not going to answer that?"

"I'm no longer here," I said.

One usually plots a route for a long journey, but there was only one place I needed to go. I opened the pristine diary before take-off, sniffed the bouquet of a fresh page, and wrote something I hoped would become infinitely profound: *take hope all ye who venture here*. It was my homage to Dante, and I looked forward to seeing his beautiful Florence, one last time.

I wondered how I would write my memoirs when there was no beginning and no end? In 1984 I lost the two loves of my life. Then, in the glorious autumn of 1985, I was further undone by a tale of star-crossed lovers. That was twenty-eight years ago.

At age sixty-four, no doubt my memories would arrive as they will, out of order. That is only proper. I have always overruled the formalities of historical timelines, having taught a relaxed version of art history. Some might even say it was fictitious, but missing facts free the creative mind to imagine the dreams of familiar strangers.

I taught my students to channel the renaissance artists and their times by putting themselves in the shoes that trod fifteenth-century soil, envisioning what might have been.

I've honed my powers of visualization by practising them regularly because mental acuity is necessary for teaching art history as a living entity. I premise that a work of art is a meeting place where reality and fantasy meet, and if one experiences it with all six senses it can be forthcoming with entertaining details. Animated visions are an added perk.

Reality is complicated. If I admitted my deepest truth, I'd have to confess I'm only brave because of Botticelli, and now I'm on my way to Florence to redeem myself.

As always, fresh pages awaited something better than my cranky opinions. I scribbled about my life for a few hours, but if truth be told, other than my success as a professor of art history, I've lived a small life – one that sprang from the petty dysfunctions of a shy youth. I never quite recovered from the whirlwind of possibilities which had overwhelmed me as a teenager.

My sister, Dorothy, had had all the attention, beaus right and left. I was the wallflower who never quite measured up to her tall blonde grace, or so I thought at the time. It's funny how the looking glass tells you false.

The could-have-dones and should-have-dones continue to nip my heels, and looking back, I realize my choices were shaped by envy. I think I'd read too many novels about black sheep and dashing suitors, and mousy cousins and star-crossed lovers, to feel at home in my own skin. For me, the real world has been the antithesis of romance and never measured up to the sort of love that takes one's breath away, although there was a time I wanted to believe it could.

I learned painfully, that romance could haunt and that it lacked sustaining power. My few disastrous confrontations via the blind dates my sister provided were enough to send me back to my books. Truer loves and greater expectations wooed me there.

I was a hand-me-down sister, and I resented that fact more than I knew at the time. It had left me with a feeling of cavernous lack. I felt I only deserved Dorothy's breadcrumbs and stepped into her shadow for some sense of relief in order to feel safe.

But I could draw. Everyone pushed me to draw, and so I was prodded into art school down in London where I could garner praise and retreat into my work. I never had to issue excuses for being an introvert again because artists have the good fortune of being admired for their eccentricities. I had found my natural world. The reclusive life was perfect.

For me, art and history was a combination made in heaven. I was expected to explore my inner-world and encouraged to plumb my fantasies. Paintings emerged from a thousand emotions held in check and their classification as art made me acceptable. The paintings I studied seduced me into the world of sensual beauty.

I had Botticelli to thank, or was it blame, for my sexual awakening when I was eighteen. It turned out to be the first of the many creative mirages which would seduce me, and eventually lead me to a happy career.

It had been my defining moment of love at first sight. The classic love-of-my-life moment, and I remember feeling quite petrified with lust when I met the most beautiful man in the world across a crowded art gallery.

I say met, but we couldn't really meet because his eyes were permanently closed, and he was a painted figure who lay sleeping inside a gold frame. I could only call out and beg entrance to his dream, and when that failed, I drew him into mine.

These sad thoughts did not a memoir make and so I was happy when the air hostess brought lunch and I could read instead.

I had left my unwieldy gift book at home and packed my portable copy of *The Divine Comedy* which had been everywhere with me. I'm still fixated on Botticelli, and since he had read these very words, I could meet him within its pages. We could be shocked and enthralled together, and in many ways we could find our way to each other, considering the whole premise of Dante was to reach Beatrice, the love of *his* life with whom he'd never spoken, but admired from afar as a teenager. The girl's early death had dashed all hope of a physical meeting. Dante and I seemed like long-distance twins.

I mused how airports are our era's equivalent of Dante's hell, and that flying was a form of purgatory. Captivity in a plane where one unwittingly contemplates life from the lofty perspective of thirty-thousand feet. But Florence was worth flying for. It was the best place on earth; it was the paradise where I first truly *met* Botticelli.

I opened my dog-eared book, as well-worn as myself, to read once more about a journey through hell and back, loves lost and found, loving from afar, and following one's dreams – a story of holding on, long after the abandonment of logic and physics. Brother Dante led me through his mystical landscape that, according to a painting by Michelino, housed an underworld that resembled a multi-tiered wedding cake. It was a place I couldn't believe in other than metaphor, nevertheless, I still understood his purgatory, the clearing house of things done and not done or left unfinished.

I welcomed the feeling when my eyes signalled the arrival of sleep, and I willingly surrendered to floating in the sky – a goddess on her throne set at cruising altitude, looking down through the clouds. I saw an island below, glorified by divine light, witnessed from being suspended inside a peach sunset. I recognized the tiny stone circle of Stonehenge, with myself, the sky goddess able to reach down at will to pick up a fallen lintel stone and replace it with ease.

And then I was suddenly looking up at my plane, with Glastonbury Tor behind me, blazing with light, silhouetted by an aurora of gold, and a circle of wolves inside the great standing stones of Salisbury Plain howled at the invisible moon.

A blast of cold wind distracted me. I heard a strange hissing noise and rose into the air towards it, buffeted from side to side by a rough updraft. A soft bell chimed above me, and I was back in the plane where passengers were buckling their seatbelts. The man next to me had turned both our air valves full-on and the cool spray revived me. The bell sounded again and the pilot's voice announced with calm authority: ladies and gentlemen, we're experiencing a pocket of slight turbulence. Sit tight. We should be through it in a few minutes.

I closed my eyes and lifted my face to the welcome air. Slight turbulence ahead seemed like an understatement.

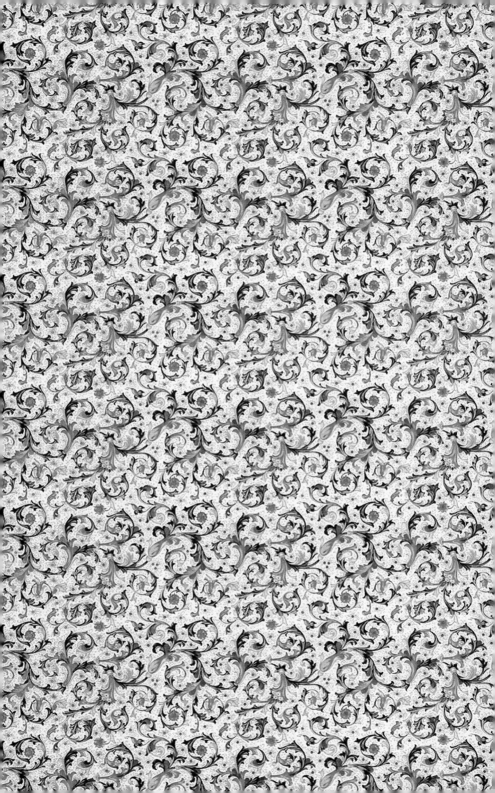

THE
INFERNO

*"There is
no greater sorrow
then to recall
our times of joy
in wretchedness"*

~ Dante Alighieri

the inferno

the first circle of hell

~ REMEMBERING THE PAST ~

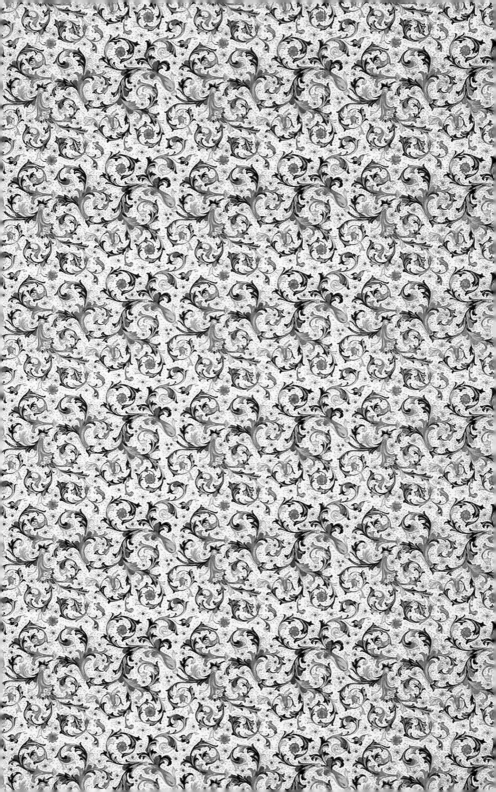

> *"I believe*
> *in the compelling power of love.*
> *I do not understand it.*
> *I believe it to be the most fragrant blossom*
> *of all this thorny existence"*
> ~ Theodore Dreiser

the thorn birds' curse

ON BOARD ALITALIA FLIGHT 101 TO FLORENCE ~
DECEMBER 29, 2013

I have decided to write my memoirs as random chapters of a story, and one particular memory begs to be heard first. It concerns an event in 1985 when I was thirty-six.

The pressure in the cabin is oppressive and I'm glad for the chill spray of air from the overhead jet. It transports me to a September dawn that held the promise of snow, the night I heard a story which turned unchecked optimism to despair. In retrospect, it had been a silly thing to take to heart but I absorbed it as if it was true, and like most unexamined truths, in the light of hindsight it was utterly insubstantial. Nevertheless, it struck a nerve and I retreated into angry hibernation that has lasted to this day.

I can see most of my fellow passengers are absorbed in an

in-flight movie which is ironic, considering the incident that so unhinged me had also been actors performing on a small screen. So I let the smell of snow take me.~ RH

Little Cobiton ~ October 1, 1985

The first night I watched old Mary Carson angling for the handsome young priest in the television adaptation of *The Thorn Birds*, I knew she was the death-crone of love.

It was twenty-eight years ago when this steely icon with papery skin the texture of boiled lace, side-swiped my hard-won expectations that true love played fair by the rules of synchronicity.

The jaunty theme music had promised all manner of fine rustic japes and the sweeping kangaroo-studded landscape portrayed the thrilling wilderness of tough untamed men. Panoramic Australia, painted from the wealthy side of the billabong, was appealing, but heartbreak lurked raw and cruel behind the red velvet curtains of Drogheda. Not only that, the surrounding countryside was inhabited by savage boars. Wild pigs that charged like mad things in a climate as hot as hell.

Knowing she's going to suicide that night, eighty-two year old Mary of the transparent blue-white hair and wallpaper-thin sexual allure, declares her desire for Father Ralph de Bricassart, fifty-years her junior, and he rebuffs her last request for a kiss:

"Kiss me goodbye Ralph."

"Mary goodnight. Sleep well."

"No. On my mouth. Kiss me on the mouth as if we were lovers."

The priest reproaches Mary for her impassioned admission of her feelings after she tells him she fell in love with him when she first saw him, long before he would become a cardinal:

"No. Not love," he says. *"I'm the goad of your old age, that's all. A reminder of what you can no longer be."*

The rejected Mary's rebuttal flashed sharp and cold, confusing everything about romance I had pretended to believe.

"Let me tell you something, Cardinal de Bricassart, about old age and about that God of yours. That vengeful God who ruins our bodies and leaves us with only enough wit for regret. Inside this stupid body I'm still young. I still feel. I still want. I still dream, and I still love you."

The electrifying scenes of a vital elderly woman desperately in love with a young man against all age-appropriate conventions was not something I could dismiss. I felt Mary's pain. I *was* Mary.

The poignant triangle of loves destined to fail, with

Father Ralph, in turn, denying his passion for Mary's young niece, Meggie, twenty-five years his junior, fairly capped the *age-old* dilemma of May-December romances.

The drama was well cast: Meggie was a paragon of classic beauty, and Ralph, Father de Bricassart, was the quintessential leading man. Tall, elegant, and handsome with the extra-attractive quality of being socially taboo.

Forbidden love. To me, it was a familiar theme of ill-fated relationships that could never be and a man all the more desirable for being unattainable.

The speed of adoration suddenly seemed intentionally wilful.

I had been deceived when the narrator first spoke the words 'love' and 'story' so close together as to seem the two elements might actually be related. They weren't. It was a saga based on fear and the chemistry of intimate obsession, and souls born too soon or too late.

Mary may even have deserved her comeuppance. She was a heartless rag of greedy power – a controlling harridan dishing pain over her thousands of square miles of cursed drought, but she was admirably feisty. I wanted so much to admire her impassioned queenly persona that tried to make up for lost time, but she was too cold. She was ice.

Mary's hired hands shivered in the heat-waves like mirages, bowing low, awaiting knighthood or the lash. Her pedigree neighbors wilted in fancy-dress at her beck and call, striking sepia poses in the dust-covered rose garden. Only the landscape was impervious to her whims. Sandblasting winds blew her starving sheep deeper into the hills where the last creek ran desperate in a long spidery crack of stagnant water, and like love, the lush grasses of Drogheda turned to a sea of ashes.

Mary presided regally over her buildings of unpainted mauve wood shimmering under a sun too high to leave shadows, and all the while, the muted colours of Drogheda's dehydrated fences rattled like bleached bones as she strained for a telltale sign of dust on the horizon kicked up by Father Ralph's car.

The Thorn Birds inspired the opposite of *schadenfreude* within me – that German word for *'harm-joy'* which describes the human pleasure of seeing beautiful people fail. I felt the opposite, in defiance of *'delectatio morosa,'* the perverse human habit of dwelling with enjoyment of evil thoughts. I jumped at the chance to process the vicarious problems of a fictitious family so I didn't have to face my own for a while.

I found nothing about young Meggie Cleary and Father Ralph's thorny affair pleasurable. I anticipated the next episode, naively expecting love to conquer all. Perhaps in a scene of denouement it would, heaven knows we viewers had earned it, but there was no sigh of relief after sweating through the Shakespearian weeks, holding out for a romantic turn of fortune. The gods of Olympus were sporting with mortals again.

I had wanted altruism to make sense. Being too impatient for a windfall, I had wanted to shake something sweet from the tree of truth. I wanted to believe in stories where intrepid lovers and self-sacrifice were rewarded with a payoff of grace, but the show was a slow striptease of love with no final reveal, and the conclusion of *The Thorn Birds* remained true to tragedy. No eleventh-hour cupid bothered to string his bow. After each hour of hope, bittersweet credits faded to black. What a terrible way to go.

I knew the life of a starving sheep all too well, and how infinitely brutal it was to be reminded of what one could no longer be.

> *"A kiss*
> *makes the heart young again*
> *and wipes out the years."*
> ~ Rupert Brooke

the peacock's blessing

ON BOARD ALITALIA FLIGHT 101 TO FLORENCE
DECEMBER 29, 2013

Sixty-four is an even number applied to my physical body. Inside, like Mary Carson, I'm in my prime. It's only the mirror which surprises me with a shock of vanity like Captain Hook's saluta-tion to an unfortunate minion: 'who is this bloated codfish I see before me?' But then, Hook was a vain thug and Peter Pan was the story of a lost boy who never had to grow up. ~ RH

Little Cobiton ~ October 1, 1985

It is difficult to process even now, how one window into a common tale may be the making or breaking of a life. A vision of an old lady caught between lust and reality. Two women, really: the passionate inner sex goddess of chemistry 101 and the physical shell at odds with gravity. When beauty fades, fame and wealth are ashes in the mouth.

Illogically, I was thirty-six going on eighty and love had never come to stay. I was young enough to be terrified of old age. To stop time one had to relive the past. Fiction and truth were equally cruel but history could be anything I wanted it to be.

Mind over body defined the need to see never-ending love and beauty. The pretty paintings which had so enthralled me seemed more like dangerous traps.

It morbid to fixate on the truth that all the renaissance artists and their models were dead, grown into silent dust. Portraits were their photographs. The Simonettas who died young were faces in amber. The most supple nudes and madonnas had been turned out to fend for themselves in the streets as soon as their flesh sagged. Movie stars trapped in celluloid became icons. All the photo albums of frozen beauties are sad commentaries of fragile human power. *The Thorn Birds* was also about vanity and vitality.

All the Alices in all the Wonderlands eventually grow up to realize that chasing childhood rabbits is only fun through the first door. After that, growing up is hard work. No wonder Peter Pan hid out in Neverland and Mary referred to the Australian outback as the 'back of the never-never.'

I knew in my heart I was already the foreshadow of

a Mary, bound for vicarious love in my dotage, out of time, the same way I had once felt in my teens, loving a man who couldn't age.

Feeling perfectly young on the inside with the irreconcilable difference of old-age on the outside was a war of physics. Mary's vulnerable confession haunted me, and like most fear-based prophecies, it was bound to be a self-fulfilling one. I was the poster girl for vicarious dreamers in love with love.

Themes of loss began to trickle down my living room walls. I watched Meggie and Ralph's unsatisfying romance the way morbidly-curious people feel compelled to slow down and circle the block to view a road accident. I wanted to know and I wanted to look away.

I craved the toady compliments from the badass queen's mirror on the wall but I wanted to be able to look into it and see warts and all without falling apart.

"Yet, love, mere love, is beautiful indeed
And worthy of acceptation. Fire is bright,
Let temple burn, or flax; an equal light
Leaps in the flame from cedar-plank or weed:
And love is fire"
~ Elizabeth Barrett Browning

the phoenix's promise

ON BOARD ALITALIA FLIGHT 101 TO FLORENCE
~DECEMBER 29, 2013

*I thought I'd found my perfect love when I was eighteen, but he
was a teenager's fantasy. By the age of thirty-six I scarred before
I'd been cut; I could bruise from an anxious thought, but my
martyrdom formally began the year before in Florence when I
betrayed an innocent man.*

*The theory of paranormal attraction was a tidy convention
to navigate the foggy territory of romantic love, but it was useful
in explaining loves' sudden appearance and the overwhelming
chemical fluctuations of arousal that seemed to exist outside of
common sense.~ RH*

adoration ~ loving Botticelli

Little Cobiton ~ September 2, 1985

After the *Thorn Birds* had done their worst, I fell asleep on the couch with the television on.

I woke fitful, my head fuzzy with static like the screen hissing its square of white noise at the end of programming. I felt gutted. Horribly mortal. I needed to speak with my angel.

I stared, dry-eyed, at Botticelli's *Venus and Mars*, and said goodbye. I was drained of the energy needed to create tears, and instead, the first sheath of toothpick arrows pricked my left eye, and I knew a migraine was in the room.

Nevertheless, I was determined to walk the regular pilgrimage to process my pain with the angel, but the nucleus of early snow hung low in the clouds, calling for a winter coat. I searched its pockets for my best gloves and was promptly stung by a tardy September wasp which must have crawled in there to die. It was a sign in the guise of a wrong-time wasp, and the sting allowed the fury within me to rage.

This time I didn't give a toss for medical intervention. I headed for the stone angel with malignant thoughts, prepared to breach his safe wrought-iron enclosure that had lost its gate long before my time. He loomed there as contemplative as ever, staring down at something only he could see, possibly some unseen dog feces I'd just stepped in that was now under my shoe. I was livid.

I stared at his mouth but there was no hint of his enigmatic Mona Lisa smile. The eyes of my divine mannequin who had been my shoulder to cry on for ten years, were sightless. No trace of empathy lingered to indicate the bond we had forged.

I felt a surge of bile rising in my throat. "Where the hell are you guys when we really need you!" I shrieked. "I mean, one favor and you're done?" Frosty silence. "Cat got your tongue?" I raised my voice in an accusation that hit the trees and flew back in my face. "I NEEDED you! And YOU left me alone!"

It felt good to rant like a madwoman. "So, what should we be mourning? " I shouted. "The death of love and beauty? The art of silence? Being left alone? You goddam mother!" Death, beauty, art, and abandonment fairly covered the four cornerstones of my repressed anger.

The light shifted, and the statue's form changed into an iconic Madonna and child, no doubt to mock me. I closed my eyes to steady myself and the mother and child vanished. My angel was back. He remained smugly stoic but I sensed a flutter of movement in his wings.

I slumped to the ground in defeat. "Okay, DON'T tell me!" I said, grabbing two handful of rotting leaves, rubbing them into my hair.

His reply came as the soft hooting of an owl that glided over us, dropping a wave of sickness over me. I leaned my forehead against the angel's marble feet and was transported to the memory of a cool washcloth being placed on my fevered brow.

The symbolic buzzing of wasps in my head was a painful enough reminder to separate me from the stone.

The aura in my left eye was stronger now, and I made my way home to the medication I stocked for such an episode. I opened the bottle and stared into a turquoise nest of gel capsules that, in my present negative state, made me think of frogspawn, and then, after staring in the mirror at the half of my face I could still see, I flushed them down the toilet. Tonight was earmarked for suffering, and who was I to deny an angel that kind of contrary satisfaction.

An hour later, I was on my knees gasping for air with my hand still on fire – the cold vitriol of panic inside my throat, rising into the base of my skull, searching for the back of my eyes where it would lay its eggs and hatch into razorblades. I retched until I was limp from trying to disgorge the bad dream I'd been carrying around since I was a teenager.

"Happy now?" I moaned to the invisible presence I imagined beside me. "So this is lovesickness."

I lay on my back and welcomed the migraine in like a tsunami, daring it to wash away the TV and its suicidal birds, and the rectory and the stone angel, and me.

The angel handed me a washcloth and led me to my bed reciting a line from a poem about promises to keep and miles to go before I could sleep.

Even fiction which I had wrongly assumed was under the control of a human pen, told the truth when it was honest. Varnished stories played nice for a while, but art history with a twist was my best solution for living vicariously. It was the sweetest form of rebirth available, time being a fractious thing to pin down.

THE DIVINE COMEDY

"The man who lies asleep will never waken fame,
and his desire and all his life drift past him like a dream,
and the traces of his memory fade from time
like smoke in air, or ripples on a stream"

~ Dante Alighieri

sophie sofia

ON BOARD ALITALIA FLIGHT 101 TO FLORENCE
DECEMBER 29, 2013

But fifteen years after 'The Thorn Birds,' on the cusp of the new millennium, Sophie arrived to enrich my self-imposed isolation. Although my days were filled with teaching a beloved subject, I was in danger of becoming a fifty-one-year-old recluse.

I once had a whimsical thought that she and I were soul mates, and now we're both age sixty-four according to the logistics of parallel life-spans. Meeting each other brought our lives into an alignment of mutual devotion.

I had intended on naming her Sophia because the day she came into my life, I'd been giving a lecture on Byzantine architecture as related to the restored Hagia Sophia Museum in old Constantinople, but my infallible filter system delivered the less formal, Sophie, instead. ~ RH

Little Cobiton ~ New Year's Day, 2000

I had listened to a Scottish woman sing *Auld Lang Sine* until the last haunting strains faded to silence and expelled a long peaceful sigh as I was released from the trance of her voice. The world felt different, better than new. I headed for my first walk of the year feeling light and hopeful even in the brisk wind which stole my breath as I opened the door. I felt the urgent need to ground the new year with my stone therapist, but what began as a wintry post-midnight stroll to the angel ended in the discovery of a frozen lump of barely-breathing grey fur stuck fast to its base.

A cat I knew instinctively as female had climbed the steps of the angel's plinth out of the wet snow to shelter in the windswept folds of his marble robes, and the physics of moisture and freezing metal had acted like glue. Her body-heat had melted the frost on the brass plaque as she huddled for warmth. Ironically, its message lay beneath her like prophecy with the words: *"Vita Nuova ~ here begins a new life."*

The north wind must have dropped the temperature while she paused to rest and sealed her to the surface. She was conscious because she responded to my voice with a feeble meow but her eyes remained closed.

"Hello. Well, you *did* get yourself in a muddle. No worries, sweetpea. You're safe now. We'll just get you lovely and warm first, shall we," I said, covering her with my scarf. "There, doesn't that feel nice?" She bleated piteously as I pried her loose, easing her from the metal plate one hair at a time the way an archaeologist a frees a precious relic.

"Who's a lucky girl?" I crooned as the angel surrendered her to my care. I felt her body relax against me, thrumming like a harp string, and I looked up into the statue's face. "Thank you," I said. "Happy New Year."

I hustled out of the metal fence with its posts that looked like spears, and faced the wind. "Happy New Year little one," I said to my charge, and cuddled her home.

By the time we'd reached my door, she was purring madly, vibrating inside a nest of red wool. I transported her to the hearth, grabbing a sofa throw on the way, and transferred her shivering body to the blanket, turned up the fire, and patted her dry. I made a well from sofa cushions and she nestled into them at once.

I stayed beside her until I was sure she had settled. "Welcome home," I said, and then something extraordinary happened. Sophie's eyes opened like emerald stars, and at first I thought she was searching my face with sentient concern, but she was blind, sniffing the air for the scent of safety.

A plaintive cry of gratitude issued from deep within her like a squeak toy when I touched her. She was not a baby, and I could see someone had taken care of her because she wore a collar, so she had either been abandoned, become lost, or run away. She needed warmth, nourishment, and affection. Things easy to supply.

My larder was well-stocked with holiday food and

yielded sardines, and I clattered around in my kitchen making us a late snack.

Sophie reminded me of a person amazed at meeting an old acquaintance after many years. "It's a small world," I told her. "Don't worry, you can stay as long as you like."

She had been through an ordeal, the pads of her paws were covered in scabs and she was thin. I chattered on while she lapped daintily at the sardine oil. "Where on earth have you been? Are you a long way from home?"

They were rhetorical questions until the dreams started.

Reluctantly, I posted a notice in the newspaper and the bulletin board in the post office that a grey short-haired female cat had been found, and visited the local vet and police to see if anyone had made enquiries. After a week, I removed the possibility she belonged with anyone other than me, and life settled into a cosy nest for two.

My flirtation with a belief in soul mates flowed errat- ically according to immediate gratification and had always been a tremendous leap of wishful thinking, so in a whimsical moment I mused that Sophie was mine, but then a ginger tom named Simkin walked in a year later to claim her as his.

Sophia is from the Latin translation of the Greek for wisdom, but since the wisdom of falling asleep in the snow seemed unlike the savvy feline instincts of sur- vival, I speculated Sophie may have been ill. The vet soon quashed that theory: she was malnourished and exhausted but otherwise healthy.

I came to believe that she'd fainted from hunger, worn out from travel. At least, that's what she told me later, in the dreamtime. She'd said she'd come a long way.

Sophie eclipsed the angel for a while as my new therapist and in return I got to provide unending supplies of fish pâté, heat, and dry shelter, and grant her pride of place on my bed. She claimed its centre, and when I called her she wouldn't come; she only answered to the special rattle of sardine keys in a glass jar.

When I was worried, Sophie guided me straight. One recurring dream took place in a familiar maze of cobblestone alleyways that led to a high stone wall with an open gate. Beyond it was a panorama of green hills and avenues of tall cypress trees like the ones I'd seen in Tuscany. Sophie invariably led me to the same gate, and when I looked back over my shoulder, I recognized the tall shape of the campanile and the red dome of Santa Maria del Fiore, so I knew we were in Florence.

I sometimes played scrabble solitaire for half an hour to unwind, and Sophie amused herself by playing with the loose letter tiles. She culled the letter B quite often, staring at it for ages as if she could see, before pushing it towards me. She also twitched her ears towards Botticelli's *Adoration* over the mantelpiece, the way a stealthy cat listens for signs of movement.

The first time I witnessed Sophie's art vigil, I thought she could hear the wasp that had landed on the picture frame, but then it buzzed right past her and she took no notice.

Sophie's concentration could be disconcerting, especially when she nattered at an empty corner as if it contained a ghost. Thankfully, I've never believed in discarnate spirits. I considered myself a tough old bird, but since I did believe in the feline's capacity to hear what I couldn't, there was a small doubt that festered on the back shelf of my mind. I've never been a woman who is afraid of the dark or being alone. I have always treasured my solitude.

⌒

Botticelli's *Venus and Mars* shows the god of war sleeping naked with his armour and weapons beside him. Several fauns are making sport with his helmet and lance, overseen by the pensive goddess, Venus, who reclines fully-clothed and expressionless. By that I mean indifferent.

One wonders if Venus can even *see* the fauns. If it was truly the post-coital scene it's touted to be, the goddess was remarkably unmoved. Literally virginal, untouched with not a hair out of place. More than that, she seemed, well, bored. It was a dispassionate representation of love's blissful aftermath.

Venus's bland expression was easily dismissed in order to study the naked, Mars, draped immodestly in a skimpy loincloth. I doubted she was daydreaming, lost to the world in a deep, dreamless slumber. I speculated the couple had only shared a partial tryst and that Venus had been left to contemplate a future consummation, perhaps miffed that her consort had been too exhausted to perform. I deduced she had been spurned because she showed no trace of a woman exhausted from carnal joy.

In a particularly lucid dream, I was sat next to the bedroom room fire knitting a red scarf as the mouse-sized fauns in the *Venus and Mars* gambled about teasing Sophie. She was keen to catch one and stared at the edge of the picture frame expecting them to run out, and they obliged. All four of them scampered through the house and out the door into the cemetery where the lychgate had become a gate in the wall of a fortified city, a gate that opened into a field of poppies. The fauns disappeared but Sophie and I followed the sound of their flutes until it became the whistling of a brisk wind that whipped the flower stalks into a moving sea.

With my back to the gate, I surveyed a vista of red and green that spread to a distant horizon with a mountain sparkling under a blue sky. The smell of sulphur wafted across a discernible pathway cut through a swath of waving red. Sophie led a path through the poppies to the banks of an effervescent stream where we sat under a shade tree.

After appearing mesmerized by the rush of sparkling water, Sophie rustled into the tall flowers and brought me a trembling mouse. It was unharmed and stayed sunning itself on a rock, happy to share a few crumbs from a picnic basket that had materialized with Sophie's favourite – a flat oval tin of sardines. For me and the mouse, there was sharp aged-cheddar, sweet golden apples, and crusty French bread.

Our dream picnic had class: a bottle of Chianti wrapped in woven straw, a crystal goblet, and a silver cheese knife with an ivory handle were provided. I concluded Sophie's philosophy was to listen to a problem, feed it, and set it free.

A shimmering turquoise peacock emerged, shrieking from the poppies to fly over us, headed for Florence, but when we followed it back to the city, we found the gate locked. Sophie manifested the picnic's sardine key on a gold chain around my neck, which opened it.

The gate was the entrance to the spirit world; the path, a journey; the key, a solution to a problem; poppies, an opiate of forgetfulness commanded: *remember this*; the stream represented the flow of life; the tree, knowledge; the mountain, a distant quest; a mouse is a persistent problem; the smell of sulphur could only mean hell; the peacock, a symbol of rebirth embodied the Renaissance; and the golden apple was the classic prize awarded by Venus. The Italian Renaissance emerging from forgetfulness was a clear metaphor, linked to a precarious journey through hell that I must take to reach happiness. All of it was blue-sky thinking.

AND DEATH
SHALL HAVE
NO DOMINION

And death
shall have no dominion.
Dead men naked
they shall be one
With the man in the wind
and the west moon;
When their bones are picked clean
and the clean bones gone,
They shall have stars
at elbow and foot;
Though they go mad
they shall be sane,
Though they sink through the sea
they shall rise again
Though lovers be lost
love shall not;
And death
shall have no dominion.

~ Dylan Thomas

"I am certain of nothing
but the holiness of the heart's affections
and the truth of the imagination."
~John Keats

everything old is new again

So many silenced thoughts are awakening from my growing desire to document my years. The irony is not lost on me, considering my past consists of unvarnished facts, and I prefer to take history with a generous helping of imaginative embellishment. The one fact that remains, is creative license cannot be applied to one's own memoirs. ~ RH

My life has been a grotesque of regrets, fear and panic attacks from feeling displaced in the wider world. I had not been emotionally brave. I retreated from the social scene in favour of evenings at home with my fantasies. It was heaven to lock the door against intruders who challenged me to participate in the unstable market-places for esteem, and power, and love. I preferred to reign quietly in a still-life painting or behind the trees of a pastoral landscape.

My imagination spent itself in my studies of art history, and I formulated a creative way of interpreting artists lives outside the context of their work.

Artists are like partially open books, and I learned to read between the lines where their innermost fears and joys lingered the same way as mine did, out of sight in case of persecution and ugly consequences. They protected themselves from far more dangerous foes than mine, but underneath the skin we were the same, vulnerable to exposure, bluffing in the games of social and emotional unease.

In my late teens, I was courted by a succession of insubstantial beaus who arrived with some urgency on the pages of romance novels. They enticed me from between the lines like sirens. None had a face – just a saturation of enough presence essential to flirt with attitude. They were fine, for a while.

The warm pulsing of courtly love was wild enough to generate enough heat to champion my nights and stoke my daydreams. Midnight usually found me in the arms of a lightly-scented ghostly lover but I grew more demanding. I needed real faces. Enter the handsome parade of actor-heroes I could see and hear who emoted their lines on screen.

I sashayed my way through an assortment of composite heroes who were always attentive and available at the dimming of a lamp.

In my mind, I was their ideal counterpart – a devastating incarnation that morphed between gaunt cover girl and curvaceous starlet. But then, at eighteen, I visited the National Gallery and fell in love with a god, then a portrait, then an artist, then a man and an angel.

Soon after, Ralph de Bricassart showed up on the small screen to break several hearts, including his own. After that... after all that hope, I settled for living alone.

Reality check: vanity, thy name is me. The truth is, I am petite – a fine upstanding word for short and slender, but being short also means I'm programmed to be *cuddly* in my later years. At sixty-four, my body has already transformed to a less dainty dish and soon it may evoke the saccharine quaintness of 'the sweet old dear.' The petite ingénue of sleek passion could become a plump Mrs. Bunny in Victorian petticoats. I didn't think I'd be bothered by it, but I am. Some mornings it takes Herculean strength to hold up enough blue sky to get up and face the mirror or fill another cold kettle.

My older sister got the height and the blonde hair. Dorothy inherited the family home; I inherited the rectory. Dorothy earned the sophistication; I won the eccentricities and the sensitivities of the artist. Dorothy wore haute-couture; I learned how to carry off flamboyant capes and scarves with boots and eclectic accessories.

I survived amongst the hot ashes of post middle-age, content to be alone, thankful to be living in a country where it rained most nights. Rural England allowed me the freedom of walking invisible under the village moon in a raincoat over a nightgown.

My professional cachet, however, had been in danger of being eclipsed by the default image of the eccentric cat lady waving an angry cane at bad boys. I couldn't endure that. I smile to think I'd never shared my home with a cat until I was fifty-one after meeting Sophie, and now I may appear to be the quintessential reclusive cat lady.

I'm carefree which is, I fear, almost the same thing as letting oneself go when fashion slips into comfort and a resignation towards self-indulgence. Fairly soon there will be less need to wear perfume and makeup, and a devotion to elastic waistbands and flat comfortable shoes as my feet widen into painful planks. If unchecked, I fear I may become a lampoon of Elizabethan dementia – the iconic parody of a queen who wanders her palace as a sad caricature.

It was inevitable that my young self-image as love's bright promise would pale with time. Versions of hot summer love always fade into watercolours, and before too long I knew I would face, 'the pallid winter of the crone,' a melodramatic generation I had coined in a low moment.

Ever since *The Thorn Birds* I have suffered nightmarish visions of being some feeble bone-loss hunchback – a dear-old-thing shuffling in bedroom slippers in the centre aisle of an all-night supermarket shopping for cat food, while Dorothy swanned about with a face-lift and the latest fashions.

One's subconscious does try hard to belabour a point. I'm in my early sixties, not a centenarian. But then, my dreams have always tried desperately to give me a shake, and thankfully, there is Sophie to counteract the lurid queen who waves to me from the bathroom mirror.

It's easy to grow up cynical when the promises of first romance break like soap bubbles on a rose thorn. Love-hunger stalks human females early, and sustaining joy is like trying to hold on to a cloud.

I began keeping a diary after Sophie arrived, so that's ten years of musing and waffling and hesitations of hedging the truth, but these last few days it's ripe with juicy foreshadowing.

'Something something burning bright in the something of the night,' I wrote yesterday, in a pique of haste.

"Oh Blake," I said out loud to the page "you are a one. How did you get there, inside my thoughts?"

I fancied I heard him. "You left your mind open," he replied, and I imagined him turning over in his grave.

*"Beauty awakens the soul
to act"*
~ Dante Alighieri

ON BOARD ALITALIA FLIGHT 101 TO FLORENCE
DECEMBER 29, 2013

*I adore Budge's dedication on the first page of this new diary
which reads: 'Happy birthday, Queenie. Life's a scrabble, so
here's a bonus of nine letters: I love you, B.' I may not be her
birthmother but she's the daughter of my heart. ~ RH*

When Dorothy's daughter, Iris, was five, she insisted I
call her Budge. It was our secret, the first of many.

I adore my niece. I was her cool aunt who lived apart
from her mother's vanity. I didn't try to be her role model,
but I was in the prime position to be more lenient, more
indulgent, and less controlling than her mother.

I've been close to Budge all her life; we were more like

sisters until she became a runaway teenager at sixteen and adopted me as her replacement mom, proclaiming my lifestyle as *radically hipsville.*

It was a temporary arrangement approved by my sister, considering the alternative was sharing digs and a range of worldly experiences guaranteed to launch a sheltered young girl into the arms of trouble.

Dorothy had been loathe to take her married name. "I refuse to be Mrs. Bird," she said.

For once, I felt superior. "Yes," I agreed smirking, "Dotty Bird *is* a bit much." She glared at me and we both collapsed into laughter. Dorothy Ross-Howard she would stay.

I disdained my sister's years in a loveless marriage, but I had opted for a parallel course, dedicating my passions to a career of academic servitude.

After I became Budge's unofficial mother in 1990, I was more responsible. More careful. Overnight, I was a traitor to the art of seeming cool, at least the variation that encompassed being an independent woman who had no plans to marry or multiply. I was hardly a party animal.

I figured my jaded outlook on love could taint Budge's romantic expectations if I wasn't a vigilant champion of the most positive thinking I could muster. That whole 'cruel to be kind' thing is overstated. I'm a crusader for historical truth, but emotional truth is different; I chose to lie to Budge about love. For three years I lied every shade of white imaginable.

By the time my niece came to live with me permanently, I was a cynical career woman of forty. Hardly a fairy godmother.

Living with Budge for four years meant reliving my buried adolescence, privy to a new generation of excessive sleepover gigglings, maxed out on cola and puppy love. I knew they were doomed.

A little girl can grow old chasing down the moon. I did. I chased the prince into the happily-ever-after ever since the time I wrote: *Dear Santa – all I want for Christmas is a pair of glass slippers.*

I wanted to tell Budge that playing the fairytale princess was dreaming with fire, but ironically, I didn't have the heart. All in Love was *not* fair, and neither was time, or should I say, timing. Lovers may meet outside their prime, and even beyond their lifespan. Falling for a man in a painting would appear to be the culmination of romantic insanity, but that's just me.

Little Cobiton, 1995

I slid onto my bed balancing a substantial tea tray and positioned it in the only spot that wasn't filled with my niece or Sophie, careful not to spill the saucer of sardines.

Budge's eyes were red from crying.

"Okay ladies, I officially call this sleepover to order," I said, banging a teaspoon on the teapot.

"And don't try to be funny," Budge said. "This is serious."

I waited for details but Budge fidgeted with a thread on her sweater and stared morosely across the room.

Sophie caught the scent of fish and stirred towards the tray.

"Okay, if you don't want to talk about it I understand, but try drinking some nice hot tea. It'll make you feel a little better," I said.

She scowled, hugging a large pillow hard enough to whiten her knuckles.

I placed the saucer under Sophie's nose. "Come on princess," I said petting her head.

"I'm not a princess. Mum always calls me that."

"I was talking to Sophie."

Budge looked at me. Her mouth was twisted into a snarl.

"You look more angry than sad.

"I did sad all day yesterday. Look at my face. I'm so ugly."

"So, how do you feel today?"

"Humiliated."

"Because?"

Her tears welled up and she looked away. "Because he didn't want to... you know, *do* it," she blurted. "How will I get a husband if I don't learn how to do it?"

I made a great display of pouring tea, wondering which of her current beaus had rebuffed her.

"Oh my god, I phoned him a dozen times and he wouldn't pick up, and then I texted him, and now I feel worse," she said, looking horrified.

I dropped two teaspoons of sugar into her cup and stirred. "A husband? I thought you wanted a career? Being a vet takes years of concentrated study? Here, drink this while its hot."

Budge took the cup and flattened her pillow into a lap tray. Her shoulders slumped and the flashes of anger in her eyes disappeared with her crestfallen expression.

"I did want to. I *do* want to, but the math says, no way."

I poured myself a cup and splashed in too much milk. "What math? Your grades are excellent."

"Life math. Rent math. Food math," Budge whined. "I need to get a job to pay the rent. Student loans are like lead balloons."

"What about our dream of opening a sanctuary for blind cats that you were going to run?" I said, stroking Sophie's back. "I've been setting aside a nest egg for that."

"Nothing ever works. Dreams don't come true."

"I agree, some don't, but you have to give each one a chance. Look, whoever he was, he may have saved your future by not having sex. I know sex feels like love but it isn't. You can't help falling in love with each boy you meet. It's natural to think each new love is forever."

"It's easy for you. Mum says you've never *been* in love."

I paused with my teacup in midair. "Well, touché. That's easy for *her* to say," I sighed. "You think I told your mum my secrets? A long time ago I was young and foolish. Then I was older and foolish, like your mum, which, by the way, is where she gets her incredibly convoluted insight on *my* life.

"Anyway, long story short, I fell for an exceptional man and at the eleventh hour I betrayed him for another. I don't actually like to dwell on it. He was the first *real* man I fell for."

"Real?"

"Not a hero in a book or a movie star or ..."

"Or a figure in a painting," Budge finished."

I snorted my tea. "Beg pardon?"

"Well you have that painting over there of a naked guy."

"Oh. Right. More tea?"

Budge got a silly grin on her face. "No thanks," she said handing me her cup. She punched her pillow into a ball and took a chocolate biscuit. "How exciting for you."

I shot her a sarcastic look. "If you think pain and guilt and shame are exciting, then yes, it was a real party."

Budge shrugged. "Didn't he forgive you?"

"I think he probably did. They both did. I was too chicken to find out, but I never forgave myself."

She tilted her head coyly. "Do you still miss him?"

I sipped my pale abandoned tea. It was lukewarm and disgusting. "Every day, but one can't go back. The past is long gone."

"How long ago was it?"

"I said I didn't want to talk about it."

I moved the tray to the floor and sat cross-legged, leaning against the headboard, gazing at the figure of Mars. "It seems like hundreds of years," I said. "Love is all about timing."

"I bet he was gorgeous wasn't he? Come on you can tell me. What was he like? Do you have his picture?"

"I do, and I'm not showing you. He was a perfect angel."

We both stared at the far wall in silence.

Budge grimaced but at least she was brighter. She tossed the pillow aside and sprawled next to Sophie. "Well, if happy-ever-after always screws up, what's a girl supposed to do? What hope is there? Mum says you're going to be in deep trouble without a man around to look after you when you're really old."

"Well, I'll let you know when I'm *really* old, but I do know that old-age is no time to be a sissy. I heard that somewhere," I said. "So it's smart for a woman to toughen up as early as possible."

Budge rolled on her back, and asked me the million dollar question: "What if she isn't very smart?"

I gave her a little nudge with my foot. "Dearest girl, wisdom comes from believing in yourself, not fairy tales. Growing up is only a start."

I laughed and threw my pillow at her, and Sophie vacated the bed for a less interactive space. "I think there's an elephant in the room," I said.

Budge groaned and made a face. "Sometimes you say the weirdest things."

"Sometimes weird things are the best way to tell the truth."

Budge clambered up next to me again and gave me the wide-eyed stare of a deer, and I wrapped an extra quilt around her shoulders. "There's no need to play innocent with me," I said. "Remember, I overheard you and your friends talking for a few years. That's quite the education you lot gave me, madam."

Budge gave me the haughty look of a peeved princess. "But I *am* innocent. I'm still a *virgin*."

"If *that's* the bar for experience, then I hope you stay ignorant for a few more years. There's an old saying, that ignorance is bliss, but as I recall, even the sweetest of days could end in emotional tears. If you're up to a game of scrabble, I wouldn't say no, or we could watch a movie."

"A movie," Budge decided, "as long as it's not *Room with a View* again."

"A thing of beauty
Is a joy for ever:
Its loveliness increases; it will never
Pass into nothingness; but still will keep
A bower quiet for us, and a sleep
Full of sweet dreams, and health,
And quiet breathing."
~ John Keats

a prisoner of war

ON BOARD ALITALIA FLIGHT 101 TO FLORENCE
DECEMBER 29, 2013

Which brings me to that beginning that never was, when I was
an art student on my first visit to the National Gallery, I thought
to spend an innocent school trip admiring the Turner's I so loved,
but nothing so simple ensued. ~ RH

Reigate, Surrey ~ 1967

Technically, I first *met* Botticelli on a warm library day
in 1967 on the pages of an art history textbook, *Janson's*

History of Art, during a research mission for a term paper titled 'The Transition of the Picture Plane as Influenced by Cimabue and Giotto.'

I treated myself to a trip through Janson's earliest chapters on primitive art to the Parisian evolution and the American revelations of abstraction. I'd had no idea of the Lascaux caves with shaman dreams splashed across their granite walls, or the nuances of the later brotherhoods from the Impressionists to the Group of Seven, but more significantly, the pre-Raphaelites who pulled Botticelli from the shadows and made him a household name.

Botticelli's colours were ceramic-bright: clear blues and pinks, trapped in images flat as wallpaper patterns. His ocean recalled the cardboard waves from the flimsy set of a budget summer-stock opera. His *Birth of Venus* reminded me of a pop-up book with missing pull-tabs to indicate where any action might be possible. Venus was beautiful yet inert. I accepted his paintings as they were: sentimental, the unique expression of a master illustrator.

But, it was Sandro's *Venus and Mars,* a metaphor of pure yin-yang, that caught my eye in spite of the sleeping god's painfully twisted limbs. Botticelli proves that the human form, if beautiful enough, can cause temporary blindness to its false anatomy. This is how a painting can hypnotize. The colours and shapes and the draperies can lead the eye into an illusion of perfection, irrespective of real space.

A two-dimensional illusion either compels one to

enter or deliberately refuses admission. Our brains *read* elbows and knees and hands making impossible gestures, rendered so tenderly that we forgive all clumsiness of form. We selectively ignore details in paintings the same way we suspend belief when we watch a movie, which is after all, a succession of a thousand paintings flashing one's retina at lightning speed.

An art gallery is a world apart from a library. It's a planet where I disengage my left-brain at the entrance and experience art in a disembodied trance, but the power of painted pheromones is underrated. Right-brain reverie once changed my life.

I wish I could state that, since art is subjective, it takes no prisoners, but I'd be wrong. If abduction can happen once, it's a fair assumption seduction can happen twice.

Botticelli had rendered a magnificent male torso, but if your eye follows the legs, they are ill-observed. It looks as if the god of war is performing tantric yoga. But beauty forgives an awkward pose. One wants to see a perfect god, and so, for as long as the hypnosis lasts, one does.

Mars lay sleeping, oblivious of his discomfort, dreaming of past victories, while Venus stared off into the future contemplating a conquest of her own. They were being investigated by four fauns.

I made the mistake of staring too long into one of the faun's demonic eyes, and for weeks afterwards I had the recurring nightmare where the sound of scuttling hooves from diminutive goat-children the size of spaniels haunted my dreams. Once they even grew into full-sized satyrs that clattered around my bed.

One fractious night when I was overtired, the posts on my bed grew into tall trees the moment I closed my eyes, and instead of a cloth ceiling, a bower of vines joined hands into a vaulted roof above me. The evening's drizzle tapped a lullaby on the window and grew impatient, evolving into a tempest where each crash of thunder drove me deeper into an antediluvian landscape. I smoothed my long flowered nightgown and reclined on a red pillow resting on the ground, sheltering under a dripping forest canopy.

My pillows and sheets became a pale flowerbed of fragrant roses and peonies. Around me lay the discarded paraphernalia of human storms: an open umbrella lay at my feet, a raincoat hung from a low branch, and a pair of tall rubber boots rested abandoned alongside my prone body. A pointy-eared faun stared curiously down one of the boots while a second faun tried to squeeze his stumpy goat-leg into the other.

My eyes were closed but I couldn't shut out the images of being examined from above as if I were also a spirit hovering above the trees. From behind my drowsing form, two more fauns appeared and scampered around me, giggling.

Multiple points of view afforded me the image of a chubby fist grabbing the handle of the umbrella. The horned creature twirled it playfully behind its grotesque head sending droplets of rain spinning with gentle centrifugal force that showered upon me in slow motion as real pearls which obscured my view. I felt the cool oiliness of rolling pearls on my face and down the neck of my nightgown.

Then I heard the rustle of umbrella silk being shaken dry and saw it being closed so the little beast could prod me with it for sport. It kept grinning and jabbing as if trying to wake me but I refused to open my eyes.

I slumbered on fitfully, a rainy-day Venus in a flowered nightshirt. But this was pre-Sophie, and I had no champion to translate a strange dream of parallel Arcadia as an encouraging nudge to pay attention.

When I woke the first thing I saw was my pearl necklace dropped into a slither of beads on the bedside table, dripping over the sides of the book I'd been reading: a pocket-sized English-Italian dictionary.

In 1967, the Reigate School of Art in Surrey where I was happily enrolled as a teenager of eighteen, was a country quilt of old mansions casually linked together on a residential stretch of Blackborough Road. It boasted an eclectic network of classrooms held together by a loose grid of modern portables and old huts that delightfully, no-one had bothered to renovate into a sterile facility. Gravel paths led from one creaking classroom to the others like a grey threadbare carpet meandering between shade trees and flowerbeds. The college had grown like a wild garden as adjacent properties and sheds had come on the market.

This, to my great good fortune, meant a less-intimidating campus and an informal style of teaching suited to the arts, one I later adapted to my own informal style of teaching.

I shared my attic rooms with Sienna – a classmate who was studying calligraphy, an exacting discipline that begged the atmosphere of a monastery. Together we created a quiet sanctuary, she the scribe, and me, the eager historian.

There was a priory nearby with a pond and swans where Sienna and I ate our bag lunches of cold scotch eggs and apples, or muffin-sized blocks of local cheddar which we consumed as if they were slices of pound cake.

We never ate proper meals; we nibbled at the groceries we dubbed mice meals. The end of the month was often reduced to creative cooking featuring drastic combinations of cheap breakfast cereals, made into mush too thick to be gruel.

The electrical heating was activated by a coin-operated meter which released heat by the minute and dictated a choice between warmth and food. Often it was neither. We were slaves to the Shilling God. Six coins meant the lights popped-off after an hour because the convection heater given to us by Sienna's well-intentioned parents, absorbed shilling-juice like a sponge.

The ticking meter changed our perception of time. "What time is it?" became more accurate when answered in financial terms: "three shillings left, maybe less."

In desperation, all we could do to stay warm was wear several layers of thin cardigans, bed socks, and fingerless gloves, and study in bed under quilts, reading by candlelight while frost gathered on the inside of the windows and ice formed in the sink.

It was all glorious fun to a teenager away from home, and apart from Botticelli's pesky goat-children with the faces of demented-looking old men, snuggling with *Janson* open to a page of Renaissance art was better than a hundred novels. Strange that such limitations are some of the happiest memories of independence.

I thought I knew the *Adoration of the Magi,* well, but I discovered Sandro Botticelli's expression was a pretext for something he held back from me. His face was rarely serious, never far from good-natured laughter. I used to imagine slipping into the crowd and circle back around the ruins to sneak up on him. I even tapped him on the shoulder a few times. Once, in a daydream when Sophie led me to his art studio on the Via Nuova, I watched him paint his self-portrait.

I often searched the face of Botticelli seeking an emotional way in because his eyes were a compelling invitation even though his overall demeanour was one of mild disdain. His eyes appraised me with intimidating perception. I even heard the taunting echo of his sensuous voice: *I defy you to look deeply, mortal. Please, step this way.*

His slight sneer showed how Sandro saw himself or perhaps wanted others to see him, and gives him an aura of slight contempt which, I had first suspected, he thought was a sign of masculinity. I wondered if he may indeed resent what he had been compelled to paint by his patrons in order to eat because this particular *Adoration* was commissioned by a corrupt businessman angling for brownie points with every artist's ultimate patron, the Medici.

I taught my students to speculate. To put themselves in the shoes of the Florentine *gods*. I asked them: who amongst us knows what an artist had to do in Sandro's day to make it to the feet of the Medici?

Botticelli seemed to lack the temperament of the ruthlessly ambitious. I had thought he was a compliant painter, likely astonished at his own spikes of success and failure. Whatever his strategy, his star was definitively aligned with the increase and decrease of the Medici and eventually, the rise of Savonarola, the fanatic Dominican whose spies stirred betrayal into a religious obligation. His followers called the piagnoni, the weepers, were the equivalent of pilgrims wearing ashes on their foreheads, ironically to show their humility. Instead, they succeeded to distinguish themselves above the general population by appearing more holy.

Secular art was in; profane art was heresy. Artists following the grind of business were fulfilling other people's agendas. Persecuting artists was as easy as shooting paintings in a barrel, and to add irony to my metaphor, the name Botticelli means little barrel. Like most child-ish nicknames it had been acquired through a slip of sib-ling one-upmanship.

I once watched an old movie: *The Agony and the Ecstasy*, and somewhere in the shadows of the Sistine I saw the actors playing the roles of people I felt I knew. So, it was inevitable for me to wax fanciful and see Botticelli teasing his fellow apprentices in the studio of Verrocchio or Leonardo pushing his flying machine off Mt Ceceri, and Raphael ogling the Sistine ceiling and the freshly-painted *Mona Lisa*, and Bramante arguing with Michelangelo. All of them manoeuvring their way through popes and other plagues as if they lived down the street. In my mind, they were as substantial as any of my neighbours whom I rarely spoke to.

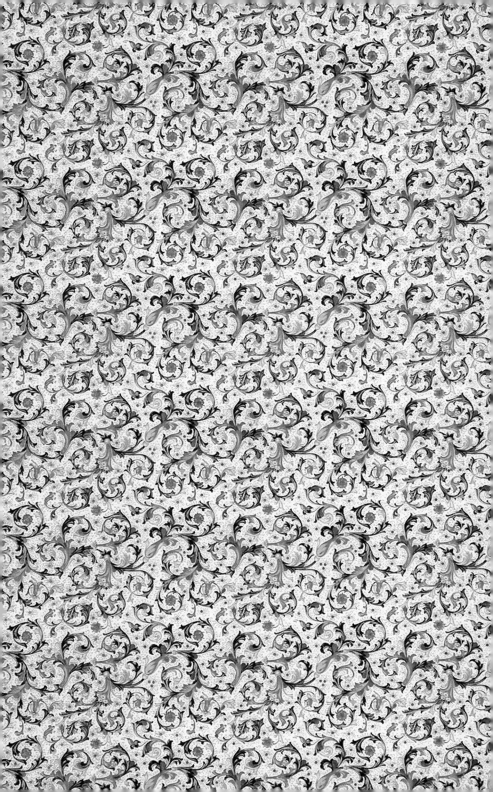

Sandro Botticelli's
Venus and Mars

"As soon go kindle fire with snow,
as seek to quench the fire of love
with words"
~William Shakespeare

meetings are such sweet sorrow

ON BOARD ALITALIA FLIGHT 101 TO FLORENCE
DECEMBER 29, 2013

When I was eighteen, I met the first love of my life in a decidedly compromising position. He was sleeping after having ravished a goddess. At least, that was the common assumption, but Venus's bored expression told a different story. I chose to believe he had rejected her and was dreaming of me.~ RH

The National Gallery, London ~ 1967

For weeks, the school trip to the National Gallery had been nothing but a benign circle on my calendar, and the scheduled Saturday arrived, normal enough, except that morning the sky was bluer, the trees more sharply outlined. At breakfast, the sugar in my tea set my nerves to trembling. I was jumpy. My skin reacted adversely to the cashmere beret I always wore. It had never felt constricted or itchy before, and I felt the need to wear sunglasses against the bright colours of the other students' clothes.

Conversation on the bus riffed around me in the usual buzz, but I heard my classmates as if they were bees in a glass jar. I was not culled out, but set apart, respectfully left to my own thoughts which lingered on an unbearable knife-edge of expectancy as my brain muddled into a storm of resistance. I was fighting with fate again.

The sound of my shoes on the stone steps of the Gallery reverberated like an echo as the vortex of air issuing from massive building sucked me towards the entrance. I could hear the loud flapping of the long display flags hanging from the windows, and the pigeons, usually in an uproar, froze silently in the square.

Once inside, I felt an odd sensation of static electricity playing over my skin and I sat on a bench hoping it would pass. Strangely, I seemed to be moving slower than everyone else, but I wasn't frightened. I raised my arm and a stream of ghost arms splayed out in a fan.

I heard the wasps, and smelled the summer grass and the sweet scent of myrtle before I saw the painting. The coolness of Botticelli's *Venus and Mars* forest glade enveloped me as I halted several feet away, entranced, but the compelling sounds of a flute and children laughing released me, and I moved closer.

The 'children' had hooves and the legs of goats. Small stumps of horns grew from their foreheads, and their grotesque faun faces and pointed ears resembled those of garden gnomes.

Mars was sleeping and I wanted to kiss him awake as a surprise. "I'm here," I whispered, but Botticelli's vapid model, Simonetta, was there, waiting for her second chance. I was invisible to them both.

I whispered again. "Wake up my angel," but Mars lay as if dead or enchanted under a curse.

Simonetta looked smug.

"What have you done?" I shouted.

She continued to look through me. "He's dreaming about me," I said. "You can ignore me if you want, but he belongs to me."

I pleaded with Mars more loudly. "Wake up! Please wake up," but he was deep in the Underworld, searching for me.

Simonetta stood and smoothed her dress. "My husband will wonder where I am," she announced to the fauns, and disappeared.

I shooed away the fauns, and lay beside Mars with my arms around him to keep him warm. My wedding gown was pure white. Its embroidered lace flowers fell from the silk and took root in the grass growing in a protective circle around us as I waited for his return.

The gallery's guide book had the iconography backwards: Botticelli had painted the 'goddess' Simonetta rather than Venus. But another banal fact served to bring me back to the speed of the twentieth-century. *Venus and Mars* was mere dabble of interior decoration – a painted panel called a *spalliera* designed to fit into the back of a sofa.

That simple domestic throwaway allowed me to breathe forward, but it was seventeen years before my lover came home.

"Has this been thus before?
And shall not thus time's eddying flight
Still with our lives our love restore
In death's despite,
And day and night yield
one delight once more"
~ Dante Gabriel Rossetti

trip of a lifetime

ON BOARD ALITALIA FLIGHT 101 TO FLORENCE
DECEMBER 29, 2013

Here I am, once again en route to my wonderful Florence, and thoughts I had wanted to remain buried have arisen from their ashes with alarming clarity.

When I was thirty-five, I travelled to Florence with a woman colleague and her sister. It was a last minute whim on my part, and I think they resented my tagging along, but I wanted Florence more than staying in their good graces. It was time for me to go.

My 1984 trip had been two weeks of anticipation and delight which collapsed into shame and regret, and the worst feeling of emptiness I have ever known, so intense, I have modelled the rest of my life to protect myself from a repeat experience.

I was harbouring beneath the most profound influence of courtly love, and my powers of imagination were so great, I had been able to convince myself that I lived under a supernatural enchantment. I was in love with love; besotted with an ideal, determined to attain a love greater than a fling with an ordinary man who could only ever be a pale imitation of a Roman god. ~ R H

Florence ~ May 1,1984

It was the summer of 84' when I first met the city of Florence and came face to face with the two other loves of my life.

I was prone to stress-induced migraines, and since flying was one of my worst fears, I arrived in Florence feeling less than vivacious. I was jet lagged, over-stimulated, punch-drunk from excitement and insomnia, and the excruciating heat of the Tuscan sun had sizzled my nerves into sharp twigs. Then, I made the mistake of celebrating my arrival by drinking the complimentary mini-bottle of sherry saved from my flight.

My friends Eda and Giovanna were Italian, and their family holiday defined our itinerary. It included a pit-stop in Milan with couple of days in Florence, and the remainder of our two weeks in Trento, visiting their grandmother. All I wanted was Florence, and I was naive enough to think three days would be enough. Like a mouse, I deferred to my travel companion's plan, but I split off on my own to visit the Uffizi, determined to view Botticelli's *Adoration* alone and have Florence to myself for as long as possible.

Against all warnings, I openly wore gold jewelry in a foreign country. I wore my gold charm bracelet every day as a talisman for love. It was unthinkable for me to leave it at home when the city of my heart had called me.

Friends teased me it was a hope chest for the wrist because it had a definitively romantic theme. My collection of love amulets jangled like a wind chime.

My first charm was a gold disc with strange markings on both sides that looked like runes. At first glance the lines made no sense but the medallion was mounted on a wire frame and spun on a pivot. When you blew on it as if you were blowing a bubble through a hoop, it spun fast enough for the runes to link together so the words *soul mate* appeared.

There was also a castle, a baby in a cradle, and two halves of a split heart. My name was engraved on one half; the other remained a clear landing pad for the name of my future husband. There were the symbols for male and female, a chess-piece knight, Cinderella's slipper, a peacock, a pair of swans with their necks entwined, an ankh, and a yin-yang representing the perfect balance of masculine to feminine. A tough combination for Venus to ignore.

I had fidgeted nervously with my bracelet all through the flight, and to distract me, Eda talked me through the plane's descent.

She clinked the ice in her Glenfiddich in my ear. "What do you want to see first?" she asked.

I looked away from the wing tip that was flexing as if it was made of rubber. "The art," I replied, closing my eyes.

"Besides that. You're not at work, you know," she said. "Come on luv, open your eyes and look. Florence is going to appear through those clouds any minute. You don't want to miss it."

"Art is my passion," I said, "and I intend to experience Florence as a native. Have I showed you my old map?"

"Many times."

"I don't know why you aren't excited by it. It's how Florence looked during the time of Leonardo and Botticelli," I said.

"I teach life-drawing, not art history, that's why. And if you'd just look out your window you'll see Florence during the time of *you*."

I took a deep breath and stared at my bracelet. Eda touched it with her plastic cup. "So, what's the significance of a peacock and the swans?"

"A peacock is a symbol of rebirth and swans mate for life," I said. "I feel queasy."

Eda handed me her scotch. "Drink this."

I tossed it back in one go and surprisingly, felt better.

Her eyes widened at her empty cup but she continued, nonplussed. "It's all very love-specific, isn't it. I still think you should've left it at home. Gold is a magnet for thieves. I'm only saying. It's in all the brochures. You should get one of those clasp thingys with a safety chain."

She stuffed her empty cup in the pouch in front of her as Giovanna craned her neck to see out my window and thought better of it. I saw her grit her teeth and clutch Eda's hand with her eyes squeezed shut.

Eda sighed "I don't know, between the two of you," she said. "Buck up the pair of you. We're having fun."

"*Trains* are fun, Giovanna replied.

"You should buy a new charm when we get there. Gold is cheaper in Italy, isn't it G," Eda nattered.

"I will if this thing ever lands," I said.

I glanced out my window as the plane banked and felt I was being tipped into Florence. Below me was Brunelleschi's red dome of its landmark cathedral, and I burst into tears.

"I have been here before,
But when or how I cannot tell:
I know the grass beyond the door,
The sweet keen smell,
The sighing sound,
the lights around the shore."
~ Dante Gabriel Rossetti

buongiorno

ON BOARD ALITALIA FLIGHT 101 TO FLORENCE
DECEMBER 29, 2013

Sandro and I first met in Florence, in 1984, on a rainy Thursday,
inside a church of sorts — a shrine of art. He was there, wrapped
in an apricot cloak, his face framed with auburn curls, apprais-
ing me with his biting blue eyes and an audacious mouth that I
suspected knew how to kiss. ~ RH

Florence ~ May 2,1984

In retrospect, it was that trick of the light moment when
the eyes in a portrait say 'stay a while and let me look
back at you.'

I had stood rooted, feeling exposed, and never flinched. Stare-for-stare, electrons danced between us. It was curiosity at first sight. And I remember hearing the distant strains of music I had never known but swore I could taste and smell.

The scent of artist's musk reached out, the worn fabric of a weathered cape slipped through my memory, imprinted warm and thick, and Italian voices collided in the dark, making sparks.

"You're awake," I said, and then a crowd of tourists separated us, and I sent Sandro a thought over my shoulder as I left. "See you tomorrow."

But something unexpected happened, and the next day another love swept me off my feet and my time in Florence ran out.

"In that book which is my memory,
On the first page of the chapter
That is the day when I first met you,
Appear the words: here begins a new life"
~ Dante Alighieri, Vita Nuova

time passages

ON BOARD ALITALIA FLIGHT 101 TO FLORENCE
DECEMBER 29, 2013

I had flown from England to Florence in a haste of passion with my mind as wide open as Pandora's box, but I made the mistake of rushing to Botticelli's side, assuming that the location of his earthly remains was the quintessential magnet for communion. I couldn't have been more wrong. I stood there shamefaced and deflated, staring down at a dull inscription of chiseled letters which proclaimed the last known address of Alessandro di Mariano Filipepi, a.k.a Sandro Botticelli. ~ RH

Florence ~ May 2, 1984

Sandro's grave was a cold church floor. No soft earthen bed, baking under the Tuscan sun where flowers could grow or the roots of a nearby tree could feel their way through the soil to embrace his soul.

The austere confines of the Church of Ognissanti was devoid of organic presence. There was no ethereal signature of heat rising to mark the aura of a vital spirit. Visitors' footsteps echoed in the freezing gloom of religion and made me want to shout a juicy obscenity to challenge the strength of its uneasy power.

I left, taking my shivers with me, and stood like a forlorn sunflower in the piazza until I felt my blood melting. 'Cold as the tomb' is real. Bone fragments bedded under a stone blanket is no fit memorial for a passionate man.

Clouds gathered and my thin dress whipped around my legs. Dust swirled low in the street, and merchants battled awnings over their stalls. I didn't care to rush back to the pensione to change, so, it was early afternoon when I walked through a thunderstorm, caught in my white dress with the dainty flowers. I passed a dozen gelato stands and coffee houses to the Uffizi, determined to see the fleshed-out Sandro, displayed more reverently, in-situ.

It was tourist season and the gallery teemed with sightseers on a tight schedule, now eager to fill the galleries to get out of the rain.

I trailed a silver puddle from the street into the passageway of the Uffizi with the single-mind to reach *The Adoration*, and as I wove through the stream of traffic intent on cramming the art of Florence into one afternoon, I sent my heart ahead of me, "I am here ... it's Linton. Where are you? Sandro? Where are you?"

There was no door, just an arched entrance, and the large salon was palpable with Botticelli's presence. Directly opposite me, the iconic *Birth of Venus* captured my attention. I felt *the Adoration* to my right but was unable to move.

"*Principessa*," he said, "I am here."

I wanted to look over my shoulder but I closed my eyes and turned around.

"Open your eyes *Mia carissima*," he said.

The bright shape of his cloak caught my eye and I slowly followed its folds to his face. "Hello," I said, my voice shaking, "you're awake."

"It is you who have been sleeping," he replied.

His smile encouraged me. "Yes," I said, "for five-hundred years. Like the proverbial princess."

A crowd of pushy Americans blurred between us. "Hey lookit, the Venus on the half shell!" one of them shouted, as he elbowed past me. "Geez, it's kinda small. Where's the *Mona Lisa*?"

I shuddered. The man's physical brush against my arm made me ache for Sandro's touch.

"It is raining," Sandro said.

I stood there, my sheer summer dress clinging like skin, and tried to smile.

"I feel dizzy."

"So close, now," he said, but his voice was sad.

"It is still too far. I will return tomorrow."

His need filled my head. I needed air. People were pressing too close.

"Promise me," he said.

I searched his face – close enough to see the corners of his mouth tense. His eyes were dark with emotion.

"I promise."

"*A domani principessa*. Tomorrow then."

"Yes, tomorrow," I repeated, and pulled myself from his imagined embrace, looking back, pausing to return and look again, before finally tearing myself away.

The rain hit my face as I emerged from the Uffizi where a sea of umbrellas still gathered around the outdoor cafe tables opposite, open for the determined few, resigned to experience the romance of Florence in the rain.

The world had not stopped. I was still breathing, and I knew it would be impossible to live happily ever after anywhere else but here. I might have dashed back inside but for the swarm of energy that swept me into a river of drenched sightseers.

So, I grabbed an espresso to-go, and returned to my pensione and my room with its black louvered shutters that now opened to a sea of glistening red tiles swimming with water. I sipped strong coffee and watched the downpour cleanse Florence, feeling like Juliet on her balcony. Below and out over the city my love waited for me. I was blissfully happy. But sadly, I did not believe in, nor count on, divine intervention.

WHAT IF I SAY

"What if I say I shall not wait?
What if I burst the fleshly gate
And pass, escaped, to thee?"
~ Emily Dickenson

ON BOARD ALITALIA FLIGHT 101 TO FLORENCE
DECEMBER 29, 2013

The next day had been a walking nightmare. I had promised to
return to Botticelli but was devastated to find the Uffizi closed. ~ RH

Florence ~ May 3,1984

In my haste to see Botticelli I'd neglected to eat but had quickly downed a glass of orange juice, and on the way to the gallery I bought a bar of dark chocolate for my breakfast.

Florence had dried to a bright shine, and to while the

time, I decided to buy a love charm for my bracelet from an up-market goldsmith on the Ponte Vecchio.

I chose a winged lion engraved with the words *pui di ieri meno di domani, per sempre* on its base: 'more than yesterday; less than tomorrow, always and forever.' The salesgirl assured me its sentiment was the classic love token an Italian suitor gives his sweetheart, and I was still an idealist, superstitious enough to think of my bracelet as a magnetic valentine – a tangible reminder, symbolic of a golden future.

Although my street-wise friends had warned me to never take it off, I wore it with renewed delight, heavier now for its latest addition, aware of the sound it made, jangling on my wrist.

I felt it's reassuring weight as I waved away a wasp which was no doubt attracted by the scent of chocolate left in my bag, so I ate the remaining pieces as I made my way over the bridge to the Boboli gardens with the wasp determined to follow and threw the wrapper into a bin. The wasp zoomed there immediately, so I was left to meander alone through the carpet of formal flow-erbeds thinking of the wasps in Botticelli's *Venus and Mars*, painted to honor the Vespucci family and their daughter of the hour, Simonetta.

An hour later, an 'official' aura began in my left eye. The pinwheel of alarming lights was the warning that pain would strike, and to find a bed in dark cool place or some painkillers before it breached the point of no return. Since neither were within my reach, I walked with one hand held over my sunglasses and wove through hoards of tourists all determined to reach the place I was trying so desperately to leave.

An internal dowsing rod led me back to the pensione near the railway station but by then I was nauseous and hallucinating. Other than a dab of Tiger Balm to my temples, it was too late for medicine. I prepared the room as best I could but fingers of light struggled through the closed shutters. The rest of a precious Florence day was wasted in a stuffy room, groaning with pain from a tempest behind my eyes which left cruel waves of broken glass breaking inside my skull.

My companions returned in the late afternoon, discussing my state in hushed voices. "She must have heat-stroke," Giovanna said.

"No, she gets these serious headaches. She'll be out of it till tomorrow."

"It's stifling in here. Open a window."

"No, it has to be dark."

I recall correcting Eda's blunder. "No, heartache," I murmured, meaning to say migraine.

"She looks feverish," Giovanna said, "should we get a doctor?"

"No, she'll be delirious for hours. I've seen her before. It's dreadful but there's nothing to do other than leave her alone, undisturbed. Too bad there isn't a bloody fan in here."

Giovanna bent down and felt my forehead. "Some people have love on the brain," she said softly, tucking the covers around me. "We'll leave you in peace, then. Lin, we'll be gone till late so don't worry. *Ciao*."

She meant no harm, but her words stung, and I was too far-gone to protest. Headaches are mild discomfort by comparison. A migraine is more like a tiny demon jabbing a sizzling trident into the frontal lobe of one's brain, and it has to run its course.

Mercifully, left alone, I listened to the relentless drone of scooters below my window which slipped into the memory of the wasp. Gradually, as I entered the worst of my pain, and evening fell, I became aware of a presence in the room who took hold of my hand. The timbre of the voice told me it was male, and at first I thought he was the kind old landlord bringing a fan, but as I soon discovered, it was not. It was an angel. I know because for an instant I was able to open my eyes and I saw his wings.

I had learned to think of my migraines as a creature taking possession, a fiend in my head who hated me passionately. It was a battle of wills lasting twelve excruciating hours or more until I claimed a weak victory, at which point I became ravenously thirsty and hungry. Sometimes stress brought them on, but I had sabotaged my gastric equilibrium by ignoring the dietary faux pas of eating both citrus and chocolate.

My angel was a mind-reader. He brought towels, a basin, and a glass of water, and didn't flinch when, at last, I disgorged the demon into a bowl, and gulped the water like a dehydrated woman stumbling from a desert.

I felt the fan of his wings soothing my face, and I opened my eyes apologetically, expecting a look of horror but instead there was a hazy young face showing concern. I only saw his eyes for an instant; it hurt to keep mine open.

He brushed the hair from my face, straightened the bedclothes like a mother, bathed my face, and administered sweet wine, allowing me only one sip at a time, speaking words of encouragement as my world came into focus.

I could smell a familiar pungent scent on his fingers I couldn't place, that served as smelling salts. I assumed it was the Tiger Balm my angel had rubbed into my temples.

He placed cool compresses on my forehead, and all the while his voice acted like a salve. I didn't have to understand what he was saying, he projected compassion, and something else I never expected, his eyes held the unmistakable look of love.

I retained the vague impression of a single dazzling strip of golden light on a collarless white shirt, olive skin, and blue eyes. Definitely blue. *Definitively* blue, and shoulder-length titian hair glowing with its own aura of red highlights. He leaned over me and I thought he was going to kiss my forehead but he kissed me tenderly on the mouth and then more passionately, whispering endearments which sounded startlingly intimate.

His blue eyes darkened with passion as he searched my face, and I felt his breath quicken as he brushed his lips against my neck. He lifted my shift, and I felt his hands push between my legs, wet with wanting him.

"I cannot wait," he said, and he lowered his body onto me.

I arched upwards to meet him as he eased into me slowly, rhythmically, both of us groaning with pleasure. I focused on his eyes. The rest of his face blurred as if he was underwater. Long curls clung damp on his forehead as he winced with each successive plunge building with intensity until I heard him cry out.

I watched him, a silhouette panting to regain his breath, the moonlight from the window playing over his wet skin, his head flung back, eyes squeezed shut. He returned to me with his hands again, whispering *t'amo* moving his fingers deeper and faster, kissing my lips, sucking the breath from my mouth, his tongue searching like his fingers until a golden spear of bliss shot through my flesh, body and soul.

For a moment I left my body and floated into his, and we flew together, conjoined, suspended, safe.

I tried to speak but he shushed me and lay down beside me, cradling me with his wings, and told me to sleep.

"When you have need of me, call," he said, kissing my hands. "You are not alone, now. We are one."

It was the most restful sleep of my life – the divine sleep of the beloved. I turned on my side, curling into him, and felt protected from the world. He stroked the back of my head and called me *mia bella principessa Orazia* – words I would remember all my life.

"I am forgetful of every thing
but seeing you again –
my life seems to stop there –
I see no further. You have absorb'd me.
I have a sensation at the present moment
as though I were dissolving"
~ John Keats

a gate closes

ON BOARD ALITALIA FLIGHT 101 TO FLORENCE
DECEMBER 29, 2013

The rest of my trip I walked on broken glass: second guessing, turning suddenly at a sound or the scent of flowers to see if I was divinely accompanied, but it was wishful dreaming. I was quite alone. ~ RH

Florence ~ May 4, 1984

In the morning, my ephemeral lover was gone and I faked sleep as my friends left a day early for the north. I mumbled something about catching them up in Trento and that I was staying on, too frail to travel. It was true.

I slept another hour before waking with a head that felt like cotton wool, and discovered my bracelet was gone. For the first while, I was too dazed and ashamed to grieve and accepted its loss as fair comeuppance for my behaviour. On the scale of things, a missing piece of jewelry paled next to losing ones virginity to a divine being, and I had betrayed my connection to Sandro. The day had no reality about it. Sunshine was lost on me. I went about reporting the theft to my landlord in a trance as if I'd been sedated.

My hosts were a sweet old couple. Lorenzo, the smiling and amiable soft-spoken slightly-henpecked husband, and Francesca, his effusive wife, the epitome of the Italian Mamma – an emotional and efficient matriarch.

It was easy to look distraught.

"I know I took my watch and gold bracelet off and laid them on the bedside table before I went to bed. This morning, my watch was still there but the bracelet was gone," I announced. "It is irreplaceable."

Cappuccino was offered to bridge the disquiet of three uncomfortable people in search of a mutually satisfactory solution.

As we talked I related the significance of each gold charm and how each one was a symbol of the love I hoped I'd find.

Francesca nodded, and showed me the back of the Madonna medallion around her neck. "He give to me," she said, nodding at Lorenzo.

The inscription gave me a chill. *'pui di ieri meno di domani per sempre.'*

"Always and forever," I said, and my eyes misted up.

Lorenzo patted my hand. "You will find," he said.

"Look, I need to settle my bill, and I am so sorry, but I think I must report the theft of my bracelet to the police and the British embassy. My bracelet was worth several hundred dollars, well, it was 18 carat gold, you see, and one of a kind, so it will be easy to identify."

"*Si, é bello molto bello,*" Mrs. Barberini agreed diplomatically, but her eyes showed horror. Yes, the bracelet had drawn her attention. "*É tragico,*" she said. "*Signorina* Howard allow me to adjust the monies. I am so sorry for your *problema* and I need no more of troubles with the *polizia.*"

I was taken aback. "You mean this has happened before?"

"Lately, *si*, there has been some breaks. The locks they are old... like me. But nothing as valuable as gold, *non non*, tourists, they do not think. They tease the fate."

I nodded gravely. "I don't want to make trouble for you. Maybe there's a way to resolve this situation between ourselves," I said.

"You want we should pay the gold? For a new bracelet?" Lorenzo asked.

I was feeling closed in. Ready to burst from conflicted emotions. An anxiety attack seemed imminent. "Look, I'm not feeling well," I said. "Let me think about it. I hate to put you out of pocket. Right now, I just need some air."

"You stay here longer. For no charge, yes?" Mrs. Barberini called after me.

Later, along with delayed shock, I felt a peculiar sense of relief that I was being punished for being unfaithful. The sacrifice of a golden keepsake dedicated to love seemed like the perfect atonement for my crime. The bracelet had ceased to feel like a treasure and more like a trinket. I was gutted to be abandoned and alone after the bliss of consummation only a few hours before.

The enormity of what had happened probably saved my sanity. I was numb from three losses. I determined to confess my infidelity to Sandro but then, cowardly shrivelled from the task.

All I knew was that I needed to be outside in the sunshine with humanity moving at a different speed than emptiness, and although they surrounded me like so much muted wallpaper, I felt stronger. My room held too many reasons to mope and cry.

The angel had left a vacuum where we'd so recently loved, and I lingered on the peripheral of that love in a fragile state of neediness. Passion burned out any sense of love for my former obsession. The angel had eclipsed Botticelli, and his pleading eyes consumed me with sadness.

I stood on a corner near the Via Nuova, shaken, but the smell of coffee brought me to earth, and I drank in deep breaths of holiday air with nowhere to go that wasn't haunted by guilt. A fog of remorse plagued me. I hadn't discouraged my ghostly lover but fallen into the moment and willingly surrendered.

The rest of my stay, I couldn't help but search the wrists of every female for a familiar glint of a gold peacock.

Botticelli was trapped in his gallery, waiting, while I had the freedom of the streets, but I was not free.

I wanted to celebrate as new lovers do, but fate was cruel. I was caught behind a couple walking hand-in-hand transfixed in a bubble of joy. He kissed the top of her head and she snuggled into his shoulder. I was locked out of their world entirely and yet I knew it intimately.

I was abandoned, left as the torn half of something indescribably wonderful and I nurtured the golden joy of the night inside me like a tender secret. I rubbed my bare wrist, beginning to understand the obsession some people have for penance. I even had the fleeting thought of slipping into a confession booth in a nearby church or at least to light three candles. One for each each of us. Botticelli, the angel, and me. The white band of skin on my tanned arm was contrition enough. It haunted me, and by the end of the day my wrist was red and sore from over-attention.

I passed the Uffizi and sent a confused message of apology: "I am lost. It's too late, now," I sent in a stream of thoughts. "I need to find someone. I need to find myself. I'm not a princess. Not who you want me to be. I am so sorry."

Even if I had conjured the angel in the midst of need, he had taught me more in the space of a moonlit hour than I could have wished, and I was changed. Too changed to regret my compliance but not enough changed to dismiss the betrayal I felt. Loyalty was not a casual promise. It would not do to mount the stairs to witness the pain of a man I still loved, or to bear the forgiveness he would surely give, or endure the embarrassed silence of being scrutinized for a faint hope of yesterday in my face.

Instead, I revisited the markets of Florence in a cruel trance, but whenever I relived the night, I knew I would welcome it back. The sad realization of continual longing becoming my *actual* fate, brought a tender comfort. I would suffer as I had made Sandro suffer.

For a nostalgic moment, anchored by the bells of the duomo, I stared dully at Il Porcellino surrounded by animated tourists being photographed in various states of self-conscious posing, when I felt the stirring of air and turned to see the promise of white wings disappearing into the crowd.

I ran past the Uffizi, glancing up at its windows, but the promise of white wings a few yards away was too enticing to stop. It was just as well, the run did me some good, although I never was able to catch him up, and he eventually melted into the never-ending crush of humanity on the Ponte Vecchio.

I continued on to the Boboli Gardens where I lay on the grass, closing my eyes against revelers, deferring to my state of melancholy to further alienate myself from the joy of others.

I first noticed the cat when I opened my eyes at the sound of flapping wings. The wings were white but it was not an angel. It was a pigeon the cat was stalking but I got the impression she was more interested in me. I called to her and she inched forward to sniff my hand. Soon, she rubbed into my legs, and I could see her eyes were infected and sore.

I felt the renewed sting of selfishness. Feeling sorry for myself when there was so many homeless cats that needed food and affection. I scratched behind her ears and between her shoulder blades, which felt too sharp. I wanted to feed her. "I'm sorry, sweetie, I don't have anything for you to eat," I said.

I scratched the top of her head. "That feels good doesn't it."

I thought how such brief touchstones are important in a strange land. For me, touching a cat made the world small enough to feel safe, but not for her. I had intruded enough to feel responsible. I stroked her nose and made a wish.

I wished someone would take her in and look after her. I wished I could help all the starving cats of the world with infected eyes. That's what I would do with lottery winnings, and so I wished for that too.

She followed me back to the pensione although I stopped several times trying to dissuade her. I worried for her, but I needn't have. She was obviously street-smart as she waited for gaps in the traffic to cross safely.

My landlord, Mr. Barberini, anxiously deferred to me and greeted her with kindness by giving her the leavings of the previous night's fish dinner. I watched her eat, wishing I could take her home with me. Obviously, an impossibility but I played the guilt card and got permission to keep the cat in my room for the night.

I sponged her eyes with warm water and patted them dry, and set her on the bed where her presence erased the memory of abandonment lingering there. She was a sad sight, and I hoped the residual love of the angel would heal her. We had dinner together and she let me cuddle her to sleep where I dreamed my own wings covered and protected her, and she told me what to do. I woke with a mission.

Florence ~ May 5, 1984

Mr. Barberini was so appalled to hear the cat had caught three mice in my room, he called his wife to calm me.

"All in one night," I repeated several times. "Thank heavens the cat was there."

They held hands and nodded in agreement.

"It is unhealthy," I said. "Not good for business."

I already had their sympathy and attention, and we got more chatty in the deserted dining room. We brushed aside the more pending problem of the missing bracelet and talked about the value of a good cat and how females were the best hunters. Lorenzo told me of the cat they once had and how they mourned her greatly. There were tears and out came the photo album and the homemade liqueur.

It was all very heartwarming and I was touched, but I steeled myself and concentrated on the plan, and the cat's hellish life in the streets. *Those eyes, her poor sore eyes. Her hunger. Her pure affection after so much suffering,* until I was ready to drop my bombshell.

"Something would make me very happy," I said. "And also solve both your problems."

Francesca relaxed. "Please how?"

"I will feel completely compensated by having the cat cared for," I said. "If you agree to give her a home, I will consider the matter of the bracelet closed. I will take great comfort knowing my bracelet will have brought her love. It's a sign, yes? So, there's no need to alert the authorities of a mouse problem because with a cat in residence, it no longer exists."

"You will do this?" Lorenzo asked looking incredulous.

"I will."

We shook hands which turned into many hugs. Lorenzo broke out his homemade wine.

Francesca beamed. "*Si*, the cat, she is a prayer, like on your bracelet."

"Her name is Angelina," I said.

~

The vet supplied some salve and gave Angelina injections of antibiotics. Surgery would be avoided and with the grace of god and Francesca's good cooking the infection would heal.

Back on the terrace of the pensione, Lorenzo brought out a bowl of sardines and we watched Angelina eat.

I felt as refreshed as I could be, considering the circumstances.

I packed my things with Angelina in the room, cleaning herself in a comfy chair like she'd lived there all her life. "You're going to be all right now, missy," I said, "Thank you for being my lifeline. Don't worry, I think you have a guardian angel here to look after you."

I took a last lingering look at the bed. It seemed like weeks had passed since I had lain there in the arms of an angel.

Florence ~ May 6, 1984

It was an emotional goodbye. A beaming Mrs. Barberini

wrung my hands, pinched my cheek, and wiped her eyes on her apron; Mr. Barberini stood at her side and declared Angelina was already their little baby *il loro piccolino.*

"My little Angelina, she is a gift of God," Francesca said, kissing her medallion. "From his love of you. Already she is at home. You can see this, no?"

Once more Lorenzo thanked me profusely. *"Stupendo bella signorina,"* he said. *"Mille grazie.* May love be near you."

I pressed my forwarding address into Lorenzo's hand. "Let me know how Angelina gets on," I said which made Francesca start to cry again.

Lorenzo continued to defend his honor and expressed his undying gratitude at my understanding and compassion, still proclaiming the world was doomed, utterly aghast that his establishment had been the scene of such unforeseen crimes of terrible people, apologizing for the entire population of his country and several generations of his family.

Much later, I remembered a man bumping into me in the street the day I'd wandered in a daze, unable to see. I had fallen to the ground in my disoriented state, and he made a great display of helping me to my feet, brushing off my clothes with a grand speech of apology. I recall his words: *"I help you... I so sorry ... please which way ... I can go with you."* I had little doubt that he was another womanizer loose on the streets hounding tourists for thrills and cash and gold bracelets.

"Time is too slow for those who wait,
too swift for those who fear,
too long for those who grieve,
too short for those who rejoice,
but for those who love,
time is eternity."
~ Henry Van Dyke

the last train

ON BOARD ALITALIA FLIGHT 101 TO FLORENCE
DECEMBER 29, 2013

My last coherent thought on the events of my holiday, my 'holy day' with an angel, was to store it away entirely, and pretend it had never happened, but this was trying beyond blue-sky thinking. As if a few mothballs could still my memory of exquisite bliss. There were times I managed to keep my longings submerged under my work, but then, most of the paintings I presented in my classes contained angels, and I found myself asking my students more loaded questions: which angels looked believable? What would you do if confronted with an angel? Has anyone experienced an angel encounter? If so, which angel in Renaissance art looked most authentic?

It was generally accepted Raphael's angels were the most

charming as they imbued personality and had soft feathery wings
that most resembled those of a great bird, and finally, there was
always the presence my angel statue of St. Mary's, waiting to
remind me that he need not be cast in stone forever but could be
granted animated flesh with needs beyond alleviating human suf-
fering. Compassion elevated to passion.

And now it's time to pay for my mistake. Botticelli has been
waiting long enough. The heart is a curious bedfellow. Love com-
pels one to do strange things. There are no exceptions. ~ RH

Florence ~ May 8, 1984

I could no longer stay in Florence, bereft that I had
betrayed a constant love while mourning the abandonment of an unearthly one. My lost bracelet kept sending
me messages I needed to hear. It now symbolized the
greater tragedy of stolen love that arrives and distracts
on the waves of physical desire. What Dante called *'the
lover's deficiency in the virtue of temperance.'*

I understood the complexities of being utterly guilt-rid-
den, but amazingly, in unexpected moments, I felt
buoyed-up with love from the persistent feeling my angel
was near, but the disparate feelings of drowning in guilt
and soaring with anticipation left me quite lightheaded.

I left Florence after making a last wish. Il Porcellino's
eyes showed no sympathy, they were cold and metallic,
devoid of animation. I had been ravenous but couldn't
face one more breakfast of sweet rolls and hot chocolate

pressed on me by my hosts. A dull hunger replaced my bones, and as I stood in the market, I felt a sudden craving for apples. Nothing else tempted me, so I bought a half-dozen for the journey north.

During the first hours on the train, I felt my ethereal lover travelling with me. I shut my eyes refusing to see Tuscany slipping away. Sadly, I lacked the temerity to dash back to Florence where I could have happily died in the street for the angel to claim me.

I remember being too exhausted to cry until I'd already reached Trento, but in a quiet hour wandering the countryside alone, I sat on an outcrop of rock in a large field picturing Angelina's eyes. The thought of how many Angelinas there were in the world hit me and the tears came. My grief disturbed a small beige snake basking near me and its beauty caused me to study its delicate markings. Time slipped sideways. I reached out for it in a daze and felt a solid hand blocking mine.

With a rush of pleasure I spun around expecting to see my angel. He was not there, but his touch had snapped me out of my fog in time to recognize the snake was a deadly viper.

The rest of the day I thought of Shakespeare's Cleopatra and the wonders of an ethereal being able to send a subliminal warning with such physical presence as the timely hand that had saved me from certain death.

Before boarding my plane to England I stopped by a jeweller in the airport duty-free and purchased a gold angel, meaning to start a new charm bracelet, but over the years I abandoned the expensive project to buy art and books, and the small charm became lost in a tangle of costume jewelry in a trinket box.

Once I was home, I visited my stone angel. "Was it you?" I asked. I took his silence for a no.

I remained devastated anew each time I thought of my missing bracelet. Not for the piece itself but because it brought back the impressions of wings and being wholly desired, enfolded in the most tender and exquisite love, and a relentless longing for physical arousal and orgasm. I continued to feel it's unhappy weight on my wrist like a phantom limb.

Naturally, I tried to recreate the experience, but the power to conjure an angel proved impossible. Then the crisis with Mary jolted me out of my nightly reveries.

Had I dreamt it all? It was easier to believe I had. Lucid dreaming was not new to me, but my guardian angel seemed more like a wish-fulfillment, and it was too painful continuing to chase another dream.

For a year, my angel seemed near, but still, he stayed out of touch, his golden aura always slightly out of reach. He appeared for an instant in the audience of one of my lectures and was gone, or slipped away through a flock of students, and even briefly materialized on the stairwell of my own house. Evasive, but never far, he left the scent of Tiger Balm in the air. For a while it was enough to bask in the peripheral presence of his shadow, and then too distracting to be healthy, but after the revelation of *The Thorn Birds*, the folly of saving myself for two non-corporeal men could not fail to lose its irony on me.

Thereafter, I only caught traces of my angel in movies, one aspect at a time: a voice, a face, a hand, shoulders, a smile, or even a colour. It wasn't long before my sweet angel merged into my stone angel, sometimes, when I remembered the wings and the red hair and the Tiger Balm and the kiss, his image came back to me, whole and pure.

"You have been mine before,
How long ago I may not know:
But just when at that swallow's soar
Your neck turned so,
Some veil did fall - I knew it all of yore."
~ Dante Gabriel Rossetti

hello again

The Uffizi Gallery, Florence ~ New Year's Eve, 2013

The present day Galleria degli Uffizi occupies twin buildings connected by a walkway which encloses three sides of a long rectangular inner courtyard with an open view of the River Arno framed by architecture. On the second floor in room ten hangs the object of my idolatry, Botticelli's *Adoration of the Magi.*

I braved the lobby of the Uffizi and formal introductions, fearlessly drinking champagne for the first hour before heading upstairs against the crush of sophisticated party guests. My body was out of sync with Florence, having landed the night before, over-excited and unable to eat or sleep.

I was irked that I'd forgotten to pack my beaded evening purse, and so I lugged my large handbag with a shoulder strap to the gala, concealing it behind me, low to the floor, as discreetly as I could.

I moved in a trance through a blur of formal dresses and tuxedos, on through the clink of glasses, inside the murmur of celebration and music. As I walked, I felt an old fear, self-conscious of my years, dreading a younger man's reaction, wishing it was 1984 again and me in my summer frock with the *Primavera* flowers, my hair wet from the rain.

It's only one hour in Florence time, before the world turns 2014 and I turn sixty-five. As always, Botticelli is thirty and has been dead for five-hundred years, and here we are on New Year's Eve after a leap of alarmingly perverse physics.

Tonight, meeting Sandro Botticelli for the second time, I allow myself to feel young again. I know I must beg his forgiveness. A crowd of guests separate me from him. I sense him waiting behind them, and I take a deep breath and cut through.

The last thirty years of my life wash away, the way Florentine rain runs off its famous bronze pig. Years of gravity lift from me as Botticelli's eyes reflect the most riveting memories of the things I had once desired and the weighty sour thoughts which had fed my fears of rejection and aging alone.

It had been a shared dream and Sandro had borne his part with infinite grace.

He looked the same.

"Principessa, where have you been?" he said.

"The face of all the world is changed, I think,
Since first I heard the footsteps of thy soul
Move still, oh, still, beside me, as they stole
Betwixt me and the dreadful outer brink
Of obvious death, where I, who thought to sink,
Was caught up into love, and taught the whole
of life in a new rhythm"

~ Elizabeth Barrett Browning

venus realigns with mars

The Uffizi Gallery, Florence ~
New Year's Eve, 2013

The throng of smiles and laughter parted in front of me as I sat on the viewing bench to study Alessandro di Mariano di Vanni Filipepi, the Master painter, Sandro Botticelli.

The large room hushed. I could hear the surrounding party as a thrum of audio fog. The guests moved slower and slower until they stopped, still as statues. The figures in the small painting enlarged to life-size, and Sandro's cloak moved as if ruffled by a gentle breeze.

He extended an arm from out of its folds, and I moved forward in a trance and accepted his hand.

He spoke four words, "you will come, yes?"

It was not a question.

There was no hesitation as I allowed Botticelli to pull me into the picture plane. I felt the same breeze tousle my hair, and I looked back over my shoulder expecting to see my shell, deceased as a discarded coat, collapsed on the bench with paramedics fluttering over me like moths, but the seat I so recently occupied was empty, and the room was once again abuzz with multiple languages blurring into each other like the vast hum of a sacred tuning fork. It sounded like a chapel echoing with Gregorian chant.

It was the last time I looked back.

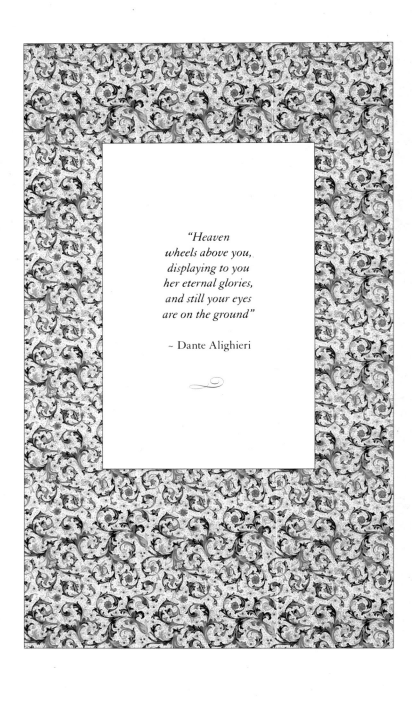

"*Heaven*
wheels above you,
displaying to you
her eternal glories,
and still your eyes
are on the ground"

~ Dante Alighieri

the purgatorio

the fifteenth cycle

~ BOTTICELLI'S CENTURY ~

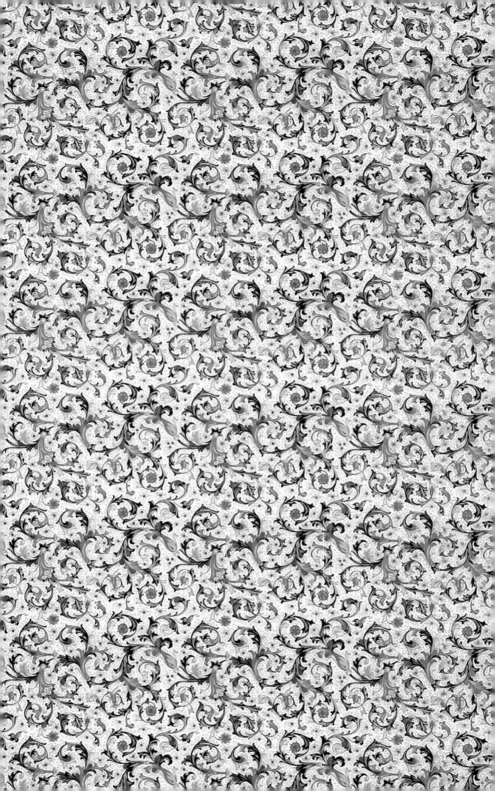

*"For love, to give up acres and degree,
I yield the grave for thy sake,
and exchange my near sweet view of heaven,
for earth with thee"*
~ Elizabeth Barrett Browning

home sweet home

Florence ~ 1480

The interior of the painting reminded me of being back
stage in a theatre. Sandro and I were separate from the
painted figures who now resembled a flat scenery prop.
We were alone, walking around them. I expected to
see the back of a raw panel braced with crossbars, but
the reverse of the figures were painted as well. Cut-out
Florentines like pressed flowers.

The peacock from the painting strutted majesti-
cally towards us and welcomed us with a hauntingly
wild shriek, sweeping our path with a brush of radiant
tail feathers that startled and then flared into a trembling fan. I looked at Sandro, wondering if he knew the
symbolic implication of the bird, and he smiled as if he
heard me.

My thoughts tripped over themselves as I corrected myself, of course he would know. Botticelli was a master artist who knew the precise identity and significance of every flower and tree in his paintings. He had strategically placed the peacock up high as the perfect observer of a momentous rebirth.

A beaming Sandro took my hand with authority and led me past the roused peacock, and we exited a stage door into the hot sunshine of Florence.

"There are only two sides to one coin," he said.

The sounds and smells of animals assaulted my senses in a delightfully-familiar way. No-one seemed to notice that I was dressed in strange clothing.

I now wore one of my favorite outfits from an old snapshot I was especially proud of: an olive-green, knitted crepe miniskirt and matching clingy stretch-silk top. Sheer taupe pantyhose and high-heeled sandals completed my costume. I was thirty-five again, back to a dainty size-six dress. Gone were my long skirt with its elastic waste-band and my sensible shoes. I became more aware that my brunette persona had revived and displaced the arthritic pains in my joints, and I kicked off my silver shoes feeling joyously free, eager to walk wherever I was being taken.

Sandro stopped and let go of my hand, then walked away with me gazing after him like a puppy learning to stay while my master tested me. Naturally, I followed disobediently until he'd teased me enough. Perhaps I had done what was expected and passed.

Sandro winked at me, and I ran into his arms. I felt like I was home inside his embrace. He laughed gently and the sound resonated within my body like a comforting echo. I surrendered. I felt the heady lack of separation from another – I was part of Botticelli and he had supplanted any sense I once harboured of being alone.

He took both my hands, grinning madly, and swung me in centre of the Piazza Signoria. There was nothing left to do but kiss. It felt like the sealing of a contract.

The year 2013 had disappeared without a trace, and I wasn't looking for the way back. I was young. I was in control of my legs. I didn't care about the rest.

"I have waiting ... *scusi*, been waiting for you," Sandro said in broken English. "Where you have been?"

I flinched at his pick up line. If he'd added 'all my life' it would have been farce, but he didn't and it wasn't.

Then he uttered an endearment, and I was his willing prisoner.

"*Mia carissima,*" he said, and pulled me into a bear hug, repeating the name *cara* over and over into my hair. He had to keep me from swooning to the ground. Sandro carried me past a fountain, and like a giddy bridegroom, he whirled me around.

I reached up and held his laughing face between my hands and kissed him deeply for what seemed like an hour. He kissed back for a couple more.

I took a moment to congratulate my powers of imagination.

He read my thoughts.

"It is real," he said, "and it's about time, *si?*"

I was thinking it was more about three glasses of champagne on jet lag, but "*Si*" was all I managed to reply.

He took off at a run again. "Come," he shouted over his shoulder. "You must make the wish with *Il Porcellino.* It is most *importante.*"

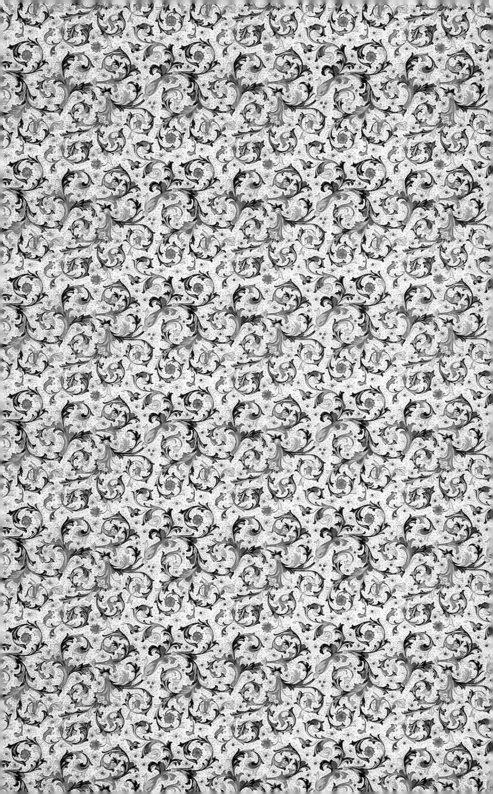

LOVE

Love is a breach in the walls, a broken gate,
Where that comes in that shall not go again;
Love sells the proud heart's citadel to Fate.
They have known shame, who love unloved. Even then,
When two mouths, thirsty each for each, find slaking,
And agony's forgot, and hushed the crying
Of credulous hearts, in heaven -- such are but taking
Their own poor dreams within their arms, and lying
Each in his lonely night, each with a ghost.
Some share that night. But they know love grows colder,
Grows false and dull, that was sweet lies at most.
Astonishment is no more in hand or shoulder,
But darkens, and dies out from kiss to kiss.
All this is love; and all love is but this.

~ Rupert Brooke

THE DIVINE COMEDY

"ma gia volgena il mio disio e'l velle
si come rota ch'igualmente e mossa,
l'amor che muove il sole e l'altre stelle"

"as a wheel turns smoothly, free from jars,
my will and my desire were turned by love,
The love that moves the sun
and the other stars"

~ Dante Alighieri, *The Paradiso* c. 1310

me-wolf

Florence ~ 1480

The streets of fifteenth-century Florence throbbed with life as Sandro Botticelli teased me with his blue-eyes and continued to run, pausing long enough for me to follow, knowing I was assessing his every animal move, tracking him like a she-wolf in my bare feet.

He scuffed his soft doeskin boots into the dust and I shouldered my purse pounding after him through the residue of mice, and the filth and dried effluvium adrift from the last rain, holding my strapless high heels that would never do in terrain such as this.

Sandro's cloak slipped around corners, disappeared down alleyways and under arches, dodging carts and street vendors, and I worried I'd lost him but even his cold trail held a vibration I could follow. I had forged a dowsing rod calibrated to this man, having loved him passionately for forty-six years, ever since I was a besotted eighteen-year-old art student in the National Gallery.

I stalked the lovely alpha-male with my newly-restored legs, exposed once more in shapely stockings under a miniskirt, eschewing the conventions of women's quattrocento fashion: overwhelmed with petticoats and corsets lined with bone, and their tresses braided into Celtic knots pulled tight enough to serve as face-lifts.

My long dark hair striped with gold swung in a casual ponytail as I experienced the returned delight of being a lithe young thing enfolded in soft clingy jersey.

The Tuscan sun felt cruel enough to bleach my hair in a matter of blocks, and I felt as if it may be turning a tawny 'Simonetta blonde' by the time the first vestiges of the market appeared past the Strozzi Palace. Perhaps this was Sandro's doing. A whim perhaps of his preference for fair beauty. Whatever it was, it did nothing to dispel my regard for him.

Sandro bowed and pointed to the familiar bronze statue of the city's mascot, the market's famous wishing-pig, and walked backwards watching me. I understood, and heard the statue give a contented metallic grunt as I rubbed its nose. Sandro nodded his approval and turned away again, increasing his pace, back the way we came, checking my progress with obvious delight.

I knew he craved attention because it was well-documented that he'd been a great tease in the studio. Now, I believed it. Those eyes said a lot more than *amuse me*; they entreated *'life is short; let's play.'* He was playing with me, now.

"Wait!" I shouted.

"*Signorina*, I have been waiting for years, now it is your turn," he called back, grinning as he continued his game.

"But, why? Why do you want to torture me?" I called after him.

At that, he stopped and turned to stare at me over his shoulder. He hesitated, and being his shadow, I stopped and stood my ground when I could easily have closed the distance between us.

He strolled towards me, appraising me, and when he was within a few yards, he stopped and winked. It was an invitation, like I needed one, but I refused. He seemed to be mocking me for pleasure.

"*Principessa*," he cajoled, in the well-rehearsed tones of an experienced seducer.

"Beast," I shouted, ready to abandon the chase and turn tail. "I understand. You have not forgiven me. Fine, I deserve that, but it's over. I made a mistake. You think it's been easy for me?"

"Come. I am still waiting. I no torture. It is enough, now, yes? I forgive."

I wanted no more of the charade. The door to the painting wasn't far, and I determined to engage what I hoped remained of my internal homing device tuned to what was most probably, now, 2014.

There was a long pause, and then Sandro laughed and held open his arms and walked towards me. But it was too late, and my deep-seated mistrust of men overruled his charm. For me, the bizarre game was over, but it was polite to let him know he'd lost.

I turned my back on him and began to double-back but his next words made me face him once more.

"*Per favore,*" he called softly. "*Io t'amo, mio tesoro, ti adoro.* Please *mia carissima.*"

His words arrived like heat. They paralyzed me before releasing me, shaken and breathless. An ensuing dizziness flooded me with overlapping memories that flapped like bright wings: Florence. Art. Rain. Death. Betrayal.

Sandro took a step closer and his eyes grew serious as he repeated his words of endearment in English: "my love, my treasure, I adore you."

It was his eyes. His gaze was a bright door that held the hope of the world. Undisguised adoration shone there, and I allowed it to approach like a forgotten dream that I had to hold at arm's length to remember. Suddenly, I wanted his teasing mouth, and his heartbeat, and to inhale the beloved musk I remembered clinging to his skin, and I knew him so utterly as to miss him, desperately.

The electrified madness between us telegraphed an ignitable message. Separation was palpable misery but I wanted to endure it longer, so I held him off. It was important to prolong it. We had been apart too long, but the bliss of reunion demanded its price in suffering.

His voice pleaded in a whisper, "*mia carrisima*. Please, I beg you, no more torture."

If Sandro hadn't closed his eyes to wish, we may still be there, waiting to be pushed together by a stranger.

I ran into his arms to be consumed by lightning. My master abductor kissed my face repeatedly and we trembled into each other until it felt safe for me to believe. Then, he gently pulled the hair elastic from my dark brown ponytail. It fell loose, still striped with gold, shoulder length, the way Botticelli loved his painted boys to look. After that, we sleepwalked most of the way home. We paused at every corner to refresh our passion and reached Sandro's rooms at a run. Tigers in the frenzy of mindful loving, we clawed our way to bliss.

Sandro was not overly gentle. His eyes had reflected truth, and I was enthralled with the return of my young body. I inhaled his Italian words and became lightheaded on the chemical language of love.

I SING THE BODY ELECTRIC

"Limitless limpid jets of love
Hot and enormous, quivering jelly of love,
White-blow and delirious juice,
Bridegroom night of love working surely
And softly into the prostrate dawn,
Undulating into the willing and yielding day,
Lost in the cleave of the clasping
And sweet-flesh'd day."
~ Walt Whitman

casper

Florence ~ 1480

Florence echoed with the blows of hammers on stone and the mad braying of traumatized donkeys. Marble dust mixed with shouted orders filled the air. It was a time of construction overload. Scaffolds covered the buildings like vines, and stone blocks and bags of sand were heaped on every corner. Men sweated into their cathedral repairs and the raising of palatial addresses for the rich, who, according to my history books, were not yet as high-profile as they were going to be.

Somewhere, the head of Michelangelo's 'David' strained to watch us over a studio wall where chisels sang with more love than could be expected twixt artist and subject.

I was reminded of Ovid's Pygmalion. The Greek myth where the besotted sculptor, Pygmalion, falls in love with his marble creation of Galatea who emerges from stone to life after his pleas to Venus. Another reminder to me of a fantasy where art wins out over reality.

Our love gibberish was as inane as any two humans urging each other to jump from a burning building. Still, the warm breathlings of double suicide murmured at the ledge were wonderful, and I remembered the lyrics from a love song: *I'm oh so glad we met, the second time around.*

I woke in a glorious nest of rumpled pillows, and savoured the morning and the wild sheets crushed with lovemaking. I closed my eyes, craving musty wine for breakfast, served in a heavy goblet of Venetian ruby glass.

My hair felt shamelessly dishevelled, and there were no mirrors to persuade me I was not thirty-something with flawless skin, and so I languished as would any self-respecting Scheherazade waiting for her master.

Sandro had gone to buy apples and bread while I delighted in the fresh sounds of Florentine horses that trotted out expectations of the enchantments ahead.

Moments after he left, a white cat ran up the stairs and leapt onto the bed, as casual as you please.

"Well, hello. Where did you spring from?" I said, smoothing a place for her next to me. I was delighted. "Is this your house?"

The realization of being in the presence of a fifteenth-century cat stunned me. She chirped a casual hello and stared at me with blasé acceptance, blinked her blue eyes once without fear or curiosity and circled her chosen spot a few times before flopping into a nesting pose. She arranged her tail neatly around her body and groomed her fur which suggested she was home after a night on the prowl, preparing to stay.

I watched her claim her space. "Do you live here? Aren't you a lovely girl," I said in a continuous croon of human nonsense.

I was in a benevolent mood, so thoughts of fur teeming with an unbridled selection of parasites never occurred. Such thoughts seemed unworthy for a first morning. Accepting fifteenth-century Florence fully-sentient would eventually introduce the organic realities of living in a city lacking sterile water, pest control, and indoor plumbing.

I scanned the room for some food to give her but thought again. This was not an era when cats would have been fed. They hunted their own food which had to be plentiful in a city overrun with unchecked vermin, and presumably, rarely allowed shelter on someone's bed.

I shuddered to think of rats and plague, and appreciated how a cat would be an asset in a place swarming with rodents, and if this wasn't Sandro's cat, it was certainly domesticated.

Cats roamed free here, and were, for the most part, feral. They were certainly not spayed and pampered and sweet-smelling as mine, but this one was clearly used to human affection with a well-advanced attitude of superiority. I was elated to have such a familiar touchstone for companionship.

I lay, savouring my new age of vitality. My century knows a woman may still be a tender nymph at thirty-five, but I had certainly forgotten. Somewhere, I still felt like an old dog breaking all the rules, barking up winter trees at wrong-time bears. Love had sloughed my years like a second skin, and happily, I discovered how much more satisfying sexual passion was than when I used to drift towards the fantasy of it in my sleep.

The world may no longer be my oyster but my dreams are, and since I've already dreamed half my life away, for act three, I intend to dream big enough to light my way past bread-and-butter physics.

'Beyond this place there be pearls' – what better map could there be than one marked with such a promise?

I had won. I had broken the *Thorn Bird* curse and my resistance to being loved.

Enter Sandro Botticelli – my very own Ralph de Bricassart, my 'chamberlain' ... my Sandro.

"Room after room,
I hunt the house through
We inhabit together.
Heart, fear nothing,
For, heart, thou shalt find her
Next time, herself
Not the trouble behind her
Left in the curtain
Or the couch's perfume."
~ Robert Browning

the second time around

A street noise awakened me. I think it was the sounds of a brawl because I heard broken glass and human voices stumbling about in the dark.

Lying awake in a foreign bed is a fine place to do some wool-gathering. I breathed fifteenth-century air and was reclining on fifteenth-century linens. An affectionate fifteenth-century body was warming the right side of mine, and not just anybody, but a master painter who lived simply with a great affinity for art and beauty, and me.

Florence gave me writing space and the carefree permission to dream an alternate future. The vast contents of my carry-on flight bag provided several pens and my diary's empty house of rooms, a toothbrush and paste, painkiller gel caps, deodorant, shampoo and soap, and *White Shoulders* cologne. In fact, I was well prepared with enough writing supplies and toiletries to serve a month of Sundays.

There were mornings I arose early from homesickness to stare at the foldout section of snapshots in my wallet in order to stay connected with a time that could no longer technically be called my past. I said hello to the image of Sophie, captured in her small window, and marveled at the substance of time and how far affection carried across the endless years of inner space.

I needed to document the incidents which indisputably led me here – back, forwards, and retrograde, traveling by sling-shot to the dark side of the moon to arrive in the brilliant Tuscan sunshine of 1476.

A few days ago I would have dawdled to the kettle and brewed a pot of tea, pressed the switches for light and heat, and the fridge would have offered me fresh milk, but I had not been loved.

I ran my hands over Sandro's back to confirm my present good fortune. I spooned him and he reached for my hand and drew it towards his lips and kept hold of it, content to cuddle it under his chin like a child with a teddy bear.

With the shutters open, a thin murk of soupy light lifted the black shapes in the room to grey. The most wonderful of these was a pair of wooden wings suspended from the ceiling like a mobile – a prop from one of the many theatricals Sandro had designed. The gold paint drew the light over the contours of its carved feathers. They swayed slightly, hovering over us like a giant protective bird.

The profiles of chairs and table and domestic objects slowly materialized. The outlines of a copper bowl and the lip of the pewter water jug draped with a slip of gauze became visible, a still-life painting in chiaroscuro, emerging slowly like an old Polaroid image.

Shadows of Florence fluttered across the ceiling as the breeze lifted the folds of Sandro's cloak hanging by the door. Sounds of wooden wheels creaking over cobbles and dogs barking drifted up from the streets.

Sandro rolled onto his back and flung his arm wide, and I gently urged him back onto his side. He smiled in his dream, and I curled myself into him, allowing his body to cradle the whole of me.

The campanile bells rang in sonorous tones, reverberating around the walls and inside my head, sending the last shadows of night, north to Fiesole. Sandro heard them in his sleep and startled but slept on the moment they stopped. For me, it was as if I was inside the bell-tower, itself. My bones vibrated with each peal, and my heart beat faster knowing the cathedral of *Santa Maria del Fiore* was a few blocks away with its new dome barely stained by time.

The duomo connected me to Little Cobiton and St. Mary's church, and as the ghosts of bells echoed around the room, I was left empty and queasy with homesickness.

I felt locked inside a time capsule, in the surreal position of being able to study a fifteenth-century wasp, now buzzing around the lip of a dirty wine glass, and suddenly the innocent hills and valleys that appeared in the bed's rumpled sheets felt like an ominous landscape. The sound of the wasp made me wish for my English garden.

I dismissed the passing thought that if I swatted it, its premature demise might alter time and everything I knew to be true, abandoned somewhere in front of the *Adoration*.

I panicked at the thought of being trapped in the purgatory of a museum diorama surrounded by the glass walls of an ancient city where I was a vulnerable foreigner. I was terrified of the next hour, and the perils of plague and poison, and living another day feeling deliriously free one moment and trapped in dangerous amber the next.

I tried to ignore the malevolent whisperings that tried to intrude – the hisses of the faces in the ceiling cracks and the mystery-lumps of unfamiliar furniture fighting their way out of the dark, and as I watched the morning come, it was hard to breathe.

Ironically, my sanity rested twinned with the life-force of the man beside me who I knew had been dead five-hundred years.

I felt Sophie jump on the bed and although I couldn't see her, I knew she was there in spirit and a sense of normalcy warmed my blood.

She was back home waiting for me. As always, we were connected, and one controlled breath after another brought me home within my own skin, as Sophie gave me leave to experience joy.

She reported her day. "I am waiting," she said. "Everything is in order. Budge is overly generous with the sardines although she uses the wrong dish. Isn't life splendid? and please don't answer."

She wished me as happy a time as she was having. "I'm sending you a friend of mine," she said, "so keep breathing."

I was comforted. Sophie still led me to higher ground. It was all good. I felt the weight of her nestle behind my knees, and was content to know she had my back.

I was able to throw off the darker shadows of my past, and lay in the arms of Botticelli where I felt, strangely, at home.

*"Love insists
the loved, loves back"*
~ Dante Alighieri

adoration of the magic

Sandro reluctantly allowed me wash his hair with my fancy shampoo and conditioner to please me. His reaction was mixed.

"Thank you *cara* for my feelings of clean, but I am smelling now like almonds. I am a new friendship of the wasps and bees," he said, pouring fresh cold water into a basin. He splashed it over his face and recoiled when I handed him my bar of perfumed soap.

"*Cara*, please no more of the smellings."

"I hope you like cats," I said. "One came in yesterday after you left, so I let her stay."

"Yes, I leave the door for her. You say you like, so..."

"Oh. So, she's not yours, then? She seemed to know her way around."

"She is cat. She owns the world, no?"

"I'd like to keep her."

"Non. That is... I mean *il gatto,* she belongs to the street," he said. "She comes and goes."

"Does she have a name?"

"Yes, after you give."

I didn't care about the skyline of Florence or the Santa Maria del Fiore's new red tiles nor its golden orb, the campanile, the giant statue of David, or any of the dozens of other landmarks I knew so well. Neither did I try to reconcile the date with Sandro's apparent age or any timeline of logic. It was now. It was Florence. And I was besotted with a man who was clearly in love with me.

The air was delightfully warm and smelled like a lemon grove. That's about all I could register. I was busy studying the gold braid on Botticelli's orange sleeve and his long tanned fingers with their slight stain of blue paint under the fingernails.

It had pleased me that he was considerably taller than his portrait implied, but then, perspective was not his finest point. The top of my head reached slightly below Sandro's chin, so I reckoned he was six-foot tall.

We fit. Perfect nuzzling height: his chest, my neck; my knee between his legs, his right leg encircling my left; arms locked waist-to-shoulder; erogenous belly-to-solar plexus. Tongue and breath, muscle to muscle, fingers entwined in each others' hair. Bound together like clockwork performing a slow ballet of sexual tension as we danced even while standing still. Time marched forwards and backwards and sideways spilling us into whatever illusion it cared to explore through our senses.

The world swam in honey. I gave in to the timbre of Sandro's voice when he spoke his slow, hypnotic Italian, which I had no way of completely understanding.

Body language perfectly expressed the intimacy we shared. It seemed as if we'd known each other for a long time because I understood the secrets of his body, and he knew everything about mine. There was never any ripping or shredding of clothes, only slow sensual dis-robings, one garment after another.

He was tender yet aggressive, and moved over me slowly with experienced calculation, but he was more than an accomplished lover; he was intuitive and instinc-tive, listening and responding to my thoughts. His pres-ence of mind and skill captured my attention. I had felt this once before, years ago with the Florentine angel, feeling so entirely adored.

Beyond our window, Florence could have burned to the ground and we wouldn't have noticed.

Afterwards, he wouldn't let me go. "No, *non ti muo-vere*, stay right here," he said drowsily when I started to rise. "I need you to stay."

"I wasn't going anywhere," I said.

"Across the room is too far."

He enfolded me in his arms, and as he slept I surveyed the room again, free of fear.

Sandro's rooms were the quintessential bachelor pad of the quattrocento. Painted screens hung slack beside the open window. Clothes hung from pegs. A candlestick was sealed to a squat central table in a sea of hardened beeswax. His bed was raised on a high box plinth used for storage.

The sound of bellowing oxen and creaking wheels reached through the window, and I didn't want to close my eyes. Some spells required one's full attention in order to hold. I wanted to imprint everything in my mind, but I gave up on the decor and gazed at Sandro instead.

If you've ever seen Botticelli's painting of the sleeping Mars, you will understand how my experience of watching Sandro's draped form slumbering on sheets was even more enticing. I started to believe in Roman gods. I drew his contours with my eyes to remember every muscle and curve and eyelash.

Lucid dreaming had never been as vivid as this. I half-expected a few fauns to appear around the bed, and was thrilled they did not.

I wished I had a camera to capture my lover's arms and chest and profile, his titian hair, his heavy eyelids, the slight cleft in his chin, and the curve of his lips in repose. His hair, curled damp from lovemaking, formed whorls on his brow and an odd spiral of strands waved into wisps with the hot air that blew across our bodies from the open window.

The white cat strolled in, leapt to the table and blinked at me with a slight look of dismay. I wanted to think she was Sophie's friend, and I appropriated a line from Dickens, deliberately misquoting: "Are you the friend who was foretold to me?"

I was working on a name for her. It had to be perfect. This ethereal creature that appeared at odd times and like a ghost, silently left as quickly as she came.

The cat blinked again, jumped to the floor, and streaked out the door.

I chided myself against any future fault-finding and breathed in the pungent odors of love exuding from Sandro's skin. "What next?" I asked the empty place where the shade of Sophie had been.

I pulled Sandro's cloak around me, moved to the window, and leaned against the shutter. The wood was cool against my cheek. I was here. This shutter was real. I could see the blistered blue paint and the green colour beneath it. I released a flake of blue with my fingernail and it landed on the orange of the cloak. It sat there, a speck of one colour against another and everything made sense.

The sun rose over the Ponte alla Carraia bridge, and I turned to glance back at the bed and suddenly the distance between my body and Sandro's was unbearable.

I crept beside him and warmed against his back. He responded to my cold skin and turned to enfold me in his arms, kissing me in his sleep.

I stayed awake, drinking in my lover's breath, watching his chest rise and fall, the rapid throb of a vein in the hollow of his collarbone timing us.

I thought I heard someone calling from outside the door but I didn't heed them. My thoughts were scattered like the night to the lemon winds of Fiesole.

Sandro Botticelli had said he wanted me to stay.

*"No sadness
is greater than in misery
to rehearse memories of joy"*
~ Dante Alighieri

nine to five-hundred

Breakfast in bed every morning was like the first: wine and bread and a handful of blue grapes, but this time the white cat had slept at our feet all night.

Sandro poured spiced wine and produced a delicate leather collar from his sleeve. "It is for a ferret, made, but I am thinking it will do for your *speciale* friend."

"I've named her Casper," I announced, "even though it's a boy's name. It's the name of a friendly ghost-child in my century. She's white as a ghost and she appears and disappears *in spirito*."

"I think you always are thinking of the *Adoration*," Sandro said, slipping the collar over Casper's head. "Casper was the name of one of the magi."

He brushed my hair and kissed the exposed nape of my neck. "*Mia carissima*, you will see my studio now?" he said, trailing a grape across my bare arm and shoulder and up into my mouth.

"What will your employ ... your apprentices say? What about your business? I don't want to disrupt your day," I said, hoping he would disagree.

He smiled at that. "It is easy to be arranged, yes? There is no-one there today, so if it would please, then we go."

"It would," I answered, a little dizzy from the early wine. "Are you sure?"

"Making your life this ... *perfetto*... it is *la mia cosa favorita*... my first thing," he announced, and lifted his glass in a toast. *"Il mio primo amore."*

"Priority," I corrected, "although I like your thought better."

"I have excitement to do this," he said, his eyes gleaming with anticipation.

Then, he braided my hair.

It was midday when we left our rooms for the sun and walked the length of the Via Ghibelina arm in arm towards the studio. Sandro wore a blue cloak of thin cotton, wrapped like a toga. The colour increased the volume of blue in his eyes, afire like sapphires.

My clothes had been replaced with a soft shift of green cotton the same colour as my old mini skirt, a long coral belt woven from straw, and flat sandals. I looked and felt like a young housewife.

We passed a slender young man in a hurry. He was stunningly beautiful with his fine features, grey eyes, shoulder-length brown hair, and immaculate rose tunic; one of the tidiest young men I had seen.

"*Buongiorno*," he said, "*come si va?*"

His warm smile took me in as he kept on his way.

"*Buongiorno*," Sandro called back over his shoulder, "it goes well, *si va bene.*"

I glanced at Sandro who was smiling to himself looking well-pleased. He lifted his eyebrows in a tease and tapped my nose with his finger.

"You like the surprise?"

I bit my tongue. There were many times when I wanted to respond with sarcasm but what followed was usually a long convoluted explanation. Our sense of humor rapport was slightly out of sync but Sandro and I were learning our own shorthand. Happily, kissing seemed to breach the language barrier enough to prove highly educational. Sandro could kiss. His lips in the portrait had promised so and they spoke the truth.

It had been a casual greeting in passing on a busy street with no time to stop for introductions. No need. Leonardo da Vinci had hurried past us, his words cut short from someone on a mission.

"We will see him again," Sandro said, squeezing my arm.

"Yes," I replied offhandedly, belaying my urge to babble about Leonardo like an art history professor.

Leonardo, circa 1470, age eighteen, was a favorite topic of discussion with my students, and for a moment, remembering them caused me physical pain.

I wondered if I may be a dreamer projecting multiple images or if Sandro was indulging my whims for his amusement.

It was unnerving when time seemed to read my mind. Dates streamed in fluid anomalies. Technically, Sandro should always be seven years older that Leonardo.

I seemed to be pre-selecting the events I wanted to see. Sandro and I remained stable, both of us thirty-five, even though he had painted the *Adoration* in 1475, at the age of thirty. I had already noted the cathedral dome of *Santa Maria del Fiore* fluctuated with various stages of construction. Today, its orb and cross were in place.

My pulse raced erratically enough for Sandro to notice, and I had to stop and gasp a few wild breaths until he asked if I was unwell. Strangely, the anxiety attack I was experiencing should have reassured me that Florence and Sandro were real, but all I felt was the sudden need to be home with Sophie and Simkin.

Sandro was worried. He sat me in the shade by the market fountain and held my hand.

"*Mia carissima*, it is soon. I understand it is much more for you. We will take slower things, yes?"

I nodded weakly.

"But, Leonardo..." I started to say and fell apart.

Through a break in a swarm of people and horses, I noticed an old man watching us. I sniffed and wiped my eyes, and looked again but he was gone. Still, his presence had stopped my outburst and proved someone other than Sandro saw me as I was.

Displaying emotions in public obviously didn't warrant a second glance. Most hours, the market was deafening from bargaining and arguing and people flailing
their arms. It was hard to separate the sounds of angry
voices from the ones overexcited from joy.

Sandro calmly wiped my tears on his cloak and sat
protectively with his arms around me until my weight
relaxed into his shoulder.

"We can go now. Home."

"Home?"

"I take."

"No," I said "please let's not spoil the day. I want to
experience real things: your studio, a painting, donkeys,
anything I can touch." I clutched the fabric of his cloak
and held it to my face. "Like this." I plunged my fingers
into the stream flowing from the fountain, "and this
water," I said, and I started to reel off solid materials:
"bricks, wood, glass, wool ..."

"And apples," he interrupted, "for later."

~

We bought apples from the old man I'd seen earlier. He
had a stall in the market piazza beside the statue of Il
Porcellino, and in the process of negotiating there was
an emotional exchange of words. Again, it wasn't clear if
Sandro was pleased or angry, but their manner seemed
more animated than the price of apples could warrant.
The man nodded vigorously and seemed agitated.

"He wants you touch the pig and wish a thing," Sandro explained. "To rub its nose."

"Please tell him I've done this," I said, smiling at the grizzled head hunched over his wares. "You had me do that on my first day."

"He says it is for him. His wish is to see you grace the piazza again. Please *cara*. He is, Melazio, an *especialle...* friend of mine."

I gave the man another smile and made an exaggerated display of rubbing the statue's bronze nose, not yet worn to brassy gold from unchecked superstition, and then took Melazio's hand which shook with palsy.

"I will see you again, Melazio," I said, patting his hand several times, and his old eyes filled with tears.

"That is my wish, also," he called after us.

"Melazio is your friend?" I asked as we walked on.

"He is an outcast, a religious fanatic bitten by sin. Let's just say, I understand him."

Being handed an apple by a wizened old man reminded me of a fairytale, and I thought it would amuse Sandro and lighten the encounter with Melazio if I told a story from my childhood.

So, I related the story of *Snow White and the Seven Dwarfs* and the poisoned apple, describing how the witchy side of the apple was a curse, and watched as Sandro's expression became increasingly confused.

"The red side," he answered. "That is the sweetest part. It would hide the taste of poison."

"No, no, a *witch*, a woman with *magico* powers. It was not a question," I replied.

"This Snow White. She is a *principessa*, yes?" he asked.

"Yes, and the apple-seller was a witch." I demonstrated with one of our apples. "This, *uno* side of the apple was poison. This other side was safe."

"*Questa parte*, this one side," Sandro said.

"Sorry?"

"The apple is a female, yes? So you say *una*.

I faced the reddest side towards him. "*This* side is poisoned."

Sandro nodded in agreement with a scowl on his face. "*Si*, the sinister side," he said.

"Yes, very." I replied, trying to look serious.

"But this poison? It did not kill?"

I gave Sandro my best grin and he pulled me into a long kiss which disoriented me so much my brain sent me a mixed message confusing Snow White with Sleeping Beauty. "She slept for one-hundred years until a prince woke her with a kiss," I said.

"Are you sure it was not the prince who slept for *five*-hundred?" he added.

"As sure as apples are female," I replied.

I gained another smother of kisses for my story.

"And now you are waking?" he asked, and I felt a chill as a cloud passed over the sun. Sandro noticed me shudder and drew me under his cloak with a reassuring kiss although he looked at the sky and continued to frown.

Five minutes or five-hundred years. We existed inside a glass prism of refracted images where a single point in time split into a spectrum of random experiences.

I finished most of my apple and stopped to share it with a donkey laden with bags of terracotta bricks.

I longed for the creature with its passive far-away eyes to be free. It's plight made me offer it another whole apple that it eagerly took from me and crunched happily.

⁓

The enormous key Sandro pulled from his pocket looked big enough to open the gates of heaven. He shouldered open the heavy door on the corner of the Via Ognisannti and the Via Nuova, then gallantly entered the dark space ahead of me.

I automatically felt around for a light switch, and oddly, light *did* appear. Sandro had propped open a high window with a long stick, and the light picked up dust particles in the air which made the room seem like the inside of a snow globe.

The studio was a long wide space with a row of sturdy trestle tables in the centre and shelves lining one wall from floor to ceiling. A tall ladder leaned against the far wall. Pottery jars of paintbrushes stood on one shelf looking like exotic vases of dried flowers, while rows of scallop shells filled with brightly-coloured powder covered another table. Sheaves of paper and books and rolled parchments arranged in a grid of cubicles were housed beside a stack of portfolios. Sketches were scattered over another of the tables. I approached to look and glimpsed a young girl's face drawn in profile, wearing a stunning necklace. Sandro blocked me and brushed them aside, but not before I caught fleeting images of a familiar face.

"Simonetta?" I said in a strained voice.

"She is not you," he said sweeping the drawings to the floor.

"No kidding."

He blushed and looked uncomfortably towards the ceiling. "No, no, I mean, not my love. Everyone thinks this... but she is nothing. She is the snow *principessa,* yes? *Biancaneve.* Signorina Snow White. She sleeps, like the Snow White, as dead, but real."

I smiled and turned away speaking towards the opposite wall. "Snow White was a bit of a pill, actually. They all were," I said, faking indifference.

Naturally, he drew a complete blank. "Pill?"

"You know, princesses," I said pointing to a different sketch of a haughty girl covered in jewels.

He sighed in recognition. "Ah, yes, a favourite *principessa* of her father."

"In my time it means more than lovely or favoured. More of a brat."

He shrugged. "A brat?"

"A manipulative little..." I searched my mind for an example he would know. "Ginevra de Benci," I blurted. "A rich girl who wants her own way all the time or she goes..." I searched for the Italian word for crazy. "*Pazzo*."

Sandro grinned and shook his head at the mention of Ginevra, a young noblewoman known for her tantrums. "Yes, this is also Simonetta. She is too-praised. This ruined her... eh, style."

"Good news for *me*, then," I said.

"And she is dead one year," he added, no doubt trying to be helpful.

I gave him a hard stare. Dead. That was a real thing. He should be dead. Maybe I was too, and my overwhelming sensations of jealousy felt embarrassingly high school.

Something Sandro said registered in my brain, and I recalled that the year of Simonetta's death was 1477, which reminded me our years here, were erratic.

"Well, she's only dead *today*," I said with my arms folded. "Who knows about tomorrow. She could be in the market buying apples."

Sandro grinned and chucked his finger under my chin. "*Mia carissima*, she was *aveva freddo*. Cold inside, yes? A cold heart. That is why I say spoiled snow *principessa*. Snow is *é fredda*."

"You're spoiling *me*," I said. "So, does that mean..."

Sandro shushed me with a savage kiss that brought the coppery taste of blood from my bottom lip into my mouth.

"*Bella mia*. You are mine. My love. *Mio amore*. This is all. You understand?"

And the newly-cleared table became the perfect place to prove that I did.

⌒

I investigated every corner of the studio like a magpie while Sandro sketched me. Every stylus and mechanical instrument, every jar of minerals and pot of ground pigment was a major discovery, and when I asked if I could watch him paint something I might know, he showed me to a recess where *The Primavera* was propped on an easel, incomplete.

I grew weary of our elastic calendar. The unfinished *Primavera* meant the year had to be close to 1483. I had to stop calculating. The fifteenth-century was apparently a hologram able to be witnessed from a thousand simultaneous perspectives. I could only assume there was a good reason why Sandro and I remained the age we had chosen for ourselves.

I stood before the painting and he came up behind me and encircled me with his arms, leaning his chin upon my head. He took my right hand in his, and I surrendered to him as he guided my hand, and together, we painted a flower in the goddess's dress. I felt like the cunning priestess, Nimue, robbing Merlin of his powers as Sandro offered up his secret techniques.

He put down the brush and left it to soak before he turned me in his arms and breathing words of love into my skin, half-chewed my flesh like a young lion.

The world outside receded into the backdrop of a mural which I guessed we could probably alter at will: cuing the wind and rain, and rearranging the stars. Day might turn to dusk with a thought, and donkeys could be set free throughout the city with baskets of apples at their feet.

One morning, while walking alone, I saw Melazio observing me from behind the statue of *David,* in the Piazza della Signoria. He stood shading his eyes, and I waved a hello. He appeared startled but raised his hand in recognition and disappeared into the mass of faces I loved to study. He was far from his usual turf, in the vicinity of Il Porcellino, but it made me feel more at home to know I knew some Florentines on a first name basis.

I always looked for him, when Sandro and I passed through the market, as we often did, commenting to Sandro when Melazio was absent, hoping he was not unwell or had perhaps, died, suggesting we visit him and take him some soup and bread.

"Melazio can't live on apples alone," I said.

"He is old," came Sandro's reply. "I have known him very long. He is shy. He moves around and I know this, he likes to be privacy. It is not *normale* for him to have made so many contacts with you. He knows me well, but he is rarely expressing himself as many times as with you."

"I see him a lot," I replied, "and he waves to me."

Sandro looked uncomfortable; he even sounded a little jealous. "There are others, why this *fascino* – this fascination with him?"

"Because I was old too and I know what it feels like, and he is your *speciale* friend," I said. "Does he live close by? We should invite him for supper."

"I know of where Melazio lives but never impose on his time. This is the friendship between us," Sandro said, and that was the matter, closed.

*"The problems of the world
cannot possibly be solved by skeptics or cynics
whose horizons are limited by the obvious realities.
We need men who can dream
of things that never were."*
~ John Keats

critical mass

We visited the church of Santa Maria Novella to view the *Adoration* in situ, while Sandro complained. "It is too high." He tipped his head sideways for a different perspective. "I tell. They do not listen."

I followed his lead and did the same. "I am more bothered that it appears in three places in the city at the same time," I said. "This church, your studio, and in the gallery that has yet to be built. I can still see the Uffizi superimposed over the present buildings."

Sandro ignored me and indicated a faint mark two feet lower on the wall and sighed. "This is where. I make this to show."

I dismissed his complaints. "The *Adoration* is still in your studio, so how can it be here?"

"This is my truth, is why."

I crossed my arms in a no-nonsense pose. "And what about mine?"

"Everything is sacred," he said, standing back, scowling at his painting as far outside the chapel as he could.

The chill of the stone church made me yearn for sunshine and I paced to keep warm. "Nothing is sacred," I replied, cupping my hands over my mouth and nose.

Sandro stared at me as if suddenly noticing I was there. "You are cold. We can go."

"We are living in a safety bubble. A sphere made of air," I added, making a circle with my arms, "but just around you and me."

"If plague or poison or a dagger does not come, then it is safe," he said.

I stopped shivering and held a fold of his cloak over my nose so it would thaw. "There are poison pens and false ears everywhere," I said. "They kill, too."

Sandro shrugged and kissed my reddened nose. "We have to live by the moment and keep a fast horse," he said, grinning.

I wanted a better answer and repeated my question. "The *Adoration* is a bit of a floating door, sometimes there, sometimes elsewhere at the same time, yet it looks solid, here," I said. "It's magical, and in English, adoration of the magi translates to adoration of the wise, but you may as well call it the worship of magic. I guess what I really want to know is, can I still go back?"

Sandro pulled me into his cloak and gently bit my ear.

His mood had lightened considerably. "I think you must be to decide this, soon," he said. "We are this magic."

I'm not bragging when I declare I have alternative inter-pretations than the standard academic opinions with regards to art. My own litmus test is organic: cold facts translated by a transfusion of warm-blooded theories.

I had guessed Botticelli's *Adoration*, was too small to have been created by more than one hand. It had always felt pure Botticelli, and I had sensed a reluctance within its elite painted crowd of Florentines on what looked to me like a forced day-trip to Bethlehem. In my earliest teaching years, I was a harsh critic of its sentiment, even though the iconography was flawless.

The holy family, depicted elevated on a rock amongst classical Roman ruins, speaks of the Neo-Platonist's view of Christianity, while the peacock of rebirth perches above, watching the proceedings with its tail significantly closed.

One or two of the faces were magnificent. One literally, being a true portrait of Lorenzo Medici, *Il Magnifico*. The other members of the family were observed with similar attention to detail, and finally, the elite front row grouping of insolent-looking Medici teenagers, appeared distinctly indifferent, if not rudely dismissive of the holy event behind them. But the generic heads of the miscellaneous onlookers were rendered with a less-exacting brush, and those were the ones I found most arresting.

There is one obscure fellow to the left of the adoring crowd, who makes eye contact with the viewer. Since his eyes lock onto ours, his inclusion could not have been incidental, and I had suspected he was fitted into the crowd for some personal reason of Botticelli's. Whoever he was, his face always sent a shiver through my entrails. The only other logical reason, was that he usurped a generic profile who had been inserted at the insistence of the patron who also eyes us, looking suitably smug. Three faces looking from history with their own stories.

I knew commissioned artist must compromise for the sake of business, and over time, paintings hold their tongue, so I found the right time to inquire.

"Why not sign it," I said.

"I think you know why."

"I know you can't sign your *name*, but there are other ways."

"We have... discussing this together. My style is to be enough."

"We?"

"My brothers. The guild of us all."

I pointed to the *Adoration's* left-hand side in the far distant background. "Who are all those miniature extras? I don't understand them. I know the main players of clan Medici. And to the right, there, is your creepy patron, himself, a parvenu of false modesty. I understand why *he's* there, but if the distant ones hold no significance, they only serve to disrupt the balance of the composition."

Sandro brooded for a moment, started to speak, then stopped.

"To defend. I will tell you. I do not do this. It is not by me."

"So, then who?"

"I do not ask."

I changed the subject since Sandro looked vexed. "Your self portrait is true," I said. "But your eyes are more blue. And your hair is longer, now."

Sandro shifted his legs to a formal position. He looked like a professor about to impart serious knowledge, and I listened carefully. He pointed to the face that disturbed me. "That one is the catamite of this one," he said, tapping the face of his patron Gaspare di Zanobi del Lama on the right. "The scoundrel banker is here who ordered the painting. He cheated me, but he made me to be seen by the Medici. So, it is not very bad. I have made them the same level, yes? To show they are in relationship."

"That catamite is the one who gives me the jeebies," I said.

"I do not know jeebies, but he should make you very uncomfortable," he said.

In my classes, anonymous characters were the most fun to interpret. I had imagined slipping into the painted crowd scenes with waiver forms and a pen, thinking how time travelers to the fifteenth-century would be smart to finagle themselves into the paintings of the day.

It might sound like a case of 'curiosity killed the painting,' but it's really not; one never intensely studies the uninteresting. I pored over details for clues. I am a detective of art, mostly to discover its soft underbelly and learn more of its creator.

I celebrated Sandro's talent irrespective of his body and heart, regardless of my harsh critiques. His work is an amazing accomplishment which stands alone as his personal style, borrowed later from Flemish influences on his travels north, and carefully filtered through his talent. He was no Leonardo, but then Leonardo was no Michelangelo and Michelangelo was no Botticelli. Masters have nothing to defend.

I am passionate about art: I gave emotional lectures celebrating the slippery brilliance of Vincent's kaleidoscopic ultramarine nights with melting lemon stars, and his black crows circling whorls of golden wheat like vultures in a frenzy of punctuation marks; I extolled the muted tones of a Turner sky seemingly painted on blotting paper, and the fury of his roiling waters and ominous shadow-clouds backlit with Naples yellow, Gentian violet, and peach light; but I questioned the liquid dribblings of Pollock, and Matisse's floating wallpaper spangles with lurching shapes and brash couplings of colours that wake the senses with clashes of reds and greens, and blues and yellows; I object to the sludge of brown paintings; and I challenge the validity of blank canvasses sporting a few hard-edged stripes.

I push the lines of objective inquiry from the sublime to the ridiculous; from Raphael to Rothko where general ignorance is supplanted by bold thoughts that outshine those of precocious student parrots. I become the devil's advocate – the child whose voice rings out over the intimidated populace, effusing about an emperor wearing no clothes, and then reverse my position to find the joy of abstraction within pretentious works. Works levitating in the stratosphere of promotions by the elite of the art world at their personal discretion. Power always rules. Art is as it is. Valued beyond subjectivity as investments with outrageous price-tags.

I taught my students to be a fly on the wall. To travel in one's easiest chair and eavesdrop and stalk, and seek under stones for the truth as it might have been, as it may still be within the infinite possibilities of imagination.

I had to remind myself of history's controlled lies. Sacred, Botticelli had said, where all possibilities are true, but nothing is real.

Animated paintings have always been an extension of my imaginative critiques. I've courted art into becoming a personal meeting place. Iconography is a symbolic language of hidden messages sent from one brain to another. There is little separation between artist and their art, not as supernatural incidents but intellectual transferences – a form of empathic incommunicado.

I believe in the benefits of studying history using imaginative past-life regressions as academic exercises in order to pry and spy like an obsessed time-traveler. I've perfected the art of intuitive listening. I've honed my powers of extra-sensory perception and visualization by practising them regularly, and because mental acuity has long-since been the basis of how I tought art history, the places where reality and fantasy meet were encouraged.

I had studied most of the Master's works in order to 'read' them, and because documentation of the renaissance period is sketchy, I chose to expand the murky details with a spicy pen to make the art and artists come alive. Otherwise, it was a drone of statistics at best, to inspire a sea of hostile faces taking my art history class for an easy 'A.'

It was a thrill to hear once-imagined conversations and traipse the footsteps over a modern map of Florence, erase the new streets and railway stations, plant a few more trees, and air a few misconceptions.

"here is the deepest secret nobody knows
here is the root of the root and the bud of the bud
and the sky of the sky of a tree called life; which grows
higher than soul can hope or mind can hide
and this is the wonder that's keeping the stars apart"

~ e.e. cummings

boboli dreamin'

The scent of jasmine and roses was intoxicating. It blew in warm gusts drenched with sunshine and spices across the carpet of rows and squares of geometric colours.

Sandro and I climbed a sweep of green velvet, away from a narrow trail cut into the grass, strolling from one jeweled flowerbed to the next. Our footsteps connected the dozens of marble planters filled with sprays of lavender, thyme, and heartsease. Five-hundred years had barely altered the landscape I visited in 1984.

Gauzy white clouds rolled overhead, lazily turning into swans and galloping horses. We lay on the orange cloak, staring at the sky, tracking the flight of each bird that flitted its brief shadow across the sun, finding new shapes in the cumulous as they morphed in and out of various animals.

We spent the day on cloud time, listening to bees. Engrossed in each others' details – an angle, a curl, the simple curve of cheek or shoulder. We held hands and compared the lengths of our fingers and our lifelines.

We counted purple dragonflies and marvelled at the microcosms of patterns in leaves, and Sandro fell asleep with his head in my lap. The colour of his hair matched my gown of amber silk and I brushed it from his face, the face of Mars blissfully separate from fighting the day to day wars he had told me about.

"I have loneliness," he had said, "and now here we are."

I wore the dress of a fine lady, bodice cut low and square, worn with a surcoat of mauve velvet embroidered with seed pearls. I had said, just once I wanted to wander as a noblewoman and feel the heaviness of formal clothes but the outfit that had materialized was soft and light as summer gauze.

Sandro must have had a bad dream because he whimpered like a child and woke startled, babbling about sacred fire. He flailed in search of my hand.

"*Mia carissima?* You are here? *Salvami.* You will save me?"

"I will never leave you," I said.

I guessed he was referring to the future when he would sacrifice his art to the Bonfire of the Vanity's flames, and I shushed him with a white lie.

"There is no fire. You are safe," I said. "There will be no fire."

Even within our waking dream the world could intrude

from the things that had already been, but if we stayed here, my younger Sandro would never fall prey to the frenzied destruction of the Dominican friar Savonarola or his street army of boy spies who considered Sandro's paintings of masques and goddesses frivolous heresy.

Savonarola preached the sinful gaieties of the noble classes led straight to hell, and the burning of secular art was a warning taste of the everlasting flames to come if one failed to submit to a life of subdued decor and fervent prayer.

Dante had made the perils of hell clear to the point of paranoia, and Sandro had illustrated the worst of them. I knew the drawings well. So detailed that one had to study them with a magnifying glass to discover the expressions of the faces twisted with suffering.

Here in our garden of Eden, living outside of time, there could be no sacrificial fire and no guilty surrender of artistic martyrdom. It was another Sandro, a later Sandro who would go on to paint madonnas to appease a religious zealot.

None of this should tarnish the silver day, so I kissed Sandro's face until he smiled in his sleep, and he drew me down on top of him inside his dream. I indulged in becoming his blanket – his shield of what was to be but never need happen so long as we stayed thirty-five.

I think we both knew our moments were rarified, and we guarded them with care. We lived inside a mirage that could dissipate if we didn't honor the weight of our new commitment.

The first capricious stage of love is like meandering through a meticulously manicured garden. Life is rosy. The art of blossoming rules the hours. The shapes are intoxicating with bright perfumes. Stretches of grass and flowerbeds are blurred with desire like a Monet dream.

The Boboli Gardens remained deserted to order. Sandro's face took on a serious demeanour.

"This will be our *speciale* place," he said. "When you are lost, I will be here. Do not forget this. It is easy to become... confusing... lost, and so you must make your way here to me for this, yes?"

I looked around at the configuration of the trees and down the direction we had come, and the only flowerbed shaped like a star. I could never mistake it. I smiled and started to move into a kiss, but he stopped me abruptly – his hand stilling my mouth. His expression was almost angry.

"*Mia carissima*. I tell you this some day it may be *importante*. Tell me you understand this."

"We have a rendezvous place right here if ... *when*, I am lost," I repeated like an obedient child.

THE DIVINE
COMEDY

"O human race,
born to fly upward,
wherefore at a little wind
dost thou so fall?"

~ Dante Alighieri

"Beloved, my Beloved, when I think
That thou wast in the world a year ago,
What time I sat alone here in the snow
And saw no footprint, and heard the silence sink"
~ Elizabeth Barrett Browning

from a to zoo

Florence is a walled city. Trade is constant, and artists retreat to the hills more often than I expected. Leonardo da Vinci had been compelled to do this; he had lived in the countryside outside Vinci until he was twelve, and harboured a primal connection to shade trees and silence, uninterrupted landscape, and skies filled with birds. I remembered the entries in his notebooks and followed his footsteps, exploring beyond the city gates, determined to find the fields of poppies Sophie had shown me.

Animals were forces to be reckoned with, from consumable livestock and the working beasts, and the horses necessary for long-distance travel, to the caged lions ... the mascots of Florence kept on public display in the Palazzo della Signoria's zoo.

Sandro had his own horse, stabled a few streets from his studio on the Via Nuova. I soon discovered this was a rare luxury for artists because it was much easier to walk within the city than ride and to rent an animal at the onset of a distant journey rather than keep them fed and groomed.

But then, I came upon the old donkey again, and changed the course of things.

He was a neglected fellow who'd worked his service to the bone and was earmarked for death.

I had made a fuss of him one afternoon after passing his long-suffering Eeyore expression.

"This one needs care," I said.

"*Si*, he has worked his share of days."

"More like he's worked the lion's share," I said, scratching between the sweet animal's ears, and I gave him part of our picnic to ease his suffering.

Sandro laughed. "He will be soon," he said.

"What's so funny? He's in torment."

"I mean he *is* lion's meat," Sandro said. "What did you think the lions eat?"

"That's his reward! Hellish cruelty to end in more suffering? Butchered?"

"*Cara*. This thing is how it must be."

"Not today it isn't," I said." But now I knew ... the lions in the zoo were well-fed on beasts of burden.

It was easy to buy the creature with the coins in Sandro's pocket, and he stepped aside with some amuse-ment allowing me to proceed. First, we led the donkey to

Sandro's stable where I had a boy bring me buckets of hot and cold water, a basket of grain, and several blankets.

The donkey munched methodically on the grain, and I cleaned every inch of his hide. Cloths soaked in warm water released masses of dirt-encrusted running sores on his back. I gently rubbed the animal down with a blanket while Sandro fetched salve from a cupboard to dress the open sores, and together we combed the matted tufts of his mane.

"He needs a name," I said hugging the donkey's neck.

"He is *asino*. It is enough, no? He is not cat."

"Nope, sorry."

The donkey sniffed at the basket and nudged me into Sandro.

"Come along sweet pea," I cooed to the beast, "I have another apple for you."

He crunched it in one bite and began to chew my basket.

I said goodbye and we left my patient standing in fresh straw with a dry blanket over his sad hide covered in old scars and open wounds.

"Sweet pea?" Sandro asked, "What is?"

"A kind of flower."

"That is sweet also, yes?"

"Not exactly. How do you say *sweetie*? As in: I am your sweetie. Your special *cara*."

Sandro gave me a look as if eyes could shrug, and smiled confirmation.

"*Carino.*"

"Thank you. Now, my friend, Carino, needs a straw hat."

"The horses will laugh," Sandro said.

"Maybe it's not to wear but to eat," I said.

"Then, we must be out of apples?"

"Am I?"

"Yes. Look. The basket; it is empty," he said.

I smothered Sandro's face in kisses, and bit his earlobe.

"No. I mean am I your *carino?*" I whispered.

He pulled me roughly into his arms and growled, "*Innamorata.*"

"Sweet-talker," I replied. "Let's find Melazio. Carino needs apples."

"Nay, things that suffer death, quench not the fire
Of deathless spirits; nor eternity
Serves sordid Time, that withers all things rare.
Not love but lawless impulse is desire:
That slays the soul; our love makes still more fair
Our friends on earth, fairer in death on high"
~ Michelangelo

the apple of his eye

I was never entirely sure of the year, but Michelangelo's *David* was still the lone inhabitant of his own planet behind the high windbreak of the artist's studio, so it could have been anytime from 1501 to 1504. I couldn't help calculating Sandro would be an old man of fifty-nine.

I had been eager to explore more of the city with my personal tour guide, but Sandro suggested I take a stroll on my own. "To feel like you belong," he said. "You know words to say I am lost," but he wrote his address on a scrap of paper and pressed it into my hand. "Show this and look helpless," he said, "then follow their pointing."

I sidled up to him with mock innocence. "*Scusi, sono io...* ah, lost," I said, "*per favore*, may I go *andare a casa* with you?"

He wrapped his orange cloak around my shoulders after kissing the hollow of my neck."*Signorina*, I am fearing if you go I shall never see you again. Maybe you stay," he teased.

"*Non*, I will go to the *mercato* like a good"... I nearly said wife but stopped, horrified, correcting myself in time with the word for servant, "*domestica*. I will cook for you."

"Go, go, Florence awaits," he said, "get dressed," and he turned me bodily, and shooed me away.

By the time I was ready the Florentine sun was unforgiving. I reached the market where quivering fingers of heat dazzled off every surface of stone and metal. I was mulling over a pungent display of fish with my nose wrinkled in disgust when a friendly voice hailed me.

Melazio was straining to pull a heavy cart, loaded with apples.

"*Signora* Linton, I must speak. *Scusi*. My friend Botticelli, he is not with you?"

"*Signorina*," I corrected.

Melazio's gaze dropped to my shoes.

"I am here alone, as you see, to buy vegetables ... *verdura*," I said, picking my way clumsily through my Italian and inanely grabbing a nearby cabbage to wave for proof.

No butchered flesh was fresh enough to warrant pur-chasing, and I was loathe to being responsible for slaugh-tering anything with fur or feathers. My sensitivities decided I would remain a vegetarian while I was here.

"He is happy now," Melazio said. "I wish to thank you for this, but I think you do not see how he adores. He lives for you, yes? You see this? You feel this?"

Melazio looked so happy, but I wasn't sure what to say, taken aback at such a forward burst of familiarity, uncomfortable without Sandro, as if I was breaching a confidence, and I have always been superstitious about declaring my joys out loud.

"Melazio, we are in love. *Innamorata*. It is a powerful time for us, yes? potent, ah, *potente*." I spread my my arms wide to encompass the sky.

"No, *donna Linton*, love is not always *adorazione*. This is different. I watch. I know this. But you do not feel?"

Melazio's face probed mine, eager for an answer. It was my turn to look at his shoes, and then up into his face. "I do feel, but it is unlucky ... ah, *sfortuna*... to talk about... *parlare* ... perfection. You understand? The fates are listening, yes?"

Melazio pointed to the Florentine pig. "Il Porcellino is not fate. He is only *uno padre*, yes? A father. He wants his children to be happy. To stay home. This is why he brings everyone back to *Firenze*. My friend is a passion-ate man. As you say *perfezione*, a perfect man. An art-ist, yes? But he feelings, they are not the same of mine – apple-seller. He is whole. All of him is yours. Sandro tells me this and I have known him long his life. I hope you to come back."

I moved to rub Il Porcellino's nose hoping this would be enough to appease him, but Melazio stayed my arm and pressed his best apple into my hand, and he kissed my cheek. "For you, eh, not donkey," he said smiling.

"I'm not going anywhere," I said.

"This is good. I am hoping this for him and for you."

"I believe I have a hope for you too," I said. "I've seen you struggling with your cart many times. Sandro and I keep a donkey who could do the pulling for you, and he could remain stabled where he is, under our expense. It would be easy work for him after what he's endured, and he can eat the apples which are not so perfect."

Melazio was delighted. "This I can afford, *signora*. I am grateful. It is not far from my home. Sandro will agree?"

"It's *signorina*, and he will be pleased," I said.

I left Melazio knowing three things: I was sure Sandro adored me as Melazio said; two, this meant he could now reject me; and three, I would have to go home to be safe.

"Show me everything twice before I go," I said, turning around, and burst into tears.

Sandro's happy expression changed to one of concern. "*Mia carissima...* please... go where? You do not want England? Home is also here, no?"

I wiped my eyes and sniffed. "I thought I *was* home. for a while I believed that but now I'm not so sure I belong. I feel displaced. I'm overwhelmed. My nerves are on fire."

"What has happened?"

"I've finally realized how much time separates us," I lied.

"Time... what is this mean?"

He covered my face with kisses muttering the word 'time' between each kiss. "This is what I think of time," he said.

"Well, what year *is* this exactly?" I asked, trying to breathe. "I will prove to you how significant it is."

"Tell me what year you want and it shall be," he said.

"It's not so much a when as a want," I replied. "I want to see Michelangelo's *David* before the first blow of a chisel, and Verrocchio's studio with the orb being made, and Leonardo as a six-year-old child. I want to talk to his mother and learn her name and who she was as a woman. I want to see you when you were fourteen and meet your brothers and sisters. And most of all, I want to show you my old world. So much will happen in the next five-hundred years."

"Five-hundred is only a number," he said.

"So is sixty-four and thirty-five," I said, "and yet they seem significant. Five-hundred is like traveling from here to the stars. Does this mean you don't want to come with me?"

Sandro drew me closer with both his hands on my hips and whispered in my ear.

"It means, little one, that where you are, I am also."

"Well, that's nice of you to say so, but poetry aside, how else I can show you who I am? I mean who I was. All the parts which make me."

"These parts. They are *non importante*, no?"

"No... I mean, yes. Not important but helpful," I tried to explain.

"I help you," Sandro said, his eyes gleaming.

He crushed my belly into his pelvis and clutched a handful of my hair, tugging it backwards to expose my ear. He nibbled my earlobe and neck, melting all need for words. Soon we were chewing each other's lips and breathing the same pocket of air.

I felt my back pressed hard against the wall and when he pulled back to give me that adorable amused look we both burst into laughter.

Smart man. He winked at me knowing the effect would be instant and rewarding. I flung myself at him full-force and ravaged him to the opposite wall, to his obvious amusement.

He scooped me off the floor and whirled me onto the bed, where we shared an intense exchange of love-starved tumble-biting until we rolled into waves of hungrier kisses, no longer aware of teeth and lips but drowning in a frenzy of being the consumer and the consumed, blurred into one animal.

An hour later, we emerged into the mainstream of midday. The narrow lanes were sweltering with hot shade as Sandro led me to the noisy work-yard behind the unfinished duomo where an enormous marble block laid, damaged and dejected.

Sandro stood in front of it in the same pose as his self-portrait in the *Adoration*, in a gesture of invitation. "The Duccio block," he said, pointing to Michelangelo's trapped giant, sleeping inside. "You want. I show."

*"Why does the eye
see a thing more clearly in dreams
than in the imagination when awake?"*
~ Leonardo da Vinci

Leonardo

The first time Sandro and I saw Leonardo he had been a teenager. This time, he was approaching his magus persona, up to his greying eyebrows in acclaim for the enigmatic *Mona Lisa*, now the centre of attention from visiting artists.

Leonardo's studio swarmed with copyists eager to absorb the maestro's innovative style – a portrait in three-quarter view making stunning eye-contact with the viewer. Before this, sitters had looked dreamily introspective or vacant or askance or studied something in their hands or were painted in profile.

Leonardo was preparing to leave for Milan which made him approximately fifty-one years of age. I also knew of Raphael's Sistine murals which would show the venerable Leonardo in his sixth decade, and yet, I had looked less weary at sixty-four, and somewhere I must surely be sixty-five, considering the new year had passed several days ago, or was it months? I couldn't tell.

Leonardo was a magnificent figure, and I felt with a sting, that by linear reckoning, Sandro would have been close to sixty at this time, so I held on to Sandro's arm extra-tightly, and gave him a kiss.

Leonardo invited us his studio where I was able to witness the crowded room of admiring copyists and meet his youngest sister, Lisabetta, his assistant, and discuss how she had posed for the Louvre's iconic *Mona Lisa*, the painting which had caused, was causing, such a stir.

The *Mona Lisa's* subversive smile was a thinly-varnished allusion to a woman's coquettish nature and a man's need to hide his emotions – a puzzle for any open mind. She is alternately lovely and plain, one of Leonardo's many unisex optical illusions of creative insight and his relentless ability to balance the complementary natures of masculine and feminine. He premised male and female were interdependent and interchangeable, yet when presented together, symbolized the completion of perfect symmetry.

There was, as I had long-speculated, a second portrait of Lisa Giocondo that my century had never seen. It was a promotional bribe from Ser Piero da Vinci, Leonardo's lawyer father, to his client Francesco Giocondo – a painting of the silk merchant's young blonde wife. Unlike the Louvre's icon, this portrait was a reveal of human openness. This shy lady had delicate, finely-arched eyebrows.

Leonardo's bushy eyebrows suggested he was deep in thought and reminded me of his deliberate scientific experiment with *La Gioconda*, the smiling woman, to prove eyebrows were the key to emotional expression. *Mona Lisa's* lack of eyebrows was a subtle game of anatomical trickery. Leonardo's forte. The secret touch which made Lisa's demeanor an eternal puzzle.

I was so happy, I sang to Sandro. *Do you smile to tempt a lover, Mona Lisa?*

Sandro looked equally elated. "I love for you to sing me more," he said.

And then, the echo of the next line in my head chilled me into silence: *or just a cold and lonely, lovely work of art?*

I stopped walking and stole a hug until I felt warm again, but thoughts of the *Adoration* in a cold gallery with Botticelli trapped and lonely inside, wouldn't leave me.

Later, we sat on the stone steps near the statue of *Il Porcellino, the piglet,* as he was euphemistically called, since in reality he was a representation of a dangerous boar with deadly tusks. Sandro pointed to the domed roof of the cathedral and trained my eyes to follow, but I still felt haunted by Nat King Cole's Mona Lisa song.

At sobering intervals throughout the day, I had experienced the subliminal messages of what had once been a delightful ballad. Now, it tainted the moment with an intrusive shadow. I must have looked serious because Sandro turned my chin towards him and gave me a wink.

"Come, *cara*. Smile. I have an art history lesson for you. You will love."

I perked up.

"Imagine that small sphere, floating off the cupola and it lands here at your feet," he said.

"A balloon?"

"*Scusi?*"

"Never mind. I will show you later," I said. "Please continue. I shall pretend the *orb* is here. Right here, right now, beside the wishing pig, all bright newly-beaten metal. You were saying?"

Sandro gave a theatrical cough. "This orb, she is *gilded bronze plates*, eight feet in wide, and the Leonardo you have met was a boy being thirteen when it was building in the studio of his master."

"Yes, I know. It was Verrocchio's."

"You do *not* know," Sandro said rapping my head lightly. "You study this thing, but maybe, some things are *vedi lose* … lost on you, yes?"

His reprimand was softened with a Botticelli smile, but he had been right. I had been an art-history snob who had spouted facts at anyone who dared broach the subject.

"Sorry, most *is* lost. I will behave. I am here to learn, and you are *my* master."

"Dear apprentice," he said, "this is a hollow thing, and

Leonardo used to hide inside here to get away from the teasing and, well, many times, me. He was easy to make *pazzo* ... crazy. I cannot help this ..." he searched for words.

"Being a practical joker?"

"I may be. I do not know this. What this means?"

"Using a person's weaknesses to make others laugh. A tease. A trickster."

"This is me. *Si.* Is true, I make. *Si é vero*, I am *buffone. Questo é vero*, is very true."

"Inside," Sandro continued, "this is bad air, it makes him see things."

"No doubt. Copper is toxic."

"No, this is *bronze*. It nearly *kills* him," Sandro said, "you are not listening."

I tried to concentrate. "Sorry, you mean, he got sick?"

"*Non* – he was inside when it was put there, up." Again, he pointed to the ball in the distance that looked like a pearl balancing on the end of my finger. "He was tricked into such by his pride. He is wanting to be the engineer, yes? He was small and light enough to be the one to help. Lorenzo, Verrocchio's catamite, tricked him. Leonardo bragged, but that was his way and not a thing of his fault. He was honest, yes? Beyond the rest of us. He stated what was true."

"How did this happen?"

"The scaffold, it was not so strong, some say it had been purposely *rotto,* damaged. It gives way, but Leonardo is tied or he would be falling."

"And the world would never have known him," I

said. "You must know of more people like this. Other artists, lost paintings, and young promising apprentices who died?"

Sandro sighed two words that said it all, "the plague, *si*, it takes."

"I understand and I don't blame you," I said, "but there are more profound ways for an artist to die. One's life's work can be erased by fire or lost through ignorance, and diminish the world of art."

"And what is happening to mine?" he asked.

"One day I will show you. You experienced a hiccup of obscurity. But as you know, some of your work made it to the Uffizi. If you'd opened your eyes as Mars you would have seen me earlier in London. People pay to visit your *Adoration* and all your other paintings that survived." I hadn't meant to reference his destroyed works sacrificed to the Vanity Fire, so I changed the subject, quickly. "You are greatly celebrated."

"A hiccup?" What this is... obscurity? But no, I am afraid to know this. Please, do not tell," he said wiping the air clean with his hands.

"How vulnerable works of art can be," I said. "How transient we humans are."

"How permanent love is," he replied, kissing my nose.

"It is so odd to think of such loss," I said. "It's easy to forget Leonardo was once a child as well as a teenager before he was a god."

"A god!"

"Yes, god, with a small 'g,' in terms of myth like your Mars and Venus."

Nat King Cole's Mona Lisa song returned to haunt me, and I addressed Sandro with my hands cupped around his beautiful face.

"Immortal master artist," I said, "you are one of the pantheon, too. But so many are missing, and so many of their works become misunderstood, lonely works of art."

⁓

With each new foray into the city, I marvelled at how many of the places I knew as traffic lights and intersections were reduced to cobblestone alleyways and picturesque low buildings, but now and then a striped awning would materialize over a building and I knew it was my time intruding from the future. The curtain between our centuries was thinning and I feared my time was running out.

⁓

Sandro woke me excitedly. "Come. I show you the world. You must see," he said.

I dressed hurriedly with Sandro's impatience growing.

"Please, *Cara*, it will be gone."

The streets were foggy, as we made our way to the

campanile and climbed to the top. We could see nothing but a layer of white cloud. It felt like I was flying.

Sandro had brought blankets. "I have seen this once before," he said, "I recognized the mist, so I think we shall see again, the same."

It was freezing, and Sandro pulled the blankets around us like a tent.

"See what? I can't see a thing," I said.

The melodic bellow of the city's bell *la Vacca*, the cow, pealed the arrival of a new day, and the mist dissipated with the deafening chime.

I shivered and gripped Sandro's hand tighter under the blanket. "No wonder you call it the cow," I said. "It's more like a bull. I feel like we're in a floating labyrinth."

I saw the first ray of sun licking the bronze orb of Santa Maria del Fiore, then under it the cupola turned gold. It looked like a gazebo in the sky, hovering beside us as liquid light trickled down further, sweeping the great dome, turning it a deep orange colour that dripped onto the streets below.

Sandro was right. It was a hologram of the world, above and below. The outlines of the streets and buildings materialized slowly, softened as if covered in snow, and a future city plan overlaid Florence like a giant sheet of tracing paper. The two street maps fluctuated as if they couldn't decide which century to be.

"*Magnifico,*" he whispered.

"*Paradiso,*" I breathed.

Narrow roads ran beneath wide modern thorough-fares and only a few famous landmarks: the bridges and the palaces, and the palazzos, and the churches, pinned the two images together. Our location in the Piazza del Duomo was clearly the heart of the grid.

"Poor old Dante," I said, "he could never have seen this. The cathedral and campanile were outlines on the ground at his death when he was fifty-six."

"He can see now. With us through," Sandro said.

Three stars on the map marked the various loca-tions of the subsequent incarnations of replacement Il Porcellino's which had been relocated over five-hundred years when each marketplace had been trimmed into parks and parking lots. Small residential streets criss-crossed into a lacework of tracks submerged a few inches underneath the sidewalks of the twenty-first century. Large shapes consumed smaller ones and reconfigured back into rows of uniform squares.

The railway station obliterated a section of coun-tryside outside the walls, devastating some historically important terrain. Few city gates remained, but from this height it was easy to trace the line where the for-tified walls had run, discernible as a serpentine shape that once enclosed the old city like a gold chain dropped from heaven.

Twenty-first century Florence overlapped its old boundaries and spilled out in all directions either side of the Arno.

Architectural outlines of ghost buildings smothered

cultivated olive groves, and the rows of cypress trees receding into the surrounding valleys fell to paved highways as far as the horizon – which promised a mythological journey to a future era.

We watched the two street maps argue until the year 2014 vaporized in a flash of white light, and the streets settled into the familiar pattern of 1480.

"We will go home, now," Sandro said, dismissing the ground by redirecting my gaze to the cupola and orb looming beside us. He held my chin, stared deeply into my eyes, and gave me one of his smouldering winks. "Where you will remember your words, that I am your *master*, yes?"

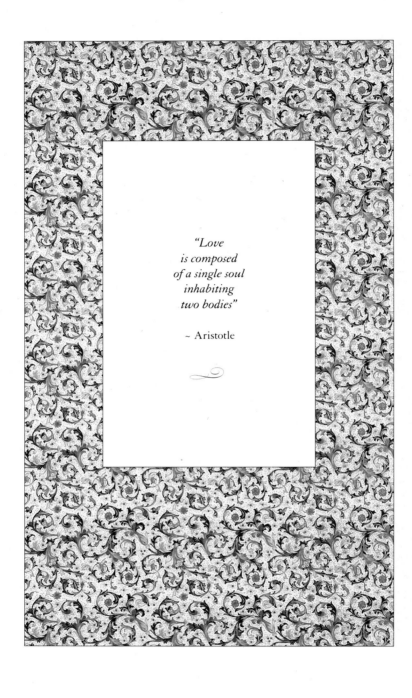

"Love
is composed
of a single soul
inhabiting
two bodies"

~ Aristotle

"Doom takes to part us, leaves thy heart in mine
With pulses that beat double. What I do
And what I dream includes thee, as the wine
Must taste of its own grapes"
~ Elizabeth Barrett Browning

signora filipepi

I am to sit for my supper. How's that for a fantasy? Being immortalized by Sandro Botticelli.

At first, it was to be an old convention – a profile, but after we had revisited the *Mona Lisa* we agreed, I will sit facing the artist.

I flouted Renaissance fashion in a crimson gown worn off the shoulder, and Sandro produced a stunning emerald, pearl, and ruby necklace from a leather pouch and fastened it around my neck.

"These were left as a guarantee for payment. A portrait of the mistress of a ... *connection*, but there was a death and they are mine to give," Sandro said, straightening the multiple strands of filigreed gold to lay flat, a brilliant collection of red and green gemstones and pearls caught in a delicate network of knots.

He stood back assessing my new image, and his eyes glistened with tears as he dropped a smaller pouch into my hand. Inside was a matching ring that I slipped onto my index finger – a central brilliant-cut ruby in a cluster of emeralds and pearls.

"How do I look?" I said.

"I cannot speak of this. I am happy," he replied.

"That good?"

Tears streamed down his face. "*Si, is* good. I am in happiness also. Forgive. I can be too much of this."

I was posed with Casper in my lap. Sandro relaxed visibly and teased that I should have Carino leaning over my shoulder.

"It would look like a nativity scene," I said.

"My little Madonna. This is not so bad, yes?"

He sketched my hair in a traditional twist of elaborate braids entwined with pearls from an existing illustration of a local beauty, so in the end I am a composite: my own face and hands, a designer dress I had once admired in a magazine, an unknown principessa's hair, and second-hand jewels, posed with Sophie's friend.

It amused Sandro to tease me, and when I had been allowed to look I saw his under-drawing portrayed me seated next to Marzocco the male lion, icon of Florence. I was enchanted. "It's Aslan," I remarked.

"Who?"

"Aslan is a mythical lion from a book," I began. "The king of a parallel world accessed through a panel of wood at the back of a wardrobe."

"So, this is fitting," he said, "your portrait is painting on the same, a panel, so, is *fortuna*, yes?"

"I have met this lion before in a lucid dream," I said, "not unlike ... well, are we sharing one now? Are we dreaming? Do you know?"

"Not to dreaming," he insisted. "You are away from England. In my country. Your bespoken rooms are vacant for a week, because you are penetrating a panel in the Uffizi, no? I can take you. You are not there, waiting. You are here, and time is going. Has passed."

"Then, I will have to go back. I have a ticket," I reasoned stupidly.

There was a brilliant silence where only the sound of scratching chalk filled the room.

"I'm not dead, then," I said. "Gosh."

"What is gosh?"

"Gosh is a god in my time," I said. "The god of surprise."

"You are not dead, *mia carissima*."

Sandro worked quickly from a red chalk drawing, and while he worked I wondered how he might appreciate acrylic paints or my oils. His medium was tempera – pigments mixed with egg yolks and vinegar water.

After three sittings there was an under-painting of odd purple skin tones and the lion was green.

"There won't be time to finish it. I hope you can work from memory."

"You are leaving so soon?"

"By my reckoning I have a couple of days before my flight," I said. "Not long enough for a portrait to be painted."

"Yes, I had forgotten you can fly," he said without a trace of sarcasm.

Sandro set aside his brush and wiped his fingers. He looked set for business. "You can move now. I think there is a matter of *importante* to discuss, no?"

I nodded. It amused me that both yes and no essentially mean the same thing in Italian: is that so?

"If what you say is true, I can come back. I have to settle some things. I have dependents and well, responsibilities."

I was not smiling. I had checked my reality at the foot of his painting, and now there were intruding images of airports and luggage tags and duty-free. If anyone asked if I had anything to declare I would be forced to say I was out of my mind, which seemed undeniably true.

"And me? I am a dependent, no?" he said walking towards me.

"I may have a choice to stay," I said, "but I should go for a while."

"Not without me," he said casually, as if traveling

five-hundred years into his future was an inconsequential matter.

I had been avoiding this discussion and was delighted.

"You want to come?" I asked, suddenly warm-blooded, again.

"I want to be with you," he countered. "But I think we will live here, yes?"

"Live?" I said, smirking. "If you say so, but I don't want to be old again."

"You are the keeper," he said.

Sandro was adamant. "We are not confined. We visit this times together. We enjoy, yes? All of them are true but mistaken... out of order," he said with a shrug. "You think this things are easy for me? They are not. For a while I am thinking I am damned to Hell. What else I could have thought? But it feels like heaven and so this I accept."

"We cherry-pick what I want to see and what you agree to show me," I said.

"Show?"

"*Dimmi*. We .... pick... harvest the best cherries, *il meglio*, selecting the choicest and leave the rest."

The obvious incomprehensible elephant in the room was ignored. Sandro and I were experiencing a journey in a labyrinthine universe and the proof was too murky to play with. As my father used to say whenever we reached a holiday destination: "we've arrived and to prove it we're here." It was enough that we were somewhere together.

I put our bizarre calendar down to sampling Sandro's century while overriding mine, and I was mortified to realize I had dismissed how our meeting was an extraordinary event for him, too.

I rationalized I could write a definitive account of the studios and the streets, and describe what people wore and the conditions, and who had painted what, and the names of the models from the alleys who found themselves upgraded to immortality, portrayed as Madonnas and saints.

It seemed that no sooner than a query formed in my head, than Sandro presented me with the answer.

"So you're able to read my mind?" I asked.

"We are sharing gifts and each one I am happy to give," he answered with a kiss. "It's your birthday every day, no?" he said.

He winked knowingly and shook his head as if to say he knew more. It was all very tantalizing.

I theorized that Sandro and I could only have experienced such a perfect relationship as ours, in hindsight-love. Love outside of time. Love that transcended time because loves in our own times either had a long time to fade, whereas true lovers in Sandro's, often parted from premature death.

I was too sleepy from the wine to clear the table. I counted the olive pits on my plate and arranged them in a circle while Sandro poured the last of the red wine. He seemed energized. "I can fill," he said, holding the empty jug.

"Please don't on my account."

He placed the ceramic jug back on the table, and to keep awake, I traced the band of grape leaves painted around its base with my finger, and studied the remnants of a typical artist's meal which was a still-life of pewter soup bowls and spoons; two plates, a pile of olive pits on Sandro's and a circle on mine, and some chunks of bread drying in the dusk. A cluster of purple grapes crowned a wooden bowl of lemons and pomegranates sitting in the center of the table next to a candle that looked more like a slowly-melting pyramid.

"I miss some of my favourite foods," I said. "I'm not a vegetarian, but I do miss the potato."

"I have not these. This is a meat?"

"It's a lumpy brown fruit like an apple that grows underground. In France it is called the apple of the earth."

"So, a tree is under the ground?"

"Just leaves above and roots and potatoes below. They're impossibly addictive."

My mouth watered like a Pavlov dog from the word potato.

"So these fruits are not ..."

"Not tomatoes. Bright red and squishy like rotten

apples that grow on vines, sweet as a grape, but..." I picked up a pomegranate from the bowl. "As big as this."

"We English like boiling and mashing things. Potatoes with butter and cream; and tomatoes with vinegar and spices that we call ketchup, which brings me to French fries. Raw strips of potato fried in a cauldron of boiling oil. Drained and sprinkled with salt. We drizzle ketchup over everything that isn't sweet."

"Like garum? The sauce of ancient Rome."

"Almost, with one exception. Ketchup is actually edible. When all your city states make one country, it will be credited with pizza and spaghetti. Two of my country's favourite foods. There are no words to describe the joy of pizza."

"You like to cook in *Inghilterra?*"

"I'm an English cook so I buy a lot of takeaway."

"Taking where?"

"Dishes cooked far away that you bring home to eat."

"You mean potatoes cooked in France?"

As it grew late, the candle spluttered out and we continued talking in the dark.

I addressed the anomaly 'elephant.' "We don't age because we met when we were thirty-five," I premised.

"Age is irrelevant here," he started to say.

"Here, being what, an altered state of bliss?"

Sandro yawned and sipped his wine. "*Si, si,* a state of *felicità,* yes?" he replied.

"Felicity, yes, happiness. We experience our shared world in vignettes," I said. "We leapfrog."

He looked puzzled, and pointed to the pattern of grape leaves. "Vines? Frogs?"

"Small bites of information."

Sandro sounded alarmed.

"I mean small ... *scenarios*." I made my fingers perform in the manner of a leaping frog from his wrist to his shoulder. He lifted my hand and kissed it, both sides, which led to a more passionate exploration up my arm.

He left the table and pulled me into an embrace.

"Now I shall turn into a beautiful princess," I said in his ear.

"You are a princess. *La mia bella principessa*."

Sandro laughed. He was a student who had just understood a complex problem. "*scenarios*... Ah yes, this is how it is, after death for me, during life for you. You may see what I can remember. I am learning too, no?"

"And what of my century?" I asked. "Will you learn there as well?"

"I have glimpsed your time from my painting. I have seen clothes change and the lights that shine from the ceiling contained in glass spheres, but little more than this. But, since we have none of the miracle lights tonight, let us go to bed."

I sent a paper airplane across the room. Then, holding another, I made flying passes in the air and brought it in for a smooth landing.

Sandro looked unimpressed. "I know of the ornithopter, he said. Leonardo's apprentices do not... hold their tongues in this."

I broke a small piece of the grape stem, and surprisingly it looked like a small stick figure, and refolded the paper so it resembled one long wing of a biplane. "This is a man flying an ornithopter," I said holding the paper and stem together. "Leonardo's ornithopter glides on the updrafts," I said, "making the wing static in the air. The air that holds the birds up when they float motionless also holds the ornithopter wings made of cloth. Later, we learned to do more than float *down* from cliffs; we learned to *lift up* from the ground. Inside silver *cilindri* with wings that hold hundreds of people. You will see."

I demonstrated. Sandro's table became a runway. "Then we did something *pazzo*." I turned the cylinder upright to represent a paper rocket and held it ready for launch. "Lift off," I said, raising it high. "We flew straight. Up, up, up." I pointed to the sky. "To *la luna*," I said.

Sandro smiled indulgently, folding his own bit of paper into a cylinder and stared at me through one end. "But you cannot."

He scrunched my rocket into a ball and tossed it at my head.

"We do many impossible things," I said, "the only

thing more impossible is describing them in words. I only inherited them. It's not like I know how they work."

I tried again, wishing I had the art of origami at my fingertips, and fashioned a crude jumbo jet from the cylinder and the long flat wing. "This is an even larger plane," I said. I picked up an olive pit from my plate. "This is a person," I said. "Hundreds of these go inside one of these, and whoosh..." My jumbo taxied and took to the air. "And that is how I got here."

"You came through my painting," Sandro said smugly. "Is whoosh!"

"Yes, I meant how I got to the gallery," I said, tapping my foot on the floor. "To the party."

I cleared a space on the table and placed a grape at one end. "We are here, and I live there," I said, placing another grape to indicate the British Isles. "Between these grapes are mountains and countries. I live further than *Francia*, yes?"

"*Gran Bretagno*," he said.

"England."

"*Scuso, Inghilterra.*"

"*Si. Bravo.*"

The tip of my finger jumped from one grape to the other.

"This is safe?" he asked.

How could I begin to explain the rest. I had inherited technology that seemed commonplace even to me.

Ideas proliferate on the shoulders of others. I lived in a world of gadgetry and electronic hocus-pocus based on knowledge that expanded separate from me. In spite of me.

I had not been a contributor; I was pure beneficiary. I had little concept how a digital camera, internal combustion engine, or television worked, let alone how the cosmos had come to be measured. I only knew that it had been because vast numbers were thrown out to wow the rest of us 'ants' with compound equations and sums so incredibly mind-numbing, they had to be labeled, astronomical. It was a daily occurrence to accept the absurd, and yet, I resisted the implausible situation of being transported five-hundred years in time and space to spend ten days with a man who once lived.

It's different when the bizarre arrives, doorstep fashion, on the periphery of one's intelligence.

I tried to translate the meaning of recorded and replayed. "The things we do loop around us," I said, gesturing with my arms, and then drew a circle and made an X on its circumference. "In circles. Birth and death," I said, tapping the X twice.

Sandro tapped the X a third time. "And birth," he said.

"And the seasons. All the time the same but different. I drew a straight line and made an X at both ends. This time here, is over. It has been and gone. Finished ... *finito*. My time is still happening, over here. *Continua*."

"*Accadendo*," he corrected with a wry expression. Enough for today. School is outside."

Smoke and mirror science was the acceptable explanation for everything, and my century had become blasé to the insane pace.

I was one of the semi-intellectual ants who accepted what was, not a changer, mover or a shaker of life. I exist in a subliminal state of subdued amazement, and after I'd tried, rather dismally, to tell Sandro of my century, I realized I'd been living in ignorance for most of it.

Higher mathematics is an alien planet for those uninitiated in a private language that converses with other galaxies in equations and proofs and geometry.

I couldn't even dogpaddle in the ocean of serious science, and the pseudo-sciences of astrology and reading horoscopes was commercial rubbish, but in the far recesses of my mind I recalled that certain illustrious physicists had proclaimed that conventional time-travel was a given of parallel universes and that all time existed simultaneously.

"you being in love
will tell who softly asks in love,
Am I separated from your body smile brain hands merely
to become the jumping puppets of a dream? oh I mean:
entirely having in my careful how
careful arms created this at length
inexcusable, this inexplicable pleasure-you go from several
persons: believe me that strangers arrive
when I have kissed you into a memory"

~ e.e. cummings

Divine feline

I called out to Sophie in my sleep to tell her I missed her and not to worry, but she didn't come. Then I remembered the sardine keys in a jar and rattled it for what felt like a long time. A transparent cat with wings dropped into my lap from the clouds above and my immediate thought was that Sophie had died in my absence and was in spirit form, so I sadly awaited her next move.

Gradually, the cat turned opaque revealing herself to be Casper, but she followed Sophie's rules and scampered off, wings folded, begging me to tag along.

"Aslan gives rides," I called after her, and she stopped. She grew to the size of a lion and unfurled her wings, so I climbed on her back and we flew. We circled an airport where I recognized various landmarks in the surrounding fields: Stonehenge, St. Mary's church, and the National Gallery. I noted the concentric circles of Dante's beehive underworld, that from above resembled a maze. Next to it was another circle, this one red, and I knew it was the roof of Florence's great cathedral. The stone lions of Trafalgar Square rose and joined us in the sky, and I heard a traffic controller shout, *love is blind, love is blind... love is blind... ready for takeoff.*

Casper was telling me to go home.

Wherever I travel I take comfort that there will always be cats. They confirm I belong. Foreign cats centre me because we communicate using the language of affection. Cats don't purr in Italian or English. Humans speak 'pigeon cat' more by gesture and funny noises and tones of voice, so I felt grounded by Casper.

I took special notice of the fifteenth-century alley-cats. So many had poor eyes. Grey tabbies are common enough, but it was still a poignant shock whenever I saw a Sophie lookalike. I fancied Casper was one of her ancestors and that by touching her I somehow touched Sophie.

Florence was home to colonies of working ferals that failed to counteract the rodent population. They reminded me of the famous cemetery cats of Pere

Lachaise in Paris, at home in every patch of sunlight, sunning themselves atop grave monuments, strolling the gravel paths, and perched on low red rooftops.

Florentine cats patrolled the marketplaces like famished security guards.

Befriending the cat in the Boboli Gardens years ago still pleased me. I thought of her still, whenever I was reminded of angels in general. She had been the positive energy to ground my disastrous love triangle. Lorenzo and Francesca Barberini had sent me many pictures of Angelina, 'the princess with the healthy eyes,' as Francesca always called her in her letters. Angelina had passed away in 2000 at the age of eighteen, a month before Mr. Barberini.

A purple shadow hung low over the city as I crossed the market square, but Melazio was still there with Carino hitched to his cart.

"*Buongiorno* Melazio. *Buongiorno* Carino," I said, giving the donkey a hug and kissing his nose. I see you are well my old friend." His hide was covered in scars, but free of sores.

"*Signora* your other old friend, I am, is also well," Melazio said, laughing.

"*Signorina*," I corrected, as usual. "I am happy to hear this."

Melazio cradled something white in his arms and I thought it was a cat, but when I peered closely I could see it was a ferret. An albino with pink eyes.

"I see you have another pet, Melazio?"

"Carino and I have an ally," he said.

I continued to scratch the donkey's ears. "How so?"

"This one keeps the rats away from Carino's apples."

"And where is Carino's hat?"

"I keep. For the sun. I am grateful. It sells the apples."

A few yards from the market, my blood froze from a familiar intrusive sound. The faint notes of a ringtone came from my basket. I searched but my phone wasn't there, no doubt it was ringing back in the hotel room I hadn't occupied since my first night. It was the last sign I needed to tell me my time was up. I was being called home.

I heard it again later, with Sandro. "This song, I have been hearing many times. It is calling us, yes? It is time to decide."

"One can't simply abandon things," Sandro declared, referring to unfinished works of art but referencing my life left behind. "They abandon you."

That made me consider. I hadn't allowed for long-term care for my pets. I'd assumed time was passing in parallel time, then and now. It was all very well to go on a lark for ten days, but I had responsibilities, and Budge had to go home.

Sandro had to go away from time to time and I had

never questioned why. Now, I knew it was time for me to put my affairs in order.

The market pig stared over our heads pretending not to care. Still, tradition said it granted travellers a return ticket, and I made Sandro rub its nose with me.

I blew Il Porcellino a kiss and said thank you, *tante grazie, mille grazie*. A million thanks.

Entering a painting is as miraculous as it gets. I had walked into the frame and past the figures, and out into the streets of Florence. Now I was ready for the return trip.

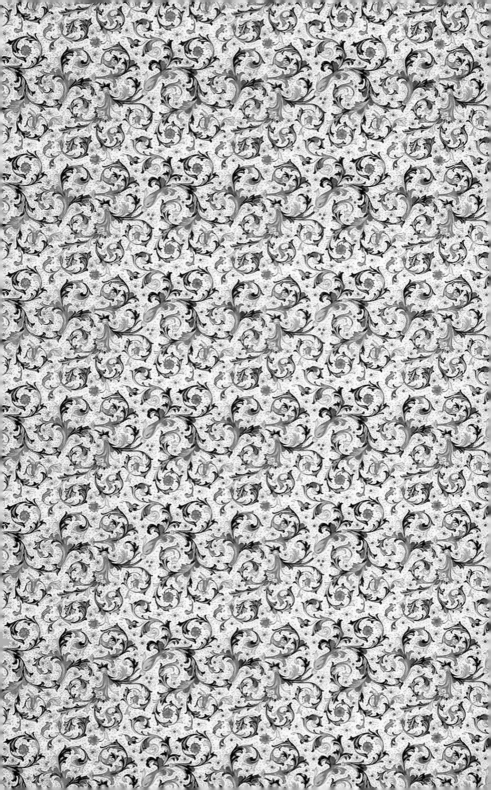

THE INFERNO

"Amor, ch'al cor gentile ratto s'apprende
prese costui de la bella persona
che mi fu tolta; e 'l modo ancor m'offende.

Amor, che a nullo amato amar perdona,
Mi prese del costui piacer sì forte,
Che, come vedi, ancor non m'abbandona..."

"Love, which quickly arrests the gentle heart,
Seized him with my beautiful form
That was taken from me,
in a manner which still grieves me.

Love, which pardons no beloved from loving,
took me so strongly with delight in him
That, as you see, it still abandons me not..."

~ Dante Alighieri

the purgatorio

the twenty-first cycle

~ LINTON'S CENTURY ~

Dante Domenico di Michelino
(1417–1491)

THE WATER IS WIDE
"The water is wide, I can't cross o'er.
And neither have I wings to fly.
give me a boat that can carry two,
And both shall row, my love and I.
~ 17th century English folk song

the enlightenment

The Uffizi had materialized, obligingly, with enough time for Sandro and I to retrace our steps through the *Adoration* to the modern city of Florence where Sandro followed me in shock. I hailed a cab to the railway station and made sure to avert his attention as we passed his own quarter of the city.

"Best not to look," I said.

"I do not recognize anyway," he said, except that." He gestured to the duomo behind us. *"Ma bella Firenze,"* he muttered. "I am glad to be dead for this." But he gamely held my hand and surrendered, allowing me to lead.

I was thrilled that I had retained my thirty-five year old body, and hustled him forward as covertly as I could, but it could never have been a seamless transition.

It was the reckless pace that shook him the most. "Everyone is running," he said. It was a perfectly accurate observation and a sad commentary on my century.

We returned to my room where I picked up my plane ticket and we tested the bed and made extensive use of soap, hot water, and room service. I purchased two train tickets to Milan, and from there it was a great deal of jostling and brazenly pushing against a school of human fish. Sandro had no credentials, so we made a stop at the Italian passport office where, amazingly, he was issued a temporary international travel permit from possibly Milan's dimmest female government clerk. But then she succumbed to much flirtation as Sandro flashed multiple smiles at the woman. I have no doubt his blue eyes had a lot to do with her swift progress from a pencilled request to the rubber stamp on her desk.

Sandro was a showstopper with his curly auburn hair, white shirt, boots and cape. A look of incredulity crept over the Milanese clerk's face as she stamped a cardboard boarding pass for a direct flight to Heathrow.

Understandably, Sandro paled at the jumbo jet, so we sat on the observation deck until he'd seen the lumbering things take off and land for an hour. He eventually entered into the spirit of our adventure and actually seemed eager to fly.

I bought a small atlas at a newsagent while Sandro examined a display of gold jewelry in a case. "Not so well made" was his verdict.

"Well, you were a goldsmith, so you're hard to please," I said.

"*Non.* I am. I was, but this things are..."

"Crude by comparison," I said, remembering the quality of my portrait jewelry.

"Careless," he said.

While we waited at the gate we studied a map of the world as a completed jigsaw puzzle with pastel countries fitted against segments of blue ocean. Sandro turned the pages until I stopped him at the map of England. "We are going here," I said pointing to the blank space below the word Cambridge. "That is Little Cobiton," I said. "That space."

"Why it is not there?"

"It's a surprise," I said.

"And I will also see a potato."

We flew over the quilted landscapes below, over mountain peaks and lakes, and I traced our route on the map of Europe. He was fascinated by his country being the shape of a boot. I pointed out Florence and Rome and Milan. Then, Flanders and Spain and France. I tapped the English Channel. "Britannia," I said.

Sandro measured the length of Italy using his finger as a ruler and compared it to my island home. "It is small, no?"

I flipped a few pages. *"Amerigo Vespucci Land,"* I quipped, pointing to the massive continent of North

America. "It was claimed in 1492, by Amerigo Vespucci. Did you know him?" but a shiver passed over my enthusiasm as I recalled Simonetta was a distant cousin of the explorer.

"I knew *of* him."

Sandro, tactfully ignored the connection with Simonetta, and after a while I relaxed. Being a professor again was like guiding a country boy through London's grand museums, and I noted with some amusement that Sandro was entirely captivated by a glass of ice-water. So much for dinosaurs and Egyptian mummies, I thought. He seemed indomitable, sitting beside me eating his first airline meal of bright red lasagne without comment. This observation made me smile; my bad English cooking would be painless by comparison.

"*Mio amore*," I said, when it got too cloudy to see from the window, "I have something for you to read," and I pulled out the *Divine Comedy*." I cannot read *Inglese*, he said, "but I remember doing the illustrations. But these are not mine."

The hall seemed strangely stale and small as I called out a greeting to Budge from the doorstep.

She came downstairs, dressed on the run with her suitcase already at the door.

"What are you doing out there?" she said, breathless from her running.

"You are also running," Sandro said.

"You look like the white rabbit late for an important date," I added.

"Well, I *am* a bit like the mad hatter today. Alice, you look well. I think you've even lost a few years. Did you bring back the painting Mr. ...?"

"Yes, yes we did," I interrupted. "Please let me introduce Mr. Filipepi from the Uffizi," I said, and turned to Sandro. "Alessandro, this is my niece, Iris."

Budge shook hands and appraised Sandro looking from him to me with an expectant expression. She must have seen her aged aunt, glowing with excitement and a handsome middle-aged Italian man dressed for Shakespeare. My head swam with excuses at the ready, but I needn't have bothered, like me in the fifteenth-century, Sandro's period clothes breached no problem.

Sandro kept hold of Budge's hand and kissed it, and when she blushed I couldn't breathe from jealousy. I felt as impaled as a thorn bird.

"We had to drop the painting in London for security," I explained. You're off already, I see."

Budge was lovely in her mini-dress and striped pashmina. A tall blonde drink of water and a dead-ringer for the Simonetta look. "Sorry to love and leave you," she said, shouldering her purse, grabbing the extended handle of her suitcase.

Sandro smiled and held open the door.

"*Ciao*, she replied. "Queenie, the cats are fine; the plants...?" She grimaced. "Sorry." She gave me a hug.

"Wow, he's a keeper," she whispered. "Must dash. I've got a bus to catch," she said to Sandro.

She faced me again as an afterthought. "And a very Merry Unbirthday to you. We'll celebrate next week. Welcome to Little Cobiton, Mr. Filipepi, I know your name from somewhere."

"I hope to see again, *signorina*," he said. "*Addio*."

"If you're going to be around, I will, she said." He watched with a little too much fascination as she wheeled her suitcase down the street.

"I think your boxes on wheels are *stupendo*. Wonders are in everywhere," he said. Your name is also mine?

"Sorry?"

"Alice. Alessandro."

"I'll explain that later. In fact I will show it to you."

Simkin slipped in the open door, streaked past Sandro, and headed for the kitchen. I followed him in search of Sophie, calling her name, and Sandro followed me.

The living room was empty but the bright grid of his Madonnas diverted him.

Sandro examined each one closely. "These are so smaller than mine, but look how perfect, this way, together."

Strangely, he made no comment of the *Adoration* over the fireplace, barely giving it a glance.

Several Leonardo's graced the hall, and in the area off the kitchen, a huge blow-up of the *Mona Lisa* filled the dining room. An exquisite miniature of Cecelia Gallerani, *Lady with an Ermine* graced the bathroom.

"And who is in your bedroom?" Sandro asked, peering

at *Venus and Mars* over the second fireplace. I see we are both sleeping in here. *Perfetto*. And this is Sofia, yes?"

Sophie paced in circles on the bed nattering towards us in a state of agitation.

"Yes, this is my Sophie," I said.

Sandro and I reached down to pet her together, and she sniffed past my hand to Sandro's. Simkin continued to prowl in the shadows, edging closer until he could resist no longer.

"Well, I'm going to put the kettle on," I said. "I can't believe how much I've missed tea."

"I will stay here with Sofia," Sandro said.

When I returned, Sandro was already cuddling a willing Sophie which shocked me. I stood back from them, happy and sad, but caught a glimpse of myself in the mirror. It reflected back a tortured woman but at least an attractive one in her mid-thirties.

"Come, we will have this *tea*," Sandro said, kissing Sophie, but when he tried to put her on a chair she clung to his cloak, snuggling into his neck, refusing to be parted.

"You're quite the charmer," I said. "I didn't know you were so fond of cats."

"I am selecting of the best. Like the harvest of the cherries. As you say, picking, yes?"

The tea tray rattled from more than fatigue. It seemed heavier than usual, and I set it down too hard. Sandro stared at two odd shapes in a small bowl.

"This is a potato," I said, holding up a spud with sprouting eyes.

He looked at it dubiously. "This is the amazing apple from the ground?" he asked.

"It tastes better than it looks," I said, "and this is a tomato."

I contrived to have Sophie on my own, feeling the old sting of rejection. I came bearing sardines. "Hussy," I said, stroking her ears. "He's mine. I thought you weren't mad at me for leaving? I called you a few times and you didn't come."

"Even cats have to sleep," she purred.

My wardrobe delivered another reality check. No size-six dresses and misshapen slippers for my new perfect bunion-free feet.

Two females had eclipsed my homecoming, and my enthusiasm shut down a little. It took the rest of the day showing off the electric marvels throughout the house to put me in a confident mood, but it was the joys of a hot soapy shower with Sandro that proved the stimulant I needed to feel like a woman worth cherishing.

By dusk, we lay drinking wine, in front of a robust fire with Sophie and Simkin basking in the heat.

"Your world is so busy with light and this feeling of dry ... and very ... very warmth," he said, indicating the discarded towels that had been handed to him straight from the tumble-dryer.

Botticelli lives with me now. The man who once recorded the delicate themes of elaborate theatrical masques in painted panels, casually slipping into the picture plane to check behind the cut-out trees, now hikes my quiet woodland trails and picnics with me on the banks of the River Ouse.

My house is his house which means my cats are his cats. Sophie followes him around as if he had sardines in his pocket.

"Ah, *ciao mia bella gattina, Sofia*," he crooned, making a fuss of her whenever he saw her.

"Sophie." I corrected. The new Sophie acted as if Sandro was made of catnip, besotted whenever she heard his voice.

"She used to be shy," I said, trying to convince myself. "Let's take her and Simkin back to Florence with us," I said.

"I think when it is time, yes," he answered, and continued to canoodle Sophie.

We could see our breath the next morning when I introduced Sandro to my stone angel. For me, it was a moment of mixed emotions that I determined to hold in check but memories of the other angel invoked him to my side. I felt the moment haunted with a tangible sensation of his benevolent presence. So *now* you come, I thought, feeling irritated.

"I have always been here," came the distinct reply.

Sandro looked up as if he'd heard and gave me a wink.

The firecracker air of October made the fallen leaves

crackle with static as we trod the path. The autumn air had a distinct nip to it that made my eyes water, and feeling them spilling with tears primed me for the real ones that seemed likely to follow.

In the distance I saw the black fence on its slight slope and the statue's white shape looming. I pointed. "He is there."

I held back and let Sandro walk ahead of me, pretending to tie my shoelace.

"*Buongiorno*," Sandro said in a crisp clear voice as if he were about to give a speech. "I hear you are an *especiale* friend to *Signorina* Linton."

I caught up and put my arm through Sandro's. We stood in silence for a heartbeat but I needed to busy myself. I felt awkward that I had admitted how I had told this sculpture my troubles. It felt as if I was bringing a beau home to meet my father. I was tongue-tied and shy. "It's no Michelangelo," I said, breaking the silence and wished I hadn't. Sandro ignored me with the tact of a greater artist to one of less talent.

I sent the angelic presence a plea. "Is there an easy way to forgiveness?"

"Wing and a prayer," he replied.

I let go of Sandro's arm and brushed the leaves from the inscription. For each time I've read it, it seemed written for me alone, and now it was for him as well.

Sandro touched the name Dante Alighieri. "Our new life starts too my old friend," he said, taking one perfect golden leaf left stuck on the angel's foot, tucking it behind my ear. Then, he kissed my nose, and noticed my red eyes.

"Come *carissima*, it is not a sad day. We are in *Inghilterra*, no?"

⁓

Our ability to momentarily stupefy and delight each other and the growing respect for the regenerative powers of desire reminded me again of eternity and Sophie biting her own tail.

We lived largest when I surrendered, but old dogs like me take time to learn new tricks. Balancing the tricks and treats of life is a delicate magic act. As always, the fears and delights are in the reveal. Reveals that can render life an immortal comedy if you let them, but both Sandro and I had to remain vigilant lest either of us drop the magic.

I heard the telephone from outside. I had coached Sandro to answer calls and he was getting better at modifying shouting into the receiver, but I rushed in and picked up on the kitchen extension.

"*Buongiorno?*" he shouted as if he were addressing someone across the room.

"Mr Fillipepi, hello, *buongiorno*, it's Iris, is my aunt home?"

"Ah, *signorina* Budge, *si*, she is. I get. *Uno momento.*"

"Telephoning is for you," he shouted out the door.

Budge's voice was animated. I could hear her

grinning."Ooh, your lovely man is still around," she said, "so how's it going over there?"

"I am well, thank you."

"I get it. He's right there, isn't he? I called to ask you what you'd like for your belated birthday?"

"A pair of rose-coloured glasses and more sherry," I said, smiling. "I have everything else a woman could want."

"No kidding."

"Exactly."

"We should throw a party?

"Absolutely not. The last one I attended was quite enough. It was an impossible act to follow, besides, we're getting close to my next one so we can celebrate two birthdays with one balloon. I like that. It's like I missed a year and I can pretend I'm still sixty-four. That way I won't miss anything."

"Trust you to celebrate the weirdest way possible."

"Too old to change now," I said.

"*Ciao*," she said, and rang off.

I approached the mound of orange I knew to be Sandro sketching the angel. My gloved hands cupped the hot drink I was carrying and my boots crunched the frost still lurking under the damp leaves. Sandro heard and turned to greet me.

"I called ahead. "Is he being quiet today?"

"*Buongiorno, Signora Filipepi*," he called back.

I reached Sandro's side grinning madly. I was pleased but had to put up a pretense of protest. "I am absolutely *not* old enough to be your mother, and where, young man, is your new coat?" I said, handing him the tea.

"*Grazie mamma.* A robe is warmer and under I have also a secret of warm."

Sandro parted the flap of his robe. "See."

Sophie's pink nose projected from the orange wool.

"There you are madam. I've been rattling the sardine jar."

"The angel he is a good model, he does not move or get tired. Not like a silly blonde principessa."

"Your mamma wants to make breakfast," I said giving him a mock stern look. "English or Italian?"

"Please fruit and bread. I am not good with your fryings."

"You mean fry-ups. I'm having eggs and bangers."

Sandro winced. "Bangers are food of the underworld," he said.

"Then, I am Beatrice, come to tempt you into sampling the morsels of hell. Mmnn. Tasty."

"We see hell differently, *cara.*"

"Everyone does. I'm sure we design our own. All things considered, Dante must have been one disturbed poet. I miss Melazio's apples, but I'd rather have a plate of fried *porcellino*, any day."

"Be careful not to tease him, *cara*. He is Italian animal and I think you will be sorry if he tears up your ticket home. Which is reminding me, I have to go home for a while. It is for *uno grande* surprise."

I stood in shock. "Yes." I replied. "It certainly is." And then, I pushed it to the back of my mind and pretended it hadn't been said.

I breathed in the cold air and let it penetrate the moment. Happily, it cooled the first selfish words that sprang to mind and so I said something inanely sensible instead. I tickled behind Sophie's ears. "Well, I'm hungry for a cooked meal even if you aren't and I know a young lady who likes *bacon*."

Sandro's eyes looked distraught. "*Cara*, I have to leave you but I will be back."

"Life goes on," I said, nodding I was fine, "pardon the pun. I've made you a fruit plate with some nice cheddar but it can wait if you're not finished here."

Sandro showed me his sketchbook. It was a priceless drawing and it's beauty threatened to sabotage my control over a calm I did not feel.

"For your niece," he said.

Analysis is the death of love, and I needed no reminding that I may have lost my mind. It is enough that our days were filled with many sizes of joy. Sandro continued to work on exorcising the last of my demons, determined that I be gremlin-free when we returned to Florence. Strangely, I think of it as my home, now.

I'm being enlightened moment by moment. A day through Sandro's eyes brings awareness, and incredibly, I now exist deeper within the Botticelli litmus test for joy. I thought I knew the meaning of the word perspective, but ironically, I'd been living an illusion. The vision of my century, now filtered through the miraculous, expanded past my original blasé acceptance and resistance. I felt like a mad scientist who had discovered the 'Botticelli Mirror Effect.'

Sandro is fascinated by the *insignificante* of life: the ice cubes at the bottom of a fat glass, ballpoint pens, coil notepads, tin foil and cling wrap, scotch tape, and the clear fishing line I used to hang a mobile of the solar system in the kitchen. He was more interested in the 'glass string' than the representations of the planets.

Showing him these things makes them wonders of the new world. It made me the goddess of running water and instant light and flush toilets, but bringing Botticelli home meant bringing home the truth. He and I live somewhere in middle-history – a better earth that now connects his astonishment with my delight, which impressed upon me that I still hadn't shown him how to inflate a party balloon or decorate a Christmas tree. But then, we'd only been back a week.

At least there are horses and carts where I live. It's an agricultural patch where cars mingle with farm vehicles and riders on horseback, so the landscape is somewhat subdued and incongruous with the space-age. I live in a solitaire pearl strung on a roman road.

Seeing my century through the eyes of a stranger from 'outer space' is like watching a planet under a microscope spinning counter-clockwise. I'm atypical; I also think in creative myopic and telescopic points of view, both introspective and subjective, but then I reside in the artist's world. With Sandro, I am always home.

My village is a veritable time-machine; it's mentioned in the Domesday book. A farmer named Cobb, in the year, 1086, held a few fields and some cattle, that, meager as they were, counted for taxable wealth. And then, slower than most places, Cobb's land grew into a settlement where a cluster of farm-related home industries struggled to eke out a living during the darknesses of troubled times. I think of my country as a network of parishes connected by priories and monasteries, belts of forest, and duck ponds with swans.

The flowers in my garden have crawled across the ground to blend with the tipsy gravestones like an impressionist painting. There is no fence that separates the properties but a bench more or less marks an unofficial boundary. It's where I go to think, and I often take a pillow and a blanket and a book to read.

The cats follow me, pied piper style. It's the least scary place imaginable.

There is a silent presence in one room of my house. It smells like the day I moved in, fresh with promises and new paint, and it has remained so. I have never used it, and as such, I go in whenever I want to remember that serene before-time when a new home is still a polite stranger.

I had placed a single chair by the window but nothing else to distinguish it as being inhabited, but inhabited it was and is. Not by a conventional ghost, but the former me, frozen and papered into the walls from when I was a late-blooming wallflower.

It lingers with the scent of psychic potpourri from that time when I was independent with attitude. It only takes a second to feel transported. Like all imprinted memories, it is cloned deep, yet as near to the surface as the fresh roses on my dining room table.

The living room has finally become the space where vitality congregates. My television's small square of flickering stories is stilled. The farcical transparency of youth and beauty's endless chase and capture is over. Flesh and blood have staked their claim. Sandro and I are lovers playing easy to get.

Together, we blocked out the sun – the total eclipsing of two young animals orbiting one another like creatures in heat. Leaping, growing, silk sheets catching fire.

Having a male companion was a new thrill. "I'm home," I shouted. "I brought dinner."

"*Cara*, I am living," Sandro called back.

"I should hope so. I think you mean the living *room*," I corrected.

"*Si*. The room of life. I have found some things."

Sandro was seated curled next to Sophie with my family photo album on his knees, open to the pictures of Angelina and the Barberinis.

I noticed Sandro's clothes had changed from the morning. Sometimes when he saw a man in the street or a magazine they would transform, and so I was treated to a delightful succession of Botticelli in blue jeans or Mars wearing T-shirts and cargo pants. Now, I found him lounging in pyjama pants and a white T-shirt, and for a moment I was overwhelmed with how much I adored him. He was a continual source of delight and surprise, literally, mine in spirit, and so even in my awe and admiration, I felt somewhat safe, some of the time.

"When is this days?" he said, and broke my abstracted reverie.

"That was after the *terribile* time," I said. When I was sure my life was over. The morning after meeting you, and ..."

"This is Florence, yes?"

I plunked down on the sofa and stared above the images, keeping them out of focus. "That was the happy ending to leaving you. I don't intend to dwell on it, so I hope you understand. It is over, now. That is Angelina. Enough said."

Sandro looked over the edge of a photo at me and shook his head. "It is not over," he said.

And then, I remembered Sandro sketching the stone angel, the afternoon he suggested he may have to go home for a few days. A big surprise, *uno grande*, he had said.

Most days we slept till noon, turning afternoons into mornings, and falling into bed at dusk. The sunset leached into the sky like blotting paper. We indulged ourselves with weeks of exploring the countryside.

I let Sandro drive my car on out of the way roads after sundown, headlights on high-beam, illuminating a strip of new world ahead of us. We counted pale-blue rabbits nibbling midnight grasses and traveled slow to allow the crossings of skittish deer, swerving carefully to the side for each hedgehog and fox.

We discussed art while peeling Jaffa oranges, drinking in the stars. We loved against my flowered wallpaper. We donned high rubber boots to trudge the low country marshes and picked mushrooms. We made daisy chains and stalked wild swans with a camera, and stole roses from walled gardens. We explored the world like children. Christopher Robin and Pooh, loosed in the hundred-acre-wood.

One afternoon we filled the backseat with armfuls of lilac boughs and drove the twisted labyrinth of narrow Cambridge streets, touring its colleges within a fragrant, mauve cloud. My little silver car cruised the outskirts of the celebrated university, past the great ivy-covered estates whose more sensitive inhabitants must surely have felt the unseen disturbance of gently-fizzing bygone electrons, displaced when Sandro Botticelli passed by.

Then I remembered it was Autumn and lilacs were out of season.

*"But love me for love's sake,
that evermore thou may'st love on,
through love's eternity"*
~ Elizabeth Barrett Browning

il magnifico

By late November and it had snowed once or twice, the way it does in England when rain turns to sleet before it can rise into flakes in a half-hearted attempt to turn a landscape white for a few hours. We had to walk under the moon to hear the crunch of the frozen leaves, hardened before the sun reduced them to a soggy mulch of brown stars.

My teeth were on edge hearing Sandro crunch ice-cubes like shelled nuts. He couldn't get enough. It was more than a novelty. After a few days he was addicted, mesmerized by the look and sound of ice clinking in a glass. He sucked ice chips like sweets and ate them with a spoon.

I tried substituting frozen popsicles, ice-cream, and sherbets but he was less keen on sugar, hooked on the refreshing feel of frozen water than fruity flavors. I treated Sandro to a snow-cone and he made a face tasting the syrup. "Please without this colour," he pleaded, but he enjoyed the ones I spiked with the juice of a fresh lemon, well enough.

He made drawings in the condensation that misted the tall chilled goblets and swirled the cubes in a ritual, holding the glass up to the light, shaking his head in admiration for the clarity of the ice.

When I showed Sandro pictures of icebergs and ice sculptures he was more enamoured than ever, especially when he had both instant flames and ice at the same time. "I must keep my feet *in caldo*," he explained, which confused me as the word calde sounded like cold but meant hot. "*Non il freddo,*" he explained, meaning not cold.

He was like a child on Christmas morning with his feet cozied up to a roaring fire, sipping chilled water and crunching the ice.

"I am seeing more. Your world is about running and soft things and also with strange togethers of cold and hot," he said.

I hesitated about letting him sip ginger ale but he insisted on opening a can. I demonstrated and he managed to negotiate his first pull tab.

Sandro showed alarm at the hiss of escaping bubbles. "What is in?"

"Gas. Never mind, it's some sort of air that makes the noise. Watch this."

I took him into the garden and shook a can of cola vigorously.

Sandro watched amused until I opened the can and sent an explosion of brown liquid into the air.

"Are you right," he said, checking my hands.

"Now, do you still want to drink it?"

"I am sorry, but why you do this?"

"It's an acquired taste."

Carbonated bubbles not being the most forgiving of inventions, I predicted an unpleasant reaction, but he gamely sampled away.

"This everything must be tried," he said, choking from the pain in his throat.

"Bravo. You were magnificent. Pop is a bit like swallowing small razor blades. I rarely drink it but Budge loves it and so I keep some on hand."

"Pop?"

"What you just drank was pop. We call it a soft drink."

"Soft? These are sharp ways to drink," he said. "Why you have?"

"To give my friends."

He laughed. "Your life is full with smellings of flower and fruit... and soft," he said. "Mashed potatoes and gravy, and drinks called soft that are not."

Tea and coffee were ignored in favor of hot apple cider, and as much as Sandro enjoyed a flirtation with French-fries and ketchup, he craved colder savories.

Sweets were low on his food list, but being so near Christmas, the shops were full of exotic delicacies: heavy pound-cakes coated with almond paste and shortbread, and fruit cakes saturated with brandy. I couldn't resist my seasonal favourites and of course, Sandro tried each of them with the enthusiasm of an explorer.

I gained a new appreciation for an endless bounty of international cuisine and the delights of refrigeration. Chilled pineapple cut into long spears became his favourite *miracolo* until I made his snow cones with pineapple juice.

The overwhelming variety of new tastes started to impress me, including Sandro's fascination with microwave dinners. I tried to separate myself from these miracles but couldn't. Feeding Sandro made every meal an event. For the sake of my health, eating in the fifteenth-century had been a bland unadventurous parade of local produce and bread.

⁓

We sat with our chairs facing the hearth-fire the way people on a sandy shore watch the waves. Beachcombers now, of small treasures. The poignant fascination over a lover's hangnail or an eyelash curved like a comma, or the shade of a soft bruise and the white pucker of a childhood scar. Shadows of pain. Reminders of being human and vulnerable during a time, when unbelievably, we had no conscious awareness of the other's existence. A chilling thought, that we might never have met.

Sandro leaned forward and the muscles of his back

flexed under clinging white cotton. I could smell the fabric softener scorched by the iron, an entirely alien fragrance to the fifteenth-century. He embraced the clothes and trappings of the civilized world with remarkable joy.

I delighted in his new image. Botticelli in faded jeans and a T-shirt; Botticelli, barefoot in sandals wearing khakis fashionably rolled once at the cuffs; Botticelli in cargo pants and a collarless blue-denim shirt, left un-tucked; Botticelli exiting the shower, naked as Mars.

Every outfit made the original 'Botticelli in a bathrobe' more exciting. He was one with my century after a few days, and yet he still hadn't been introduced to the joys of a twenty-first century Christmas.

After a theatrical production, opening a bottle of champagne, Sandro was reluctant to accept a glass and drank Chianti instead.

I drank too much, and the champagne's soporific effects dragged me to the bottom of a turquoise sea where Sandro swam towards me. He tied a rope around my waist, and we let the current take us. The journey was pleasant until we were beached on a wintry shore, with cliffs of ice-covered rock looming over us.

Sandro pointed to a black shape. He uttered only one word as a declaration. It was both destination and invitation: "there," he said, "the inferno."

The cave entrance yawned with jagged teeth from

high above a ledge in the rock face. Stale air steamed from its throat, an odoriferous entrance to hell. Sulphuric stenches punctuated the air, yet we clambered towards it in a frenzy to be inside.

I skinned my knees; blood dripped down my legs like a stigmata turning them into red stockings. Snow blew in chills of stinging starflakes. Some caught on Sandro's cloak forming a frosty pattern of white embroidery. He reached down and hauled me up the last few feet until we sat, huddled together, exhausted and sweaty from our climb.

As always, Sandro's cloak enclosed both of us in a warm embrace and our combined body heat generated the restorative magic to explore the cave.

It was like being inside a crown. A circle of stalagmites rose in crystal spires. The earth's mineral blood seeped from the crevices, dripping into frozen fangs and sharp prison bars. We wound through them, drawn inwards towards the hiss of two green dragons.

They belched small coughs of fire in their sleep, and seemed to stir, their great scaly eyelids twitched from dreaming. There was no danger. The beasts were us, and I felt a delicious sense of physical arousal. Sandro squeezed my hand, and an internal glow fluttered into life as if a great love quickened in my womb.

I woke with a message from Dante in my mind: "The path to paradise begins in hell."

"Please to look over and away," Sandro said. "I have a surprise to hide."

"There is a closet in my spare room. The one I showed you, with the chair. I won't look. I promise."

"This is good. It is a large box. You can help me lift this but you must not look until the day."

"Christmas?"

"*Non*, of your beginning day." he replied, "as you call birthday."

*"Grow old along with me
the best is yet to be.
The last of life
for which the first was made."*
~ Robert Browning

room with a point of view

Sandro burst into the bedroom, trailing ozone and sunshine. "From Melazio," he said, presenting me with a perfect peach.

"He's expanding his business, then."

"He misses you."

I did a double take. "Wait, you've been to Florence without me? *Uno Momento,*" I said, trying to sound calm. "You said you would stay with me. You made the *grande promessa.*"

"Speak English in front of the cats, it's impolite to pretend to be someone you're not," he said. Then, he laughed. "I have to go for the surprising. Your birthday is coming up, no?"

I grinned. "Well, some days I want to be Italian," I said.

"*Brava.* This is good because we will live in *Firenze,* and I will never want to be *Inglese.*"

"Christmas here, then, and New Year's Eve in Florence," I said.

Our evening walks usually began and ended at the lych-gate of St Mary's churchyard a few yards from my door.

"This is such a strange ... eh... *lych building*," he said.

I had to agree. With its rickety thatched roof, it looked like an ancient bus shelter.

Sandro looked behind him and smiled. "Where is the gate?"

"It's not a real gate."

"I can see this."

"It's a resting place for pallbearers. The men carrying a coffin. They get a chance to pause here and rest before the long walk to the altar."

Sandro shivered. "I am freezing out here. You *Inglesi*, you do not miss the sun?"

"It's surreal that you can feel the cold when you're dead. Don't you think?" I said in a matter of fact tone, not meaning to be flip.

Sandro's brows knitted together, and he surprised me by jumping to his feet, heading down the path towards the church door. But he changed his mind, and for a moment he stomped about hugging himself, pacing a few steps towards the street, then returning. He made a display of blowing his fingers warm as an obvious exaggeration. When he stopped to stare down at me, there were tears in his eyes. He looked away, up to the stars beginning to shine, as if asking for help.

After a few minutes, he stood between two of the upright posts and stretched his arms leaning his hands on the wood, posed like a mythical hero supporting the pillars of Hercules, and I saw the muscles in his arms tense as he clenched his fists. I thought he was going to shout, and I stood to face his black glare, hoping I was wrong.

His words came, calm and sad, and his eyes burned through my thoughtless blunder. He sighed, and when he spoke, it was as if he was explaining gently to a child.

"*Mia carissima*. Linton! Look at me. I was not dead at thirty. This is who I was," he said, touching his chest.

His use of my Christian name shocked me. "Then I guess I'm not dead either," I said, trying to ease the tension.

"You were alive at thirty also, no?"

His eyes still said he was angry, and his hands stayed agitated, making sweeping melodramatic gestures that punctuated the air.

For a moment my mind went blank and then it all made sense and I let out a huge sigh.

"Oh. I see. Yes of course. I see. We are each who we *were*. Alive and sentient. Cognisant."

"This is not, as you say, a *repeating*," he said. "It is a new... a different way, yes? A *seconda*... a better chance. New. You will see."

"I am trying. I'm so sorry. I didn't think. I'm always so afraid. Being in love is as terrifying as it is wonderful.

I'm delirious to have met you, but I wonder if that's the proper emotion to have when in love? It's not very stable is it? But then, love is a sort of insanity."

There was anger behind his eyes and he pursed his lips, but let me snuggle into his chest so that my next words were muffled into a fold of apricot wool.

"I don't want to lose this ... to lose you. I've never had ... I read that you... oh, never mind."

"I mind," he said. "Say it... please to say everything. *Grazie.*"

He looked apprehensive and his breath came in short spasms.

"You hate marriage!" I blurted, not daring a vision of his tormented blue eyes, "and you *kept* a boy. Those are just two of the disparaging anecdotes written about you by an artist named Vasari who came after you. After you died. And you do look horrified, so... I thought... so..."

He lifted my chin and I shut my eyes, and after he kissed my eyelids, they fluttered open. I was humiliated. Standing as vulnerable as I had ever been, disgusted at being such a *girl*.

"This is the truth," he said waving his arm at the day. "And this, you and me, is not a repeating. So... now I am this man and not the other. Yes? I want you. I *kept* boy servants and apprentices as was natural. *Naturale!* Do you hear? Not sexual. I wait for you. I demand to marry only you. Does this help?"

"Yes," I said into his shoulder.

"*Mia carrissima.* Come, we will walk some more."

I wiped my nose on his cloak and he laughed. "*Grazie*," he said. "You are feeling better?"

"I feel stupid but wonderfully stupid," I said. "Sheepish, we call it."

"*Stupido,*" he said. "I have learned this word."

"Love is the last relay
and ultimate outposts of eternity"
~ Dante Gabriel Rossetti

the annunciation

"I am having to leave, now."

Sandro announced these six words quite abruptly and unexpectedly, just as I was pouring cream into his tea, and I experienced a small death in the pit of my stomach. The cup rattled against the saucer.

"I tell you this, so I might."

"Oh," I said, feigning calm, sure the colour of living flesh had drained from my face, "will you be gone long?"

"I think perhaps a *momento*. Hardly more than this."

"You are speaking in metaphor I think. Can you be more..."

"More real?" he interrupted.

"That would be nice."

Sandro stared hard at my face, searching for clues. "*Mia carissima*, you are reading again."

His admonishment was true. Most of the time I lived between the lines, reading into what Sandro said and what I believed he was saying. I was more comfortable between the pages of art history, between the pages of a novel, and between the pages of my own diary. Too in my head.

"It's what I do," I said, as if that justified my predisposition to question all things delivered in a rainbow.

"I know this about you, but, it is time for you to trust me. I am as *confuso* as you are about what has happened. I have wondered if I had been sent to the *purgatorio* of Dante, but, the first time I saw you it was, as you say, a presentation."

"A visitation," I corrected.

"*Si,* a visit. A gentle visit. A sign of good. There was no malefic... nothing sinister. I was filled with light."

"Sometimes I think you're the goad of my old age and that Ralph was right. You're my Ralph. Sandro de Bricassart," I said.

"Now, you are making a nonsense, *sciocheze*. This is who?"

"Loving a phantom is confusing."

Sandro grabbed my shoulders and lifted my chin so I had to close my eyes to avoid his face.

"*Caramia*, open your eyes."

"They are open. I can see a lot of things this way," I said. "You'd be surprised."

"I mean now. Your eyes, here. Open them for me."

I could only oblige. His grip told me he was not going to let me run. His face was full of concern, so much so, that I wanted to comfort him.

"I'm ..."

"*Silenzio*, little one. You must listen. I am... finding something. I cannot express this. I am knowing something which is significant, yes? It is calling to me."

It was one time I was pleased to have been told not to respond. I didn't want to ask any more questions or especially be pressured to answer, and most of all, I didn't want to cry.

"How this can be? I can only wonder," he said. "It is something which must be done. It does not please me to leave you. You want to be with us, yes?"

"Us?"

I nodded even though I had no idea what he meant, and looked down at his feet. I could feel that burning of the nose and eyes which precedes the floodgate of trapped tears. He kissed the top of my head and rubbed my back, and whispered what sounded like an incantation, into my ear. That was when I felt it appropriate to sob into his chest.

So much for Shakespeare's 'parting is sweet sorrow,' I thought.

Sandro was smart. He allowed me to cry and played the soothing lover, kissing my wet face and teasing small kisses between my sobs until I felt the warmth of desire overtake my fear and opened to him. So, he loved me out of my sorrow, and it was sweet, and maybe, in the end, Shakespeare had the right attitude. I just didn't want the ending of offending shadows he wrote about. I didn't want any ending at all.

"So, how I can be a phantom? I am as you see, young and alive, no? I died when I was an old man. So, as you see, I cannot be a phantom. I could only be this after I am old. Somehow I, we, have been taken. Moved from here and there. *The Adoration* is our door. We live in front of it and behind it. Where are the young ones of us who we know? I ask myself this, and then I stop because it does not matter. This now is what matters."

Sandro's words cut through my over-thinking. The same mistaken way Mary Carson's words had been taken to heart without filtering them through kindness. I had ignored the fact that life had some guarantees of love to offer. Sandro was not the goad of my old age – I was.

I took Sandro's hand. "Come. Bring your tea," I said, and pulled him into the living room. I positioned us in front of *The Adoration* and sat him on the sofa. I stood facing him, underneath the painting while he looked on, sipping his tea.

Naturally, Sophie joined him.

The two of them became my students. *The Adoration* was my 'slide' on a projector screen in a lecture theatre. Suddenly I knew what to say and why I needed to say it as a teacher and the historian of my own life.

"This painting has a lot to say," I said. I pointed to several faces in turn. "These are real people. Flesh and blood. "What is going on here? What do you see? What is the artist telling us?"

Sandro set his tea aside and gently lifted Sophie to

the warm spot he vacated, making sure she was settled. Sophie immediately curled back into a default position of contentment and started to groom her tail.

It was my turn to be the student. I passed Sandro and he put both his hands on my shoulders.

"Thank you for this," he said. "I will talk now, and you will see truth, yes?"

"That's all I want. Now please tell me how this painting is a door."

"This is what must be I think," he said.

I poured a glass of sherry and sat next to Sophie, and she snuggled into my lap like the old days. It was surreal to see the two Sandros together. The one frozen in miniature and the one vital and living. The same face and titian hair. The same sense of overwhelming masculine power.

Sandro took a deep breath and smiled. "I am sorry in the first, to tell I may only say some things. But I can give how this is magical to me. How this did happen? This is the most I am able to tell."

"It will be enough," I said. "The rest will fill in later." I smiled and saw him visibly relax. "That I know for certain."

Sandro inclined his lovely red curls towards the painting behind him. "It is a bribe. A meeting place of power. The power of god and the power of the Medici. The magi are the first witnesses, the first guests selected from everyone to be a family of adoration.

"It was in my studio. You saw where. It consumed

me while I painted but I was not obsessed. I painted a contract, yes? Some *importante* persons who I need to please to stay eating. But it did not keep like this. I see something which makes me afraid that catches at my soul. Power comes into my brush and this is different from anything."

Sandro turned and touched the centre of the painting. Then addressed me staring into my eyes.

"I feel I may join... them. This is seems natural to be, and not a dream.

"I want to join this meeting, to have been invited. To walk in and turn around, showing I am there and I am as powerful as they, and as I paint I feel power entering the painting. Real power through me. It fills me and the work goes fast. I cannot say all, but I paint more.

"Suddenly I am there with the crowd. It is real. I am hearing, and smelling the air: the horses, the spices of the magi, and the perfumes of the finery. The others are talking with each other. The peacock calls and the horse bolts. He must be calmed by several men. The baby starts to cry and Mary suckles him. Lorenzo and Piero begin to talk business. My patron approaches me and asks when my work will be done. He tells me he will not pay. He joins his catamite and the young cousins go behind the holy shelter to gamble. I look out to my studio and then I am back.

"I find I can enter and return to the studio whenever I need and so I play, and when it is hanging in the chapel I can go inside and back out into the chapel. It is a door, yes, but there is nothing in there to stay. When I am dying I know I will be there. I just know. Wherever the painting is I am there also. I can enter where it is."

Sandro gestured again to the *Adoration*. "Now that I see it here, I must tell you a secret. I can go in this small thing and leave you and be there in *Firenze*, and I can return the same, to this room. This is how I will go."

Sandro touched his self-portrait and spoke into the painting. "You will see me here and know I am safe in *Firenze* where time has stayed mine, and now, yours."

He sighed and turned towards me.

I leaned forward causing Sophie to protest. "Then I can go through it too."

"*Non, mia carissima*, you must go through the one in *Firenze*. I am not knowing why but this is."

The dark churchyard was still vibrating with the absorbed heat of the day but I shivered uncontrollably as we ambled through the gravestones. The steeple clock struck the midnight hour and a flurry of bats swarmed out of the tower. We stopped near the bench on a smooth bank of grass. Sandro looked down and firmly took my hand.

"You are a brave woman, *cara*."

I gritted my mind against what he was going to tell me even though I knew it was here, on this earthy plot, where I would be buried. He heard my thoughts.

"It is so bad?"

"It is ... odd."

"I have died. You know this. It was natural, *mia carissima*. A breath. Then it was over, and now this after, with you, so what is there but hope? Come, there is no need to shiver."

"I'm not sure what I want for my epitaph. I wrote down one or two thoughts. I rather liked a quote from Dante: *the straightway is found*, but it doesn't matter. Shall we dance on my grave, then," I said, denying my discomfort.

He stepped gingerly into the unmarked space and pulled me in, and we locked in an embrace. I was enveloped in cloak love, and slowly he paraded me in a formal Renaissance dance, exposing me to the stars at arms length, but held hand-fast as he led me in a circle. The look of adoration in his eyes made me wish for an afterlife of such overwhelming bliss that a deserted body seemed like nothing. A feather-life. I was not alone.

"I am also not alone," he said, and we stood there under the moon and the memories, and a lifetime of unfulfilled expectations.

"I will know when it's time for me to go," he said. "I promise you we will not be parted for long."

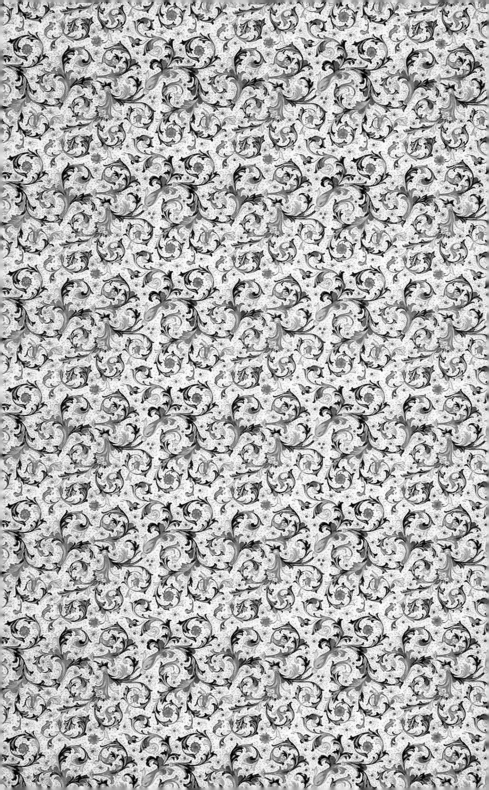

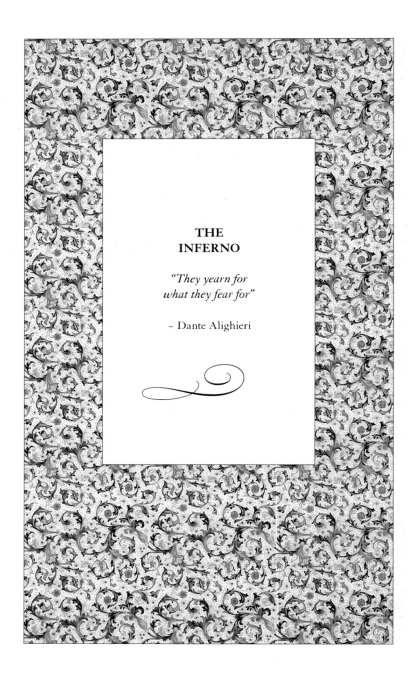

THE
INFERNO

*"They yearn for
what they fear for"*

~ Dante Alighieri

*"My own Beloved, who hast lifted me
From this drear flat of earth where I was thrown,
And, in betwixt the languid ringlets, blown
A life-breath, till the forehead hopefully
Shines out again, as all the angels see,
Before thy saving kiss. My own, my own,
Who camest to me when the world was gone"*

~ Elizabeth Barrett Browning

land escapes

There was a senior citizen, very much the worse for wear, wearily pushing a shopping cart in the super-market. The rusty wheels squealed an inch at a time and finally paused at a tall display of baked beans. He squinted at a brand out of reach and then at Sandro. The man was nonplussed, considering he was eyeing Sandro's cloak with a look of obvious admiration. He nodded to me.

"D'you think your husband could reach that tin for me," he asked. "The one with the green label."

It was within easy grasp but Sandro obliged, smiling.

The old eyes darted from Sandro to me and back to Sandro.*"Grazie tante,"* he said in an unlikely Manchester accent, and shuffled on.

Sandro looked uncomfortable. "I looked like that at the end," he said.

⁓

I could only guess how Sandro's time accelerated aging. Leonardo's last portrait in Raphael's *School of Athens* presented a man in his sixties who resembled the persona of a venerable Merlin, so Sandro's self-assessment may well have been accurate.

Sandro and I came face to face when both of us were thirty-five, but there was another reason we chose to paint ourselves in our prime. Those were the years where we were physically mature. After that, it was only our bodies that aged, just like Mary Carson had said. She had been especially right in her rage against timing and her angst over a younger man. I had heard her correctly which was why I'd been so angry. Mary had spoken the truth. Clearly, I was never going to relive my horror of such an insensitive summer/winter encounter without a fight.

⁓

Giorgio Vasari, the painter, born forty years after Sandro's death, was a sly storyteller who embellished his own versions of the truth. In his book *Lives of the Artists*, he wrote to entertain, supplying colourful data, conveniently after a generation of eye-witnesses had passed on.

He passed on a despairing account of Sandro's final

years that, due to the latest fad, the printed word, eclipsed the indelible truth. Such is the power of one man's ambition to document his profession by freezing the anecdotes of his day into a commercial froth of mythology.

His cavalier attitude towards evidence served his agenda of producing a salable book, which sadly, became one of the only sources we art historians have, in which to dip our toes. But the power of judgemental memories is a poor substitute for history, and so Vasari's account isn't much better than a dogpaddle in Hell's River Styx – the river of forgetfulness.

Vasari was manipulatively cavalier about reporting the facts. He was a gossip columnist with biased opinions and an agenda selective enough to promote or condemn each artist as would render himself the expert. Today's equivalent publication would end with the disclaimer, 'believe it or not.'

Giorgio's biographical profile did much to tarnish Botticelli's legacy as much as his others crowned an elite of favorites with laurels of sycophantic pomp. Individual artists were either granted short shrift or awarded the immortality of inflated hero worship.

Varari ignored the power of Sandro's vital years, and gathered instead, the controversial scraps that lingered concerning his public decline. Fragments which amounted to a fabrication of superstitious hearsay on the tail-end of the Savonarola inquisition and its fallout of creative upheaval.

Sandro Botticelli's chapter was an unfortunate

summary of an artist's life, somewhere between ignorance and fiction.

Vasari's definitive caricature of the aging Sandro as a frantic zealot, a spent sinner grovelling at heaven's gate, was more than melodramatic license, as was the vision of him devolving into a destitute raggedy door-to-door icon peddler.

Botticelli was a man of property when he died, but this had not been interesting enough for Vasari to mention, and his padded treatise went unchallenged.

I am the companion of Botticelli's middle-years and not the frail lunatic who, according to Vasari, Sandro would become when he reached sixty-five. The same milestone I so recently cornered somewhere in the year 2014.

Outwardly, Sandro's later works compromised a religion's fervour he could fake. Times were too tough to play the slighted artiste. Inwardly, he fumed but his natural penchant for jest covered his tracks. Being known as a *studio clown* served him well.

Sandro needed commissions and the subject matter was irrelevant to him, as long they could be couched in metaphors underneath the celebration of martyrdoms or adorations under the watchful eyes of unlikely-looking holy infants. Appearances were everything. Competition was fierce. I wouldn't prevent him burning his works on Savonarola's vanity fire, even if I could. Such a deed was his right, besides it was a 'done.' Part of history.

I shouted I love you, my words piercing the slashings of vertical rain between us, my voice gathering the weight of water like a sponge. Sandro's facial expression was obscured by silvery sheets of transparent foil. Trying to be heard over the din of weather like the roar of restaurant babble.

Love underwater. I adored my face being wet and my words delivered louder than intimacy.

We talked through the late afternoon hours of rumbling dry thunder before the rains came, then, back by the fire, long into the dusk after our own outpourings of love. I was filled with light. Botticelli loved me. My world was hallowed with grass-scented rain, bouquets of ozone, and crackled with the magic of split atoms.

Cobalt flames still played over the ceramic logs in the fireplace. Sandro spoke suddenly, his voice husky with emotion. "You were soaked through. Do you remember?"

Images of an awkward meeting replayed in my mind. I felt consumed with guilt. Flooded with conflicting emotions of shame and longing, and I couldn't bear to look into his eyes. "How could I forget."

"It is all right, *mia carissima*, it is gone now. I only meant the rain reminded me of your dress and how I could see your skin through the thin cotton, and how I wanted you."

"It was a wonderful day. I was so nervous and in love. And then such a devastating ... event. I wanted to die. Anything to remove what I'd done. My actions ... there was no way to make things right."

"I would have understood."

"I was in no condition to face you. I had betrayed everything I thought to be true about myself. I didn't understand love. I'm not sure I understand it now."

He pulled me close and smoothed my hair. "Yes, you do. You teach me this."

The night dropped quickly, and the rain fell stronger turning the crimson room into a burgundy cave. I gave in to primal feelings and relaxed like never before. It felt safe to allow spontaneous images to play in my mind. I dreamed the stirrings of stone-age fire with slabs of damp peat sending smoke into a cave's mouth, and the scent of tar pits and danger, and the sprites of primal beings dancing from the flames and up the walls like a shaman's painting while magenta light licked the contours of our hips and thighs.

We slept on bearskin hides pungent with recent life, feet warmed with hot stones wrapped in deerskin. I felt magnificently feral, but the stars frightened me.

The French doors were open to the garden, elemental, teeming with water and howling trees. Wind flared the long white curtains marking the thin veil between our centuries.

We explored our young flesh with slow kisses, old love fused together, slowly dissolving, chemical to chemical, bones heated to melting point.

Dawn brought the aftermath of two bodies cooled to warm wax.

The rain stopped. Drips from the eaves fell on the patio tiles like the ticking of a clock.

"Where will we live?" I asked.

"Florence," he answered drowsily. "Not here."

"No, I mean after."

"There is no after."

"Not even a hereafter?"

"We will see," he said. "Now, my *principessa*, it is time for dreaming.

WILD NIGHTS
"Wild nights. Wild nights.
Were I with thee,
Wild nights should be our luxury.
Futile the winds to a heart in port.
Done with the compass. Done with the chart.
Rowing in Eden. Ah, the sea.
Might I but moor tonight with thee"

~ Emily Dickenson

love underground

The London tube station made the old market of Florence seem like a small Sunday swell of placid folk on an afternoon picnic.

Steam issued from the entrance, like a stage set of Dante's Inferno, Hell's pit below stairs. I thought my advanced description of all things pertaining to the world underground had been thorough, if not excessive, but as we descended into the low pressure vacuum of stifled air, I saw the muscles in Sandro's face flinch.

The platform was the calm before the storm and the echoes of deep reptilian sighs amid the rattle of distant metal tumbled out into the cloying atmosphere of dead wind. I held Sandro's arm tightly, ready to guide him onto the train.

Trapped greasy air swirled from the tunnel's mouth, of what could easily be taken for the entrance to a monster's cave. Sandro looked uneasy from the sounds issuing forth from it like the stirrings of an awakening dragon, and I began to view my world as if I'd been dropped from the sky. An abducted alien unceremoniously subjected to an age of overpopulated mayhem.

The approaching roar from the tunnel pushed hot air ahead of itself – a silver worm emerged full of half-ingested frantic-eyed victims clamoring for escape.

I could see Sandro's expression in the reflection of the train's windows as it streaked by carrying multiple images of his anxiety. The train's breath surrounded us and belched to a stop before we were assaulted by the ugly stench of commuters: women's cheap perfume, men's liberal applications of aftershave, tobacco smoke, coffee and fast food, all mixed with mechanical grease and oil.

"Come on, that's us," I said, propelling Sandro towards what must have seemed like an army of attackers.

The belly of the beast slid open regurgitating a spill of bodies rushing for freedom. Escapees surged forward. We parted them where we stood. Either side of us they made for the sunlight like blind moles.

I urged Sandro toward the narrowing gap of the sliding doorway and dragged him closer, but his reluctance took precious seconds and the doors of the train began to close.

"It's safe," I said as I plowed on, pushing my way through the crowd, pulling him after me. "Darling, hurry it's about to leave."

For a brief instant the inside of the carriage had been empty, having disgorged itself of its last 'meal,' and I realized what I had asked this innocent man to do.

The doors whooshed softly behind us gently nipping Sandro's sleeve, and the exasperated expressions of the slowpokes left behind retreated at nightmarish speed. Resigned and irritated faces disappeared swiftly in a blur.

The usual confinement of sardine humanity enveloped us. Slick lights dimmed and flickered with the each successive contact with a new connecting rail. Traction gripped the wheels as we hurtled along propelled lurching tossed us into each other. Sandro caught me and I could feel his rapid breathing.

I transferred his hands to a metal pole and motioned Sandro to a newly vacated seat.

Sandro's voice seemed strangled. "*Cara.* We are inside the *inferno?*"

"No, not quite yet," I said, and squeezed his arm. "That's where we're going. It's called Picadilly. We're nearly there."

Naively, I had assumed he would be enchanted with

our modes of travel. I had the fleeting impression of taking Sandro on a playground carousel, and then working my up through tricycles, to jet planes and moon rockets. I overlooked the hellish atmosphere of the London underground.

I had been too eager, and now my sweetheart stared helplessly as we sped madly past bright squares of advertising into a maze of green tiles, rocking in time to rhythmic clacks, bouncing off dead-air pockets that must have seemed like we were entering the second level of hell. I half-expected to see red demons myself.

I chastised myself for not being more sensitive. I had been bragging. Throwing him into my world. Overselling. I was proud of our evolution: fast cars, flying high, electric treats, fast food, computers, smart cameras, and phones that can make small perfect paintings in a nanosecond. It was understandably overwhelming. Seeing a strange place through the innocent eyes of an 'old child' offered me a new perspective.

Sandro had shown me surprises, but nothing I didn't almost know. I was obsessed by little things: his art supplies and fresh pomegranates and the sweet liqueur he made from hanging bottles over the budding lemons so the fruit grew inside them.

I was submitting Sandro to moving pictures with special effects, rocket ships, photography and the internet. His circuits were reeling whereas mine had been pleasantly excited, and I realized how brave he was.

A straggle of bored travelers had carefully spaced themselves as far apart from each other as they could. Most were reading. One had taken the opportunity to close his eyes and sprawled as if dead, looking ironically like a clad Mars. Another stared hypnotically into the glow of a laptop. Several clung to overhead straps.

We hissed to a stop several times to exchange commuters, and I rubbed Sandro's back vigorously, whispering words of praise meant to comfort.

"Our stop is next," I said. "Hell."

He followed me enthusiastically to the doors, eager to disembark.

The train jerked us sideways as it stopped. The doors hissed open and he leapt onto the platform, pulling me after him and enfolded me in his arms.

"There. I comforted. You did it. Was it so bad?"

His grim expression said that it was.

The stairs offered a square of blue sky as bait, and Sandro slipped ahead of me, pulling me towards fresh air and the noise of traffic. A double-decker bus swerved past us, and a huddle of solemn-faced people swarmed across the street like one animal.

I had drawn Sandro a picture of the walk-sign man and explained the procedure of surviving the road. It felt very military. Walk. Halt. Walk again. Red light. Green light. Trooping in file and dodging cars. I longed for Florence and the smell of horse droppings. Such nostalgic teasing as this made me realize I was leaving my edge of the planet willingly.

The idleness of strolling is lost on London. We hustled with the human river of impatience known as the masses. Most were texting each other in a frenzy of strange new words – a language reduced to emoticons of thought, no deeper than a cat-scratch.

"You were marvellous," I said, "that couldn't have been easy."

"We do not have to stay?" Sandro said, sounding hopeful.

"No. I only have a few things to do," I replied, "and we can go, soon."

He watched me at the bank and the post office, looking more and more out of place, although he sent me dazzling smiles whenever I made eye contact.

I felt like a mother who had neglected the welfare of her child, so when I saw the balloon vendor I pulled Sandro over. To Sandro he was a man holding a cluster of colourful floating grapes

"They are filled with air," I said. "What colour do you want?"

"That and this."

"We'll take them all," I said.

We gave some away as we made our way to the bus stop, and one burst which must have been heart-stopping for him, and when we saw the bus approaching, I was excited to give him helium's parting gift. I told him to release the strings, and he gaped dumbstruck as they ascended to the clouds.

"They are reaching to heaven," he said.

"Lucky them," I said,

"*Mia carissima* we are there also very soon."

We took a late bus back to Little Cobiton. Sandro had the window seat, and I leaned my head on his shoulder, homesick for the fifteenth-century.

"We'll grab some burgers," I said. It seemed too 'coals to Newcastle' to offer him pizza although his Florence had never seen the stuff.

It began to drizzle.

"I have a surprise for you," I said as umbrellas exploded all over the streets below. I pulled mine from my purse and showed him how it extended.

"This is a special umbrella for you. It's one of my favorites." And when we were back on the streets, I pressed his finger on the button to release it.

The small tug as it flared open amused him, but the design of his *Birth of Venus* made him gasp.

"It is my own sky," he said, looking amazed. "I... *grazie*." He hugged me. "You are my goddess."

He held the dome of his painting over us and we took our time breathing in the country quiet.

Our churchyard was deserted. The rain pelted down in a refreshing song, washing the stain of London from our day.

I had one more goddess-like deed to perform. I unlocked my car with the opener from across the street. It sprang to life with a flash of headlights and a loud chirp.

Sandro behaved like a sedated child and obediently sat in the passenger seat marvelling how the umbrella collapsed.

It was a seven mile drive to the Burger King in Saffron Walden where I ordered from the car by shouting into a mesh box. A garbled voice confirmed I desired two whoppers, an extra-large order of fries, two small iced teas, and an extra cup of ice.

The girl at the first window took my money in a trance, and I handed an odoriferous bag of grease to my astonished guest, a few feet further on.

Sandro held the warm paper bag and a drink tray all the way home, probing inside the smell to pull out the occasional French-fry. They were hot and crisp. He crunched one and nodded approvingly.

"*Fantastico*," he uttered with each one. "You are right. Words are not possible for these French things."

By the time I'd parked the car, Sandro was munching happily, saying fries were *molto gustoso il meglio delizioso*, or as I gathered from his enthusiasm, tasty.

We dashed inside without the umbrella and I locked the car with a beep that made him jump.

"*Mio Dio!* I am forgetting you do this."

"Sorry, I should have warned you. I didn't think. You've heard it before."

And I hadn't been thinking. I'd been revelling in my role as the quintessential tour guide, bragging like a kid: I bet my century can beat your century.

In the end it was a 'draw.' Each time was unique unto itself. There were things to boast about, and then there were the oils of art and science that were unable to mix that we set aside.

We filled two plates with burgers and fries and I held up a packet triumphantly.

"And this is?"

"Ketchup!" he answered.

"Excellent," I said and tore open the plastic pouch.

Sandro looked dubious as it squirted sideways over-top my fries, barely missing his hand.

I turned the thermostat dial so flames leapt from a scant flicker into a purple roar.

Sandro grinned and pulled a soft throw over our legs and admired the instant appearance of ersatz fire. He picked up the remote for the television and examined it closely before setting it down gingerly as if it might explode.

"For all our miracles," I said. "I'd settle for the real thing when it comes to fire."

"Heat is real," he said warming his hands.

"Only medicine. We've made leaps. That's a given. Pain is controlled here."

I stopped myself and took a breath. I had been about to explain quantum physics which would have been con-voluted since I knew nothing other than Star Trek ter-minology and a few loose facts from the reader-friendly side of Stephen Hawking.

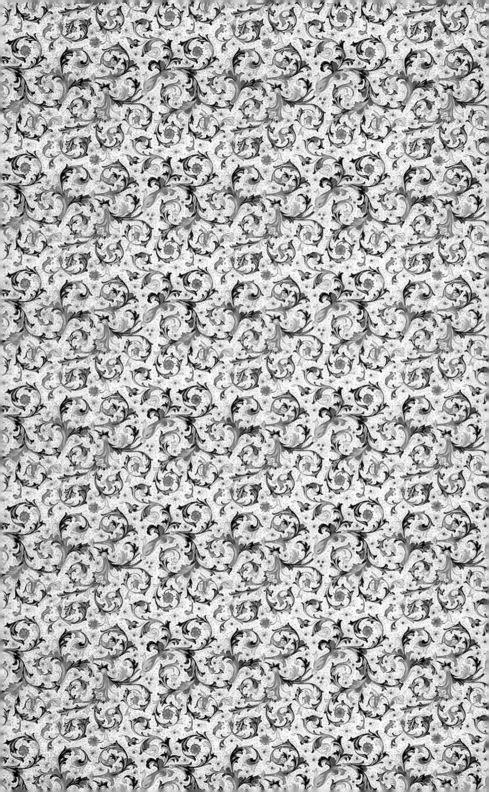

THE LOVE-SONG
of J. ALFRED PRUFROCK

"Would it have been worthwhile,
After the sunsets and the dooryards
and the sprinkled streets,
After the novels, after the teacups,
after the skirts that trail along the floor
And this, and so much more?
It is impossible to say just what I mean.
But as if a magic lantern
threw the nerves in patterns on a screen.
Would it have been worth while?
If one, settling a pillow or throwing off a shawl,
And turning toward the window, should say:
"That is not it at all,
That is not what I meant, at all"

~ T.S. Elliott

A ship there is and she sails the seas.
She's loaded deep, as deep can be;
But not as deep as the love I'm in
I know not how I sink or swim."

~ 17th century English folk song

searching for botticelli

Historically, the only facts I knew for sure was that Sandro Botticelli fell into relative obscurity late in life to be re-discovered in the 19th century by the Pre-Raphaelites — a poetic brotherhood of romantic idealists, and that he openly expressed a fear of marriage.

When I had first read of his disenchantment it had made me smile. He and I were related in one of the small ways that mattered. That historic slip had made him real to me. We shared a doomed vision from some passing impression that had affected us somewhere along the road to adulthood.

I thought I understood him and had said so to my class when I was a professor, rattling on that the stickiness of emotional life were quicksands of personal war. People cleaved to each other for better and worse. I used the example of artist's wives mentioned in passing and their mothers, never at all. Marriage to one's muse seemed the highest form of matrimony.

I showed Sandro online images of the Louvre and *The Mona Lisa*, and his own goddesses emblazoned on tote bags. We were having fun with an interactive map of the world to plot the places he'd been and the ones he could never have known.

Then, I asked him what death was like.

"For this we must go for a walk," he said.

A conversation about death meant a stroll through the graveyard. We kept on walking so he didn't have to face me while he explained. "*Mi amore cara mia* it was ... I am being *painted* in light. A falling, but to never hit the ground," he said. "*Capisci?*"

I must have looked worried.

"Do not look so, *mi amore*. This thing is an instant. Small." He made a gesture with his fingers measuring an inch apart. "*Piccolo*."

He waved life away in a sweep of his arm.

"But dying; dying is not," I said feeling perverse.

"*Cara mia*, this is not a *unico momento*. It is going, yes? And then ... anything. You, me, everything."

"You and me?" I said.

"Perhaps not to see in so disagreeably. We are no less

real. This is real. *Firenze* is real. You see. You touch. These 'things' are as they were. You do not change them."

"But they're out of order," I said.

"Which is?"

"Chronological. Time."

"You have one last demon *mia carrisima*. More on Maestro Death, then, eh. Then it will finish. But you want so I tell. *Mia carissima*, you let go. Love leads. There are trails of love. I connect with you, yes? I have no more words for 'this.' This ... things."

"You mean wishes?"

"*Non*. Whole loving," he said. "*Amare a fondo*. Entire loving. We are not without choices. In the centre of, as you call, 'things' there is a need to match. This is not desire but a making of a shape – a mould. A retuning, *si?*"

I struck a pose of martyrdom by crossing my arms in self-defense in a half-hearted attempt to generate sympathy.

"We must have been or we would not now be," he said. "*Comprendi?*"

"Fated lovers?" I asked, hopefully.

"I think more joyous connectings," he replied with a shrug.

I had been unravelling again but it was entirely necessary. The demon on my shoulder insisted I was on a joyride. Nothing but a bed of straw and a warm blanket, it hissed. It spat more iceberg words from hell. I saw them shining dangerously above the waterline concealing the sweet hooks of matrimony I had tried not to crave.

I turned for the rectory but Sandro grabbed my arm to stay. He took me by the shoulders and searched my eyes, not with anger, but the most profound hurt I had ever seen on a human face.

"*Niente*," he repeated in a restrained shout, forming his fingers together to show a small size. "How can you be this? Joy is nothing? So little?"

"Joy is everything which is why it scares me. It teases and then... I'm sorry, it is one of my demons."

"Sorry! *Ti dispiace?* You are sorry? Life is less true than you think. Do you not suppose I have thought these, as you say, *things?*"

"I supposed a lot of things in my life. I was living many lies. How may I help you? Do you have needs? Or is it all you helping me?"

Sandro looked momentarily defeated.

"Well, in death, *cara*, one learns the truth. Consider this. Consider for a moment that I know more than you, of this. Consider I am more than I was. And consider that I am yours. Consider I have this needs to understand. Then speak to me of sorry."

Naturally, my apology stuck in my throat, sounding forced under the circumstances.

"I lost you once," I said, and he understood, as one who was mine would. I became again, enfolded in my favourite place, held tight against his heart.

His words rumbled into my ears.

"*Mio amore*. I have lost also. Believe in yourself as good. For once, eh? You are not a visitation. I am no phantom. Somewhere we meet here for a reason. Words can only explain so, where we go is not for language. I held my hand to lead you, not to enchant. I think I called. You came. That is who we are. A completing, yes?"

My feeble reply 'yes' stained his shirt with tears. What more did I need? *Simpatico enfatico?* It was only our timing that was off. Only.

"*Mia carrisima* there is only one last demon. I help to show but you must cut him yourself."

If I was insane then it was a deception of brilliant compassion – a kind and considerate altered state.

Sandro was my home, now. A benevolent hospice where I was the student who needed compassionate intervention. I felt gathered in. My ongoing lesson of letting go was slowly progressing and then it advanced to the speed of light.

ECCLESIASTES 3: 1: 8
"To everything there is a season
And a time for every purpose under heaven
A time to be born and a time to die."
~ attributed to King Solomon

tis the season

I floated above Budge, waiting in the family room of the Grey Nuns Hospital pretending to read magazines. She flipped through glossy pages of the *Wall Street Tycoon* across from a silver Christmas tree dressed in all-blue ornaments and lights, pausing to rest her eyes on the ads for office supplies, the only form of literary relief. It was that or one of the stack of Dr. Seuss books piled in a corner.

She'd always loathed the illustrations and the text so blatantly condescending of an adult trying to write with the mind of a child. I had agreed, it would have to have been a deranged child with peanut butter for brains when it came to appreciating that level of poetry. The text was inane, hardly the quality to stand next to the lyricists Edward Lear and Lewis Carroll.

'The Jaberwocky' had been Budge's favourite bedtime

story whenever she had been with me for a weekend so her parents could argue guilt-free.

I weaned her on Renaissance art and Dante mixed with *Winnie the Pooh*. The illustrations of Edward Gorey ranked highest with his tales of emaciated Victorian children with dark circles under their eyes meeting fates in the darkness of gas-lamps and fog, It was this gloom that contrasted so gloriously against our electric blankets, fresh sheets, and bedtime snacks of hot milk and toasted teacakes that rendered them so satisfying.

Sometime, circa six-years-old, I had asked her what kind of bird she'd rather be, since disliking her name, Iris Bird, had become a continuing lament. It was the perfect question. The sort children are infinitely more capable of answering than adults, and relief had shone in her eyes. A budgie, she had piped up without hesitation. A blue one, she added as an afterthought. Then, after a brief pause while she consulted her blue-word list, she announced: ultramarine, not the turquoise ones.

The name Budge was approved with enthusiasm between her and me, the one adult she trusted.

Her mother had left home when Budge reached thirteen and she was left with her father who, being of scholarly mind, allowed me more hands-on time than before. Three years later, I effectively became the sole custody of a minor.

Budge at sweet sixteen, had been too big to leave in a basket on the doorstep so she had arrived at my house in a taxi with a small van of personal effects to follow.

I remembered the time Budge audited one of my 'Renaissance 101' courses. She was nineteen, her face shining in the centre of the row, half way up the stairs to the slide projector.

I gave the assembly my famous smile and asked, "Can you imagine?" with the conviction that we could and better had.

"Any student who cares to indulge," I said, "I award extra marks for ingenuity. You will have to make believe and make *me* believe."

I watched them shift in their seats. Sometimes for the surprise of an offbeat class, but mostly because they thought an 'easy A' was in the bag.

"Since art history fails as a closed book it can celebrate creativity," I told them.

"I shall read you my creed because I insist you learn how to travel in time. To stalk and interview the past with the heart of a ferret. To listen for the sounds within the heartbeat of alien traffic and to observe the street-life found there. I charge you to suspend all analysis until after cross-referencing the same event from several subjective viewpoints."

At this point there were a few nervous titters.

"I make these requests: use your natural gifts of perspective. Think of the Renaissance as a movie. It can be a romantic chick-flick or a thriller. Consider yourself the director of a documentary. Remove paintings from their frames. Study the sides that have faced the wall for centuries. They are clues. There are bloodstains on the floors and plague fires burning outside your window.

"Artists are flesh and bone travellers who lived outside their flat panels of wood and blocks of marble. They fell in love with their sculptures and models. They starved. They surpassed their professional reputations and survived their enemies which were many: revenge, jealousy, shame, disease, war, religious persecution, heresy, hate and love. Break their molds.

"The flavors of the renaissance have to be savored. The prolific Leonardo, is a rich stew, I said. Consider the raw and flinty Michelangelo as the best steak tartare."

"And Botticelli?" Budge called out.

I had sent her a wide smile. "Botticelli is strawberries dipped in dark chocolate," I replied, leaving no doubt of my addiction.

*"And we came forth
to contemplate the stars"*
~ Dante Alighieri

making a scene

I know the absolute truth of only one thing. It concerns the rise and fall of things: inevitably, everything breakable will eventually break.

My medical episode while Christmas shopping in a wild mall had been very elegant. I heard Sandro whisper "someone is coming, I have to go," and I swooned like a Victorian lady. One minute I was leaning over a fountain aiming a wishing coin at a painted goldfish, listening to a choir singing 'Hark the Herald Angels ...' and after the word angels, I was slumped gracefully, having been caught and lowered to the floor and more or less artistically arranged to look as if I was sleeping.

I awoke feeling like I was floating underwater. The room was an aquarium draped in white. A bank of machines with rows of multi-coloured fairy-lights hovered and blinked beside the bed below me. Very Christmassy, I thought, but either side of me there were rails fencing me, in.

Two nurses entered the room. The elder was in charge, and she peered at me, dictating to the younger, who made notations on a chart. Matron Nurse uttered things I didn't understand. "Patient still unconscious," she said. "No signs of REM." She tapped my elbow with a tiny rubber mallet the size of a pencil. "No reflex," she added, casually.

Clipboard Nurse copied everything onto a graph. Judging from the downward spikes dipping below the horizon line, the prognosis looked grim.

I tried to make contact. "But my eyes are open," I said to Matron. "Can't you see? I'm looking right at you. I feel a little dizzy, is all, but I haven't eaten, and what with the meds ... Perhaps some chicken soup," I suggested hopefully. "I need to get out of this bed. I have a houseguest. Look, he's very famous and I can't simply desert the man." I felt the twinge of guilt. Again.

I stared at the vital check marks cancelled by a red column of crosses on the clipboard.

"No, no no, you're not paying attention," I whispered over the clipboard minion's shoulder. "Can't you feel me breathing on you?" I spoke a little louder into her ear. "Fetch a doctor." Then, I shouted, "Sandro!"

It was obvious that I, the form on the bed, could not be the person behind Matron, as well as the body staring up at her from the bed, and also the one casting a shadow over Nurse Clipboard's last testament.

Even I could see my eyes were closed.

For a delirious moment, I believed I was dead but then I downgraded it to insane.

Something told me Sandro had returned to his world because mine had now defaulted to its customary hollow shell. I lifted my hand and saw the beginnings of familiar age spots. I was old, but I remembered what Sandro had said, determined to trust him: I promise you we will not be parted for long.

Budge entered the room with a look of concern. I watched the staff herd her into an alcove where she was read some riot act regarding my condition. She would have none of it and insisted on seeing me regardless of my being described derogatively as 'all that is *left* of her.'

Naturally, my eyes opened for Budge, and I glared past her into Matron's starched consternation. "Sometimes they recover," she said, mildly piqued, negating all her previous assurances to the contrary. She cooed at me. "Do you know where you are Miss Howard?"

"I'm lucky you're not an undertaker," I replied.

Budge snickered behind her. "Morning Queenie," she said. "Merry Christmas."

I've always stayed clear of hospitals, and I willed myself well so I could go home. I mentioned I wanted to fly to Italy and was given the thumbs down from everyone. The authorities felt I should be monitored for a long time and flatly refused to discharge me even if I passed my tests from here to eternity: psychological, physical, and mental.

I complained to Budge. It felt criminal to be forced to stay when I no longer required their care.

I edited everything I said in case I sabotaged any chance for freedom. It was best to smile and let everyone know how much I knew about current affairs as a demonstration of rational behaviour.

I asked Budge to bring me my laptop and my *Jansen*, and overindulged in much searching for Botticelli. I stared at a reproduction of his *Adoration* until my eyes felt like red Jell-O. I begged him to come out, but to no avail.

I left the book open to the page and tried to sleep.

My beloved rain splashed the hospital windows, pitter-spattering in Morse code: he loves me; he loves me not; he loves me.

Watching endless hours of *Tea with Mussolini* and *Room with a View* was slow torture, but it was the meds that kept me from Sandro. The prospect of his permanent loss was agony, so instead I made the raindrops say: he loves me; he loves me; he loves me, but I missed his eyes. Those blue Sandro Botticelli eyes.

THE
DIVINE COMEDY

*"Into the eternal darkness,
into fire and into ice"*

~ Dante Alighieri

"I saw, in gradual vision through my tears,
The sweet, sad years, the melancholy years,
Those of my own life, who by turns had flung
A shadow across me"

~ Elizabeth Barrett Browning

the agony

I probably asked one too many nurses if they'd seen a red-haired man wearing an orange cape, in the halls. 'He's Italian,' I had added for even less credibility.

"What made you ask such a mad thing?" Budge asked.

"I was tripped out on meds. It seemed logical at the time," I answered.

I was deemed of sound-enough mind to be taken into the surgeon's den and given the news of my impending demise. It seemed, I was not immortal.

A solemn face gave me the news ... *one year, Miss Howard* it said with grave concern.

I chuckled and referred to the event as *Howard's End*. It was meant as a joke, but the man had never heard of E.M. Forster. It was my luck to get stuck with a physician with no sense of flippancy about death and dying.

He added that the migraines I'd had for years were the symptoms of an inoperable brain tumour, and that he was amazed I'd survived this long considering the state of my MRI.

Despite the seriousness of the situation, I couldn't take my eyes from the nativity figurines on the edge of his desk, right under my nose. The figures were in the wrong place.

"Your Adoration isn't quite right," I said.

"My what?"

I pointed to the ornaments. "Your nativity. The Adoration." My hand poised over the figurines. "Would you mind?" I asked.

"Not at all." He gestured with his pen. "Go ahead."

He watched me curiously as I moved the figure of the kneeling magi in front of Mary and removed all the animals but one horse. I spaced the other two magi to form a triangle. "It's a bit like playing chess," I said.

I couldn't help but stare at the place Sandro should have been. "What do you see?" he asked.

I wiped an invisible tear. "An empty space. A huge empty space. Big as the pit of hell. There should be a peacock somewhere," I said, sorting through the figures of camels and sheep. "This is my friend Carino," I said, holding up a donkey, pocketing it. "He will keep me company."

The doctor raised an eyebrow. "Your chart mentions

hallucinations. I wonder if you can tell me more about that."

I looked back with a blank stare. "I saw an angel once," I said.

He scribbled something on his clipboard. "And when would this have been?" he asked.

"I can give you the exact hour," I said, "but it wasn't an hallucination. I saw his wings. I wonder why there are no princesses in chess."

I had Budge hang mistletoe over my bed and told the orderly it was angel bait, but the joke backfired; they watched me more closely.

My niece humoured me, trying to keep my mind on art. "Whatever happened to that lost Botticelli?" she asked over a mug of hospital tea, and hearing his name out of the blue with the word lost made me splutter hot tea down my nightdress.

"It's in storage."

"Did that Alessandro chap go home?"

"He did. The painting is still in dispute," I said. "It may be for a long time. It's a waiting game, not my favorite pastime."

"Speaking of Botticelli, that print in your living room is freaking me out. Every now and then, I think I can see your face in the crowd, and I swear the people move."

I missed Botticelli's kisses, and the straightjacket of healthcare was holding me hostage. I was being detained for further observation, so hospital jail required the cunning of a determined crow to escape. Of course, they thought I was bonkers. I thought I was bonkers.

They told Budge that an early form of dementia was common with my condition; I protested, saying the only thing crazy would be wasting away for months when one could die in one fell swoop. Not the smartest remark to make to a clipboard with power.

Psych staff visited me, and I behaved bland as milquetoast. I think I earned a star for my exam paper. I was sane, they told me and I tried not to look surprised. Budge smiled at me behind their backs. She knew.

Being judged of sound mind, I was sure of imminent release, but I was wrong. The measure of me was subject to the output numbers from the machines which did nothing lovely to my blood pressure.

"If you want to get out of here you should stop being so temperamental," Budge urged, but all I heard was the words tempera and mental in her suggestion which was a cruel jest. The universe seemed as perverse as ever.

Budge shmoozed my stony doctor, telling him that my irrational outbursts were utterances of artistic temperament and therefore an asset worth celebrating rather than something to penalize. I also explained, that I was writing my memoirs and that writers are partly and benignly schizophrenic in a good way when recalling their past, and didn't he appreciate great fiction?

Budge sprang me on a Tuesday. I wore my game face all the way home, feeling like a traitor for what I planned next. That's as far as I would allow myself to revert to being a sissy

I stayed compliant on the outside, devious as a spy, and faked swallowing pills like a pro. Budge left me 'sleeping' with Sophie and Simkin kneading away at my quilt in a room vibrating with feline power.

Telling massive lies made me hungry, so I got up and made tea, toast, and over-easy eggs with bacon. Sophie was partial to egg yolks, so she was given a sticky yellow glob diced small along with her share of crumbled bacon bits.

I couldn't imagine my life without her and I cried when she thanked me for her treat. It felt a little maudlin realizing this may be one of our last meals together, but I dismissed the thought, reminding myself that the cats delighted in each other, besides, I would bring Sandro back, soon.

"I'm going to take you and Simkin to Florence," I said. "Your friend misses you."

I came over dizzy while watching *Tea with Mussolini* for the umpteenth time, and told myself it was the bitter sauce of guilt. I may be about to take the freedom which belongs to me but I had to betray all my loved ones in the process. Budge gave me the inch to get home, and I was taking 1200 miles.

"Because thou art more noble and like a king,
Thou canst prevail against my fears and fling
Thy purple round me, till my heart shall grow
Too close against thine heart henceforth to know
How it shook when alone"
~ Elizabeth Barrett Browning

time after time

Waiting for Botticelli after he'd gone for a *momento* had been a nightmare, but he was still gone, and I felt the queasiness of emotion sickness, trembling like the last leaf from the tree of good and evil. I felt like an old scold who had neglected to count the hours of previous happiness as a blessing. They were never going to be enough. Earthly bliss is never enough. I longed for the sunshine of Florence and I longed for English rain.

I've never understood why people fail to express gratitude for rain. There's nothing to equal the therapy of a ferocious downpour to clear the air of lonely shadows.

The wind roared in a muffled whisper that I felt more than heard, and I checked the colour of the skies through a small, round, bevelled window, high over the front door. It was in the shape of a fan that always reminded me of a clear protractor I'd had in a grade-school math class. It looked wet, so I opened the door a crack and smelled rain through the two inch gap. Once I knew rain was falling, I could hear it – a gentle shooshing sound infused with the fragrance of a windswept sky and drenched stars.

I faced the *Adoration* and willed myself inside until I broke out in a sweat. I felt faint. Weak as a blade of grass. The painting my be a portal for Sandro but it was having no part of me.

I needed sleep. I needed to sleep outside, and my French doors offered the next best thing. I bundled up in blankets and faced the spectacle of rain, torrenting down like a beaded curtain in the open doorway. Rain drummed the patio tiles in hypnotic timpani, and the earthen embankment of gravestones and monuments either side of the garden absorbed the rest.

I slept with Sophie as a hot water bottle and under the guardianship of Simkin, that no creepy uninviteds would roam my nocturnal floors and shelter in the toes of my shoes. I surrendered to the elementals of cool flames and rain-song.

⌒

Some nights I wished for blanket rain which always pulled me into the dreamtime, hoping Sophie would lead me into a more recuperative nothingness.

I woke one midnight to distant rumbles that sounded like a heavy truck rolling through the street, but it had proven to be a thunderstorm. I wrapped myself in a raincoat and sat in my car to absorb it's white-noise, but a car seat was no match for a memory-foam mattress and a down quilt, so after a few exhilarating crashes, I abandoned the weather, made a pot of tea, turned off the lights, opened my living room curtains wide, and watched the spectacle of lightning as if I was in a darkened theatre. There I hunkered down, lonely and bereft, wrapped in blankets like a queen in her robes and viewed the command performance.

Life trickled away, sluicing towards the horizon like the runoff of old-age where I had unconsciously become comfortable, absentmindedly reworking the memory of an apricot cloak into a bridal veil.

THE LOVE-SONG
of J. ALFRED PRUFROCK
"There will be time to murder and create,
And time for all the works and days of hands
That lift and drop a question on your plate;
Time for you and time for me,
And time yet for a hundred indecisions,
And for a hundred visions and revisions,
Before the taking of a toast and tea"

~ T.S. Eliot

I dreamed the skyline of Florence was missing the bronze orb atop the Santa Maria del Fiore, so, I knew Sandro could be not much older than a teenager. From the progress of the dome, it was 1465. I ran through streets slick with rain, following Casper down an alley that opened into the field of poppies where I'd picnicked with Sophie. Delightfully, the poppy stalks turned into a sea of peacock feathers. I was overjoyed to be home, and when I woke I knew it was time to go back.

Budge was my only human dependent, so we had spoken of my last wishes in the hospital. She had been flippant.

"I have a small nest egg," I had said.

"Then you make a nice omelette for yourself. I will be fine."

"But Sophie and Simkin?"

"I am their Aunt Budge, so, no worries there," she said.

Leaving Sophie was a concern, but I rationalized her bliss with Simkin and their care to Budge. Sandro and I would return for them soon enough.

I booked my ticket and the dizzy spells retreated with my excitement. The worst case scenario would be reaching a ghastly dead end in a Florentine gallery.

I had two days to sort and pack my personal effects for the charity shops and make sure everything legal was in triplicate. Budge came with me to the bank to sign some papers.

Facing mortality gave me a twisted sense of humour. I enjoyed the kamikaze appeal of 'death by painting.' How apropos for me to dive into *The Adoration* and expire at the feet of art. To this end, I needed no telltale luggage to alert the neighbours or the taxi driver.

Renaissance artists had taught me to hide relevant things under an observer's nose where they would never see it, so I traveled incognito, artfully disguised as an aging woman with a cane meeting someone at the airport.

Sophie knew I was dying. She mewed pitifully and followed me from room to room. "I'll bring Sandro back," I told her. "We can live out our days in Florence. And after I die, between you and me, I can be the 'ghost in the gallery.' Either way, you and I and Simkin are family. You must understand, Sandro is my Simkin. You'll have to comfort Budge for a while; she's going to think this is her fault."

Sophie blinked like an owl without moving her head.

The room was settled. The cats had each found a Shan-gri-la spot, and my cup of Earl Grey was within arm's reach. I unplugged the telephone and curled up with Sophie and Simkin. Neither stirred. The *Venus and Mars* print was an empty spring landscape with a few fauns. The lovers had gone.

The house seemed cloaked in peace as I drank my tea. Leaving for Florence like a fugitive seemed a tad melodramatic. I could hardly wait.

I popped in a DVD: *Room with a View,* Forster's take on nineteenth-century tourists succumbing to the heady magic of poppies in Florence. The film Sandro had watched with his beloved city invaded by Edwardians.

"This is what years?" he had asked.

I gestured to the stainless steel kitchen and the telephone.

"A hundred years in the past," I replied. "Before all this."

"Everything is now," he had insisted.

*"You were made perfectly
To be loved
And surely I have loved you
In the idea of you
My whole life long. "*
~ Elizabeth Barrett Browning

buona notte sweet prince

I wrote a goodbye.

Dearest Budge ~

If I was out of my mind, I'd have been the first to tell you it wasn't for the want of trying. Besides, what is dementia for but to remove oneself from being old and useless? You know I'm of perfectly sound mind for a creative spirit.

Some take their last ride over the moon on a magic carpet, and I guess that about sums up this last journey of mine. There is more work to do with the Botticelli portrait and Alessandro is waiting in Florence, in need of my expertise, and every day counts, now.

I couldn't take the chance of you stopping me. Studying a great painting until the last moment is an extraordinary way to go. I won't be denied my last requests.

Now to the part where I apologize: I had to go. I wouldn't have blamed you for putting me in leg irons, I've been saying a lot of crazy things. You'll just have to trust me. They were all true.

Top drawer, inside my writing desk, there's a key to my safety deposit box. It's best you open it before you alert the bank I'm gone, otherwise it will be merry hell to get to the paperwork: my living will of course, and insurance policy, and the deeds to the house.

It's all yours now. The deeds to the cats come with the deal. You're name is as good as mine, so no worries there, you will have immediate access with your new card. When the time comes, I want the cheapest funeral. You will only be burying my past. ~ Love Q

P S ~ There is a large box in the closet of the spare room that is very special. Please, PLEASE make sure it isn't sent to a charity shop by mistake with my other things. This is extremely important. It is yours, now. Open it with Alessandro's and my love.

I imagined the jet's captain uttering the word *engage* or some equally starting-pistol order to get underway. The engines whined into a storm of killer bees and sent my bones thrumming against my seat. The point of no return was imminent: I had beaten the system that treated the elderly and dying like fragile imbeciles, a victory for the aged and infirm.

I waited for the moment. That, being shoved into one's seat by invisible hands moment, when momentum shifts. It was delightful to close my eyes and savour my last contact with the island of Great Britain, counting the slickety wet yards of the seams in the blurring concrete below, sensing that last second before lifting at last, pinned like a willing butterfly, rising, leaving, heading, climbing dreamward into a vast blue time-tunnel sky.

I gave the stewardess my best Garbo stare, peering over large sunglasses. My eyes grew heavy from the effects of neat brandy on an empty stomach at ten-thousand feet. I ordered another brandy and cut it with ginger ale.

In the meantime, I kept watch on the narrow theatre curtain from which a sandwich trolley might emerge before I passed out from hunger.

I tossed back the last of the ginger ale remembering how Sandro had reacted to his first taste of a fizzy drink and was left to contemplate a glass of nervous ice cubes. I crunched the smallest one in memory of him, and steeled myself as a tear escaped and rolled down my cheek. It felt as if his cold finger traced a line from my eyes to my chin, and I knew I was dangerously close to losing it.

I heard a voice say, may I take that from you, and sniffed brightly. The stewardess pointed to my glass.

I looked up startled. "No no, I need them," said rather shrilly. "That is, they help me."

"Are you are feeling unwell?"

"Not at all. I just... like ice."

I needn't have worried. She moved on with a blank expression on her face and beamed at a handsome man across the aisle. Amazingly, for once I was grateful for the anonymity that comes with grey hair.

An hour into the flight, I probably looked as if I was dozing, but I was alert with my magnifying glass almost touching my dog-eared map. I was transfixed leaning over a transparent street map of Florence under which lay a reproduction of the famous *Veduta della Catena* chain map of 1485 Firenze with its walls and gates. It showed the beginnings of a famously recognizable skyline whose forever skyscrapers were still the ancient campanile and the red dome of the cathedral of *Santa Maria del Fiore...* *Saint Mary of the flowers*, with its cross and golden orb. It reminded me of the 'Where's Waldo' illustrations I used to search with Budge, as if we were slightly levitating over a city like a seagull. It was easy to imagine I was wandering inside the antique map behind one of the illustrated buildings where I had so recently been happy.

In my mind I walked the pathways Sandro and I had taken, footstep for footstep, across a landscape imprisoned in a bubble of time like a diorama in a museum.

I could smell the sunlight glinting off freshly-exposed marble crystals and polished bronze. Old Florence had been an open art gallery with clouds for a ceiling and works left unguarded at night. Famous paintings still hung on crude nails and sculptures were left exposed to the elements. The air resounded with volatile trading, street-bargaining, and the turning of wooden wheels creaking like old ships. The backs of oxen heaved groaning carts of stone blocks, bags of sand, and treated timbers.

I had crushed an old straw summer hat into my capacious handbag for Carino.

I whispered goodnight Prince Sandro and fell into a disturbed dream where the old apple-vendor morphed into a witch, and I saw myself in the magic mirror as an old crone, an Elizabethan 'Queenie' wearing a wild red wig surrounding a lead-white clown face with blackened teeth. A woman who wore a fanned collar, the shape of a peacock's tail. "Who is the fairest of them all?" I heard myself ask.

"Simonetta," came the bored reply, and the mirror shattered.

I woke with the ice cubes in my lap and thought at first they were shards of glass.

THE PARADISO

"The world, when still in peril,

thought that, wheeling,
in the third epicycle, Cyprian
the fair sent down her rays of frenzied love,

... and gave the name of her
with whom I have begun this canto, to
the planet that is courted by the sun,
at times behind her and at times in front."

~ Dante Alighieri

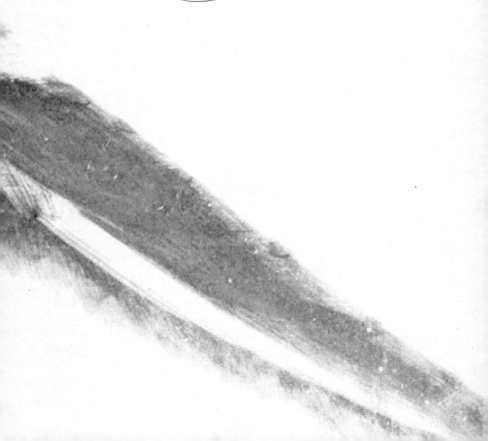

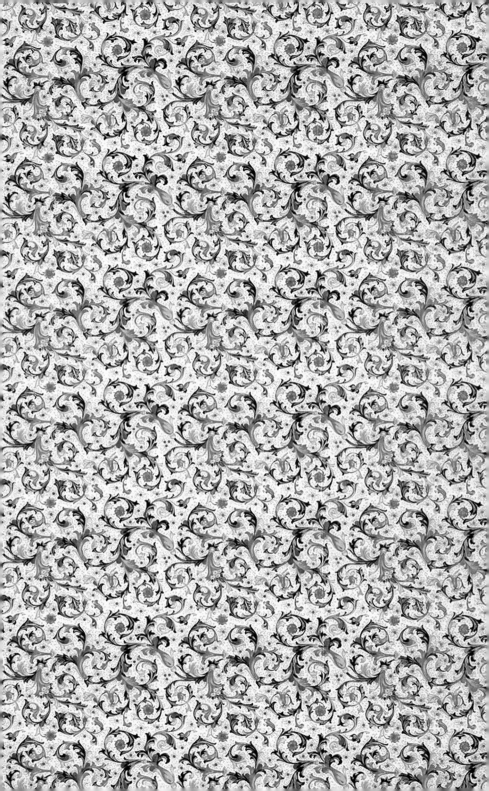

the paradiso

the morning star

~ ETERNITY ~

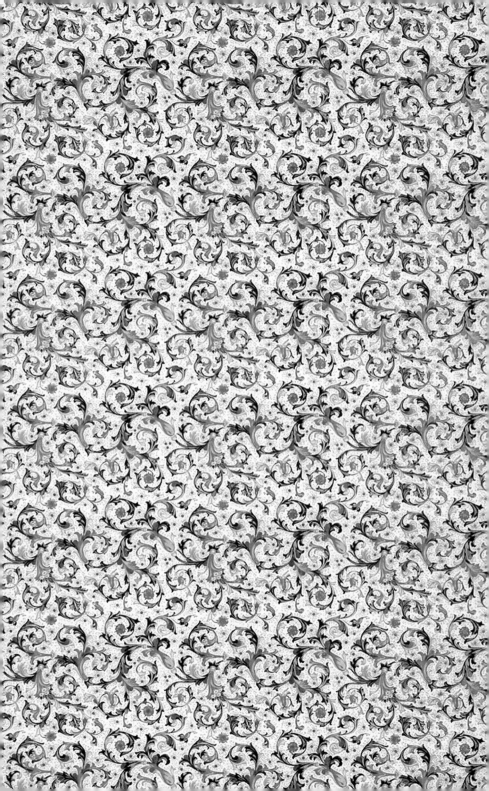

> *"Darkling I listen; and, for many a time*
> *I have been half in love with easeful Death,*
> *Call'd him soft names in many a musèd rhyme,*
> *To take into the air my quiet breath;*
> *Now more than ever seems it rich to die,*
> *To cease upon the midnight with no pain,*
> *While thou art pouring forth thy soul abroad*
> *In such an ecstasy"*
> ~ John Keats

the ecstasy

It was six o-clock in the afternoon when I hailed a taxi from the airport terminal in Florence. The roads were choked with cars. The word terminal rang in my head.

The traffic slowed to a stop near the market and I searched the square for Sandro or his old friend, Melazio, selling apples. Of course, neither of them could have been there. I recognized the latest statue of Il Porcellino guarding the fountain. I wasn't senile, I knew it was the twenty-first century.

I caught the movement of an apricot cloak, and begged the driver to wait, slipping from the vehicle as if hypnotized, with his protestations of *stupido Inglesi* mixed with an Italian invective of swearing that bellowed behind me.

The bright colour was absorbed by the crowd until I glimpsed it briefly, flickering like a light in front of me. I became obsessed with the vanishing sliver of an orange hem which continued to flash between a crush of tourists who had been reduced to a black and white postcard. The orange fabric evaded me, until I lost all sense of direction. It was useless to find another taxi, but I was within walking distance of the Uffizi.

⌒

I heard the eerie shriek of a peacock as I entered the Uffizi, and ran towards it shivering from a sudden chill. The bird's anxious cries echoed around the walls as I paused to compose myself in readiness for the stairs. My doctors had expressly forbidden stairs but there was a queue at the elevator and I couldn't wait.

I silently screamed Sandro's name every few steps, and in response the peacock answered, its calls growing ever more faint.

At the top of the stairs I saw the sweep of turquoise tail feathers disappearing around a corner, and I followed. My pulse quickened menacingly, but I hobbled as fast as I could with my cane. The soles of my running shoes made squeaking noises on the marble floor.

A uniformed woman approached me, looking concerned. "*Signora* you are looking for someone?"

"A painting," I managed to wheeze. "I'm looking for Sandro ..."

"Ah, Botticelli... he is there. To the right. Room ten. But you need a wheelchair. For you, I will get. You wait, eh?"

I had no choice but to wait. The walls were moving and I knew the earthquake was inside me.

The woman returned and installed my feet with restraints. I tried to remain calm but my cane clattered to the floor where it rolled in a circle, pinned at one end by its carved lion's head. It was retrieved and I took a few deep breaths, but I felt heat rising up my arms and into my face. The corridor was stifling. A tidal wave of human resistance pushed against my chair.

Phantom tourists surged past, rushing in a warm wind over and through me, but the wheelchair glided smoothly enough towards *The Adoration*. I held my breath.

"*Scusi Signora*. Permit me to ..."

"NO!" I felt the breath go out of me as I interrupted her rehearsed patter. I was suddenly frantic. "Where is it?" I shouted, gesturing frantically to the empty space on the wall.

"*Scusi?*"

The Adoration was gone.

I had to speak in spasms. "Where is ... the painting ... that goes ... here?"

The woman shrugged. "Ah, that one. Yes, it is away," she said with the casual efficiency of memorized English.

I swallowed painfully. "How far! ... How far away?"

She paused and looked up to the right as if consulting a chart. "I think ... in the building," she said. "It is time for the cleaning and the examine. For the back, eh? To make it safe," she replied, checking her wristwatch.

My voice was overly shrill. I could feel my body shaking, and my nerves were snapping like old wires in a suspension bridge. "Can I see it? I must see it!"

"It is not permitted. There are many others..."

"No, you don't understand," I interrupted. "I've come a *very* long way to see it."

I was exhausted and the tears started to stream down my face without any effort from me. In fact they surprised me. I hadn't planned crying as a ruse, but my expression moved her. She looked over her shoulder for enemies.

"You are alone?" she asked.

"Abandoned."

"Come," she said. "I take. We tell no-one."

"Not a living soul," I said.

~

The staff elevator dropped agonizingly slowly to the basement of the gallery. It felt like Dante's descent into the bowels of hell, and the enclosed space threatened to suffocate me. When its ancient cage creaked to a stop, I was greeted by a maze of corridors, and I thought for a horrified moment I had been dreaming and was back in the hospital. The ankle cuffs on my chair reminded me of a gurney but my nurse was dressed in navy-blue serge and wore an official Uffizi badge emblazoned with the word *personale*.

She seemed to know where she was going, but it felt like we were laboring our way to the center of a cold labyrinth, and once again I heard the mournful cry of a peacock, but this time I knew it was inside my head.

And then he was there. Botticelli, my haughty guide gesturing to step this way as if to say, welcome home, I have been waiting years for this moment.

I heard the faint sounds of the campanile bells yet the figure of Botticelli remained frozen. The woman left me then, with an Italian phrase of formal retreat relieving herself of further responsibility.

The painting was leaning against a wall easel. The perfect height for standing face to face.

"*Mia carissima* you are here at last," a voice said, but the painting remained static. I looked for signs of a gentle breeze in the draperies but there was nothing. Just a yellowed patina of surface cracks and a light bouncing off the varnish, now that it was subjected to harsh florescent lighting. *The Adoration* grew into a life-size billboard. I had a flashback of Sandro's underground excursion to Victoria station, and a scene from the movie where Harry Potter runs towards a train-station wall.

My fall from grace arrived as a sharp intake of breath. Nothing more outrageous than that. I recall leaping out of the wheelchair, slipping awkwardly to the floor, and picking up my dignity, running hell-bent towards the painting. I tripped over the hem of my long red gown, headlong into the *Adoration* as if it was an open gateway, and to accentuate my entrance, I heard the sound effect of rusty hinges, like the door of a haunted house. Melazio's voice called out, are you free? ... are you free? ... are you free?

A memory screen-door swung at the whim of hot gypsy breezes. A threshold keeping time to an old summer in the season of lemonade and coconut tans. My formal gown was replaced by a well-remembered light cotton dress with primavera flowers, its hem lifting as I walked my imaginary past life, pretending I was a glamourous runway model. Long effortless strides in painless red high heels that sank into the dirt of the Via Ognissanti.

"*Men could not part us with their worldly jars,*
Nor the seas change us, nor the tempests bend;
Our hands would touch for all the mountain-bars:
And, heaven being rolled between us at the end,
We should but vow the faster for the stars"
~ Elizabeth Barrett Browning

i'll be home for christmas

My body knows this light. It's imprinted over crisp autumn days that smell of incoming snow and red apples.

I ran through the streets of Florence, my brain on fire, and saw buildings which shouldn't be there, superimposed over Sandro's time. I passed through the stone walls of the campanile and felt a cool tugging as if someone had hold of my shadow. But I moved on and let it be stretched from me. I no longer needed to cast a persona of self.

The obstacle between me and Sandro felt like a tangle of gossamer. Sheer theatre curtains fluttered like so many layers of flat ghosts floating in liquid silk – a 13 denier mist clung to my face like a wet spider web.

It turned opaque which reminded me of milky gauze bandages and diaphanous transparent shrouds like the coffins of silkworms. Otherworldly ether threatened to smother me. I felt saturated with fear. A freak snowstorm blew across my path and compressed into a bridal veil. I had the impression of white flakes in my hair like fallen stars.

I stopped running to skim the surface of velvet paving stones, and the other people had stopped moving. A business woman in a grey suit holding a black umbrella mingled with a principessa wearing a wedding gown and glass slippers. Did I need to choose a world or was it choosing me? I saw a vision of myself in my crimson couturier portrait dress racing a few steps ahead of me, under a *Birth of Venus* umbrella. I needed to follow her. Cinderella racing towards midnight.

The campanile pealed the dying moments of a dream.

My slippers were filling with blood and I remembered the fairytale of the enchanted red shoes that had danced a girl to death. They turned into pink carpet slippers that bulged with bunions, and I was immediately the death crone, the Baba Yaga, hunched and hobbling. Then I was a child skipping over hopscotch numbers chalked on the cobblestones of the Piazza della Signoria, and the Uffizi was far behind me. One -- four -- eight -- zero -- one -- nine -- eight -- four, and as I played I was a teenager -- 18 -- hop -- and a young woman -- hop -- and the number 35 flashed like a lightning bolt, and my life continued to spin on a creaky spool, and a bank of gossamer theatre curtains opened to a view of the Ponte Vecchio.

For a moment my head was a tangle of directions. Botticelli could be anywhere. And then as the sun retreated into midnight, I remembered the gardens of the Boboli.

A sickening feeling enveloped me as I sped towards the Arno. The dark river moved slowly, shimmering under the moon, a fluid ribbon of greasy blue slipping beneath the Ponte Vecchio like a silent oil slick.

The bridge was rife with damn tourists. Terribly wrong. But then, I saw parading horses and banners too, and the lyrics of a sad song filtered through my fear: *I'll be home for Christmas, if only in my dreams.* I paused from a wave of nausea and was sick over the railings.

The night closed quickly, severing my century and Botticelli's. I felt leaden with terror as I reached the line of trees below the Boboli Palace.

The star flowerbed was there, and I stopped to catch my breath, visualizing the scene where Sandro and I had sat on our sweet slope of grass.

Sandro didn't come. Reluctantly, I made my way back to the market. Maybe, I thought irrationally, the bronze pig knew where to look. Maybe if I rubbed its nose. It was a silly thought, but I had no other recourse that made sense. Then I heard the name Melazio whispered in my ear. It was Sandro's voice.

The moment I stepped from the narrow street into the market square, I heard my name being called. It was Melazio, the old apple-seller, but today he had no cart. He stood alone looking ill and afraid. He was wearing Sandro's orange cloak.

"You came back," he said, trying to smile.

"I am looking..." I gasped, breathless with fear.

"For Botticelli," he finished.

"Have you ... do you know where ..."

"He is here."

My soul caught in my throat. "Can you tell me ... please ... where?"

He shrugged apologetically. "Here. I am here," he said. "In front of you. As you see."

The ghost of Sandro's familiar expression flickered behind the rheumy eyes of the old man. My screams reverberated throughout the square and morphed into the terrified squeal of a charging boar. I saw the bronze wishing pig raise its snout in triumph. "Oh my God, Sandro!"

"I have been waiting a long time, *mia carissima*. Please to go to my studio in the Via Nuova. Hurry, it is time. I will meet you there. I am so sorry, *scusi*, but I cannot stay."

He grew taller and wings appeared behind him. I covered my face with my hands, and dropped to my knees. When I felt strong enough, I looked, but he had gone.

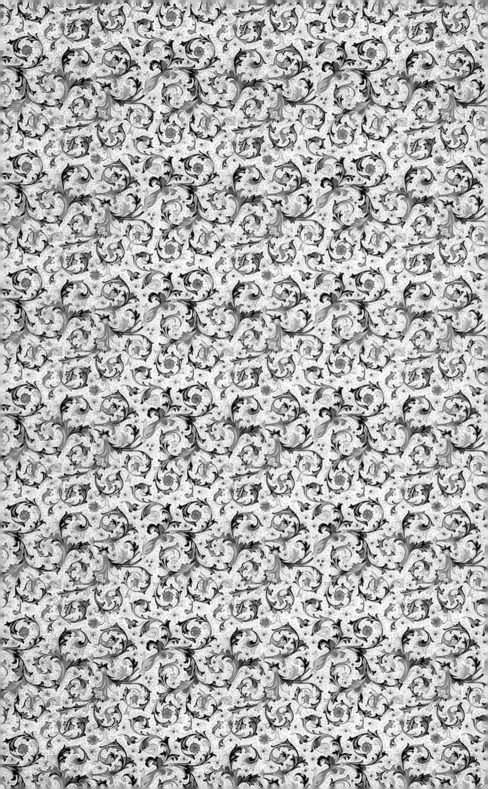

THE
INFERNO

*"In the middle
of the journey
of our life
I found myself
within a dark woods
where the straight way
was lost"*

~ Dante Alighieri

YOU BEING IN LOVE
"slowly, oh seriously
-that since and if you disappear
solemnly my selves ask "life, the question
how do I drink a dream smile
and how do I prefer this face to another and
why do I weep eat sleep- what does the whole intend"
they wonder. Oh and they cry "to be, being, that I am alive
this absurd fraction in its lowest terms
with everything cancelled but shadows"
~ e.e. cummings

fools rush in

I was lightheaded, as insubstantial as a swirl of dust particles, but I managed to stumble through the streets. I noted the only objects which inhibited my progress were fifteenth-century objects, but I was still alarmed by time-slipping, careening towards the madness of what I would do if there were no way home. Separation anxiety overwhelmed me.

In desperation, I shouted for Sophie, and felt a soft purring sensation in my throat as if I was wearing a live fur scarf.

I ran madly to the Via Nuova to find the studio door locked, but I hammered away until my strength evaporated and leaned on the wood against the memory of a modern brass plate that read Pensione Angelus, sobbing, scratching at it with bleeding fingers until it evaporated from view.

I felt displaced. The years were random numbers parading fast. It was 2013, 1475 and 1984. I heard my voice muttering: *you are a reminder of what I can no longer be. Let me tell you something, Cardinal de Bricassart, about old age and about that God of yours. That vengeful God who ruins our bodies and leaves us with only enough wit for regret. Inside this stupid body I'm still young. I still feel. I still want. I still dream, and I still love you.*

I slumped to the ground in a faint as Casper unwound herself from my neck and dropped into my lap.

I regained consciousness feeling the first symptoms of plague. Casper was gone and I was too weak to do anything but lean against the door and silently wish for death. I closed my eyes, entirely forsaken, and felt the morning warmth caress my face. But it was not the sun, it was Sandro's hand. My Sandro ... and I broke into hysterics as he lifted me from the street.

"*Mia carissima*, I am not expecting you so soon," he said in surprise, that I immediately mistook for displeasure.

"You are displeased," I said.

"I am amazed, *stupito*," he answered.

He kissed me, and caught me as the world went cold and white.

"I have been working, and you know time ... how you always say it flies, yes? Art is a prisoner of time and you and I are prisoners of art, no? Come, you are not well."

"I want to die."

I drank broth from a stoneware cup while Sandro rubbed life back into my feet and shoulders. He draped me in his orange cloak, and I surrendered. I remember being carried to a pallet in the back room with his cloak as a blanket, and slept inside the familiar protection of my lover's scent.

I felt like a baby wrapped in loosened swaddling and dreamed I rode a peacock across the sky that circled Florence in concentric circles around the orb of the Santa Maria del Fiore. It deposited me on the cathedral's cupola, and the magnificent red dome turned into the bleached straw roof of the lychgate of St. Mary's Church, and I knew I'd gone home to a place where angels feared to tread.

"Do not go gentle into that good night,
Old age should burn and rave at close of day;
Rage, rage against the dying of the light"
~ Dylan Thomas

the transfiguration

I felt Sophie jump onto my bed and begin to paw my face, and I turned away from her and slept. All was lost.

I expected the damp of England to greet me, but I awoke in Botticelli's studio on the straw pallet with Casper, and was persuaded to take a little more soup with bread. An hour later, I felt slightly restored and Sandro said he had a surprise for me.

"This is why I had to leave you so many times," he said. It is for your birthday."

My portrait was finished. Sandro had painted me as a goddess of grace and light. I shone. Behind me was a grove of apple trees. My scarlet dress looked as real as a photograph. My face glowed with the radiance of a woman staring at her beloved. Each emerald and pearl and ruby-trapped gold loop refracted the light from the necklace. Casper's painted eyes changed from blue to green and back again, welcoming me, staring back at me, from my lap. The Marzocco lion had wings folded protectively, and his right paw was raised to rest upon a golden apple instead of the classic Florentine sphere.

"You captured my soul," I said. "Thank you."

I clung to Sandro like a frightened child all that day, trying to talk. "I met Melazio... he ..." but, I could say no more. I hated the world for its convoluted physics.

Sandro was contrite. "The old man *is* me," he said. "He was always me. When you first met him, it was my last day on earth. We... that is, he and I, had to make sure you would return before he could go. He is gone now, and it is well. Perfecto, yes?

"That day, in my house. The day when you came from the Boboli with the black headache. It was ... something happened. I ..." Sandro paused and listened to something inaudible to me.

"Wait, we must go," he said. "Quickly. Come." And with that, he dragged me to the Uffizi that could not be there, but our feet flew over the route which was still a streamlined twenty-first century map overlaying the fifteenth like a rushing river. In the distance, the image of the transparent gallery flickered like a lantern.

We hastened up the stairs to salon ten, behind *the Adoration*, and he pushed me through the crowd he had painted until I could see into the gallery.

Sandro pointed to the bench. "Look," he demanded. "It is well. You are safe."

I tried to turn away, but he made me watch as paramedics covered my body with a sheet and wheeled me away.

"Now. Come," he said. "We can go."

"Home?" I asked.

He sighed and rubbed his eyes nodding, yes. "Happy Birthday, *mia amore*."

"Happy New Year, Sandro."

Sophie was waiting in the window of Botticelli's house. I saw her from the street and ran up the stairs, finally letting go of Sandro's hand. She shimmered like a mirage, and I saw her mouth open in a silent meow as she disappeared like the Cheshire Cat, except it was her blind eyes that were the last to dematerialize. Blue eyes replaced her green ones as Casper sat in her place.

I was distraught with guilt. "Sophie must have followed me here. Can she get home? I called out to her. What have I done?"

"Cats do this things all the time," Sandro said. "She is sleeping. I know this. I have seen her here many many times. And you met her years ago in Florence, no?"

"Loving me was impossible until you learned to trust me," Sandro said. We, that is the *whole* of me, the old man, Melazio, had to wait. We tried but you were as stubborn as your donkey friend, Carino, and so the studio door was my last hope. I am sorry I did not run to open it as I desired. It was Melazio who made me wait."

"You are two people then?"

He put both hands on his chest. "Well I am many, of course, I am an artist, no? But who you mean is Melazio."

Sandro sighed deeply, led me to a chair, and paced in front of me, looking nervous. "We are two ages, Melazio and I. Mela; this means apple. Zio is uncle, I make this name to cover me."

"The old you, bitten by sin?" I said. "The apple symbol. You should have been selling pomegranates for Persephone, the maiden abducted into hell. The one who must return one day each year to keep the balance in the world."

"My principessa."

"I'm not a real principessa. My name is Queenie."

"*Si, Regina* is the most powerful piece in chess, no? Above all others, she stands best. But Linton, you are another, also."

He smiled shyly and took my hand, staring into my face with an expression of resignation, and sighed. "Sofia." He said the name softly. "Sofia is Casper's real name. This name means wise, yes? Which means also magi."

I was stunned. "Sophie is Casper?"

"*Non*, Casper is your Simkin. This is why you give her the name of a boy. Sophie is Angelina, the cat who followed you that day after the terrible pain." He pointed to his head.

"So, you sent Angelina to me?"

"No *cara*, she finds you in the market when you were in mourning of me. She followed you, remember? She is our angel, yes? She comes and goes as she is. I did not send. Not then. Sometimes she finds you; sometimes to me she finds, but always to join us. She was with me when you shut me out. And then I send her back to you when the special year opened another door."

"2000," I whispered.

"There were three doors. The first was in my *Adoration*. It was exactly that, the door to me. My way of adoring you. I painted this me looking at you after I first have seen you. I painted the peacock to tell you of rebirth, your word for the Renaissance, but mine for second born. I also paint a phoenix in that corner you said is not in balance, but someone takes this away many years later. This was a double of reminding for you to believe in two lives."

"Yours and mine?" I said.

Sandro kissed me slowly and kept hold of my hand. His eyes never left mine.

"*Non, mia carissima*, yours. You have lived before. Your name was Orazia. It means the keeper of time, and you were my love. You saw a sketch of her in my studio."

I should have felt more shocked but a calm washed over me like warm water.

"The girl with the braided hair and the jewels? The one you copied for my hair?"

"*Si*. My brother, Antonio, made the jewels for his rich patron and I was making to paint a daughter's portrait with these jewels on her. It was a wedding gift from her father to the future husband. Only she did not marry. She sickened of plague and died ..."

"Let me guess, at eighteen?"

"Yes, it was, of course, yes. We were both eighteen. I am an artist in apprenticing with Fra Filippo Lippi, and she is the noble daughter of my brother's patron. A warm *principessa*, yes?"

"And you kept the jewels?"

"The father did not want. He forgets and I keep and I have removed them later from the eyes of Savonarola's fire. I am only right they belong to your Budge, and also that I make a portrait with you wearing the jewels to honour Orazia. Also, to me it was a completing. Completings are *importante*. I have learned this. You had your completings to become mine, yes?"

Time being slippery, I was still not sure about the inconsistencies of the two variations of 'our' *Adoration*. "But, you painted the *Adoration* in 1475, so how could you have been thirty-five?"

"There are two times, and also, time is liquid. I know *what* I see, not when. There is a beautiful woman is in my room and I think, an angel, but then no, it is a dreaming of Orazia. A sending, yes? and I feel love so big I am possessed to finding her, but the painting is finished being some last touchings and repairs from damage in the chapel. So it is bring to me after five years, and I see something new can be there. I can be there staring out at her. This woman, she can meet me in this sacred space I have made for others. It can be our new birth. And so I paint. I send a boy to say the painting is not ready for another months. I paint over a man who is looking at the holy family. I paint over his clothes and his face and instead I paint who I am that day. The orange robe I am wearing and the look of puzzling on my face when I saw myself through your eyes. Your eyes, Linton. The eyes of Orazia Vespucci."

"And the wasps were no accidents."

"They remind you of who is your name."

"And one stung me after I shut love out, that day in the cemetery with my stone angel."

"There is a dream I have with Sofia. She takes me to the graves and you are there, sitting very still in the snow. Then you have anger, and I think at first above you is a Madonna because I hear the words in your head shouting mother, but no, she is a female angel holding a child. I have never seen this – a pieta with wings."

"My statue was male. There was no child," I said. "You're looking at *me* in your self-portrait? How?"

"I studied in my mirror. It was meant to interest, no capture you with my eyes. Did you not feel? But it was not ... *whole*... Not enough for you to stay. This first door was the threshold you have been avoiding. The door to me. And who am I? I am the safe lover you can deny. I am dead, no?

"The second door was, as you say, a chance of time,

the shift in the thousand years that was the door for Angelina. I sent her as my messenger, *my* angel. So, then, that leaves my studio; it is death's door. Do you really trust me?"

"You've been my guide through everything. Steadfast. I trust myself with you," I replied. "Isn't that better? I trust what I feel with you. You should have smiled. In your portrait. You should have smiled."

Sandro obliged me with a dazzling living smile. "You were ... no... smiles were too easy to you. You would not believe. You mistrusted them, no? And so I challenge. I dared you to know more of me. So, now you think you deserve me?"

"I think you deserve *me*."

"You are so sure, and yet you do not deserve the pain killers of your time?"

"What?"

"I saw you make the pain worse. I was with you a whole year, until that day of the thorns. You blocked me out. It was me, not you, who was sent to hell. So you see, I know all about doors and locks."

"I am so sorry. I didn't know."

"You knew; you did not trust. This is different."

Sandro pulled me close with a face so serious I thought he was angry, then he released me so I could see his smile. "You have time to console me now."

"Can you explain what happened?" I asked, some-what relieved to finally be dead.

"Now I think I may do this," he said. "I did not mean

to frighten you. I had to show you the rest of me, and now it is complete, we can begin as we did in the pensione when you had your *malady*."

He made it sound like *my lady* and I suppressed a remark.

"That was you? My guardian angel? You're the angel from my past?"

"No, *Caramia*. You were mine. My ghost. Because of you, I would not marry. I feared it would destroy us, and so, I waited. And it became known how I feared marriage. I could not tell my friends why. This thing of *seeing* is heresy, yes? You understand?

"This is the house where I was born. I was here, the day you were *in delirio*."

Sandro walked to the far wall and tapped the plaster.

"You ran through the wall, here, and I followed. Your hotel room, it was mine, and I administered ..."

"I remember the scent of Tiger Balm."

"It was the linseed oil on my skin. It goes with me everywhere, it is the shadow of a painter."

"And the wings?"

"You saw my wooden model. You know the one. It was hanging from the ceiling in my room. You saw the wings behind me when you looked up from the bed."

He gave up talking, reached into his pocket, and handed me my gold charm bracelet. It sported thee new charms: the angel I'd misplaced, a sleeping cat, and an apple with a bite missing.

"You were wearing this. I am regretting. I have guilt

for this. And for ... not waiting. I could not wait for you and so I make love to you, and for this, I have to wait longer, until you are to die. But this is not all. There is fear. You may die without your realization. It was a thing of great timing. It was not fate; it was destiny. How I can explain these two things are different? Fate; this means unchanging. You had choice. Do you see? Destiny is not this. Destiny is becoming grown. Growing to a higher you. This can take hundreds of years. I am this.

"I am so sorry. I took your amulets as a talisman. I had to have something of you. I am once apprenticed as a goldsmith, so... this, I take." He fingered the apple charm. "I have made this apple in my own hands. It means of Venus. Like the one in your portrait under the paw of Il Marzocco."

"My bracelet. I... the day in the field with the viper?"

"I could not let you die too soon."

"So, you... we, were both phantoms? How long have I been here?"

"It is the... divine math, yes? We met in 1984 and 1480 the same; we were both thirty-five. I have finish this *Adoration* in 1475, but after I saw you, I added myself to show, yes? We have to wait until you were sixty-five. *Cara,* your visit, it has lasted one hour."

"So, divine math?"

"*Sì.*"

"Now that I'm free ... can I stay?"

"You were always here," he said.

THE INFERNO

"Do not be afraid;
our fate
cannot be taken
from us;
it is a gift."

~ Dante Alighieri

the denouement

the evening star

~ DESTINY ~

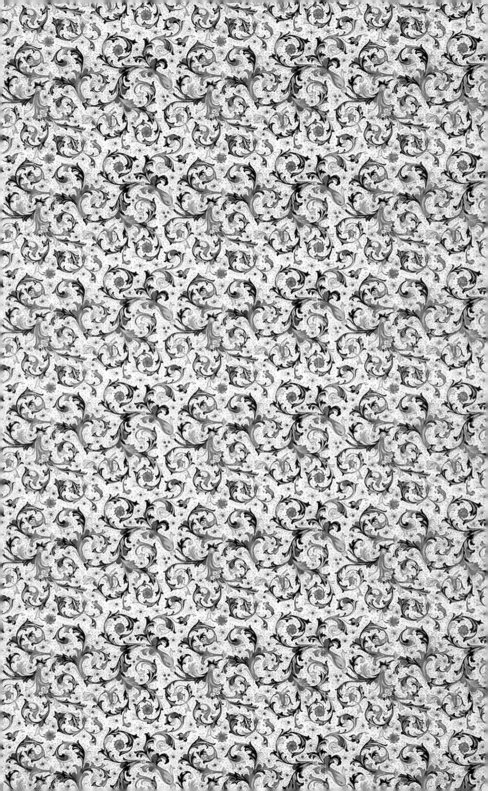

IF I BELIEVE

*and when   I have
offered up each   fragrant night
when all my days shall have before
a certain face become white perfume
only, from the ashes then thou wilt rise
and thou wilt come to her and brush
the mischief from her eyes and fold
her mouth the   new flower with
t h y unimaginable w i n g s,
where dwells the breath
of all persisting
s t a r s*

~ e.e. cummings

another door; another painting

Budge found my second letter wedged into one of the
pigeonholes of my writing desk.

The envelope read, in case of my death, in archaic
cursive script embellished with flamboyant loops flanked
with ornate flourishes. Two separately folded papers and
a key were inside. *In coso di morte.* In case of my death.

Darling Budge ~

In case I don't return, let ours be an informal parting. No goodbyes but a cheery wave from a departing train which promises tea and cakes and a slideshow of my trip when I return. And no, I don't mean to haunt you, although I think I could.

Please read out the enclosed poem to our guests, and indulge the cats to wander freely amongst them if that is their will.

Sophie knows more than you could imagine. Did you know the word Sophia means pure wisdom? Well, our Sophie is smarter than that. Here's something else to ponder that I hope you'll discover in a new career pursuit. Remember that book you brought home when you were researching the field of veterinary medicine? Well, I flipped through it one night and read that an adult female cat is called a queen. How cool is that!

Regarding the box I mentioned in the closet of the spare room, in it you'll find the business card of an appraiser who Mr. Filipepi and I have been using. He is in touch with the right people who knows of these things. Go to him. The art world is a notorious scam. The artefacts, drawings, and painting are authentic. They are my half-share of an investment with Mr. Filipepi. Protect them. Keep them or sell them to a major gallery.

Use some of the money to set up that care centre for feral and blind cats I was always on about. There will be more than enough to send you to veterinary college so you can run the place, but please, for my sake and Sophie's, stay living in my little house until she and Simkin pass on. I couldn't bear thinking of her bashing into strange walls at her age. Remember, in cat years she is quite ancient.

You know I would not ask this if it wasn't important.

Lately, I've learned a great many oddities that I'd

pooh-poohed all my life, and no, I didn't find religion. Please don't ever think that. ~ Q

The key unlocked a large trunk that contained two small packets of jewellery wrapped in silk, many notebooks, one 1481 illustrated first edition of Dante, and several bundles of yellowed drawings, some of a young lady with ornately coiffed hair, and a painted panel, all signed: Alessandro Filipepi — Sandro Botticelli. Along with them was a conté sketch on a page from a spiral notebook of the angel in St. Mary's churchyard, obviously a forgery but stylistically correct.

Budge alerted the auction houses and I was delighted she kept the ornate ruby and emerald ring for herself. The jeweller appraised the age of the golden pieces as five-hundred years old. Art dealers authenticated the drawings and confirmed *The Divine Comedy* was a rare copy illustrated by Botticelli himself.

Unbeknownst to me, Sandro had gathered a goldmine of priceless historical evidence and stashed them in my closet as my birthday surprise. Later, he explained: *"This things I will be burning, scusi, have burned already for Savonarola and so they are better to help the new 'Angelinas,' no? They have disappeared for time, and so the world will not change from this moving."*

Budge told the press that her windfall would finance a network of animal sanctuaries, and the career she had always wanted.

As my will requested, the network of cat sanctuaries for blind and feral cats is to be called LIFELINE. I had even designed the logo of a winged lion with the word feline inside the word L**ifeline** picked out in bold.

The small portfolio held many studies of a beautiful woman who reminded Budge of me. My portrait, a small painted panel, 21 inches x 15 inches, showed me wearing a red dress with a necklace of emeralds and rubies set in gold. I was posed with a white cat in the manner of Leonardo da Vinci's portrait of Cecilia Gallerani holding a ferret, but with a winged lion at my feet.

The portrait necklace was easily identified as the one wrapped in a decaying scrap of blue velvet emblazoned with the Vespucci wasp embroidered in gold.

My last diary entry perplexed Budge because it was a continuation of the tale of my ghostly lover, but she was pleased to know that at the end I had a fantasy world to dream out my life. She'd never seen me so happy as the time when I came home from Florence.

⌒

Dear Budge's memorial article was short and sweet:

My Aunt Linton held open forums hoping for the best guesses from her students. It was her mission to encourage art history majors to speculate somewhere over the moon. She kidded that her classes were engaged in forensic 'artopsy.'

Many of her student's will have fond recollections of her classes which evolved into pep rallies, as far as an academic setting would allow. She led gentle games of free-association that grew wilder once the ice was broken, and Aunt Linton did that from day one.

A few of her starter questions sounded like this: What artist had a hand in this? Was this choice a reflection of the church's impenetrable fences or a wilful deviation into heresy?

Her puzzles quickly expanded into what-ifs: Could this work have been the passing expression of a private mystery-moment? What if the artist had a toothache the day this was painted? What if he owed money to a desperado or had been tossed aside by a lover, or had the first symptoms of plague? What if he/she was under-fire for an impossible deadline or ordered to flatter the portrait of a homely wife or spoiled daughter or a vain queen, or under a desperate financial obligation? What if the artist was an incorrigible jokester intent on proving a point?

And this question which she premised as a given: What if the artist had never held a baby for more than a few fleeting moments but was commissioned to paint the holiest baby of all? These were the questions that she knew would bring an artist home to us, to live again as one of us. These were the things that begged the light of day.

She challenged her classes with new what-ifs every day. "What if a master teacher had never seen a lion or had passed on an obsessive penchant for the colour blue? What if you were a twelve-year-old apprentice abandoned by your family? What if you were a child prodigy? What if you had high-functioning autism? Where did social compromise eclipse the art of free-expression?

Where indeed. My aunt wasn't fishing for the outrageous; she was reaching for the humanity ... the elusive element missing from dry statistics, propaganda, and hearsay.

She once explained: 'Humans get into scrapes: time-sensitive, love-seeking, heart-thumping, blatant creative scrapes, but only if they're lucky.'

Let me read from one of her transcripts about the Italian Renaissance:

Our century is digitally chaotic with too much information and frozen with traffic jams; the fifteenth was rampant with fast daggers and slow poison. In the fifteenth-century, the artful skill of murder was rated spontaneous and high. Punishments were unsentimentally fluid as well as selective. Every action served the many 'popes' of power and salvation from their relative religions changed with each successor.

Infancy was a 'snakes and ladders' journey. It was survival of the luckiest. 'Deaths by love,' flourished, as did the tragic effects of enforcing childbirth on preteen girls or successive ones on the mothers who lived, the hasty romantic duels of rival lovers, sexually-transmitted diseases without antibiotics, jealous come-uppances, and melodramatic suicides. Dying came earlier in infinitely more theatrical ways. But then, souls were less troubled with their soul's destination. They were all determined to reach heaven. Dante's vision of hell made sure of that.

My aunt taught me that all roads led directly to Heaven or Hell in those days. And then, after a deep sigh... she always said: well ... so much for Rome.

*"So we beat on.
Boats against the current
Borne back ceaselessly
into the past."*

from 'The Great Gatsby'
~ F. Scott Fitzgerald

"Can miles truly separate you from a friend?
If you want to be with someone you love,
aren't you already there?"
~ Richard Bach

the revelation

Loving Botticelli throughout my early years had been a self-imposed purgatory. We exist now, in a paradise of our own making. I had been too blind to accept my worthiness, and so, I arrived there the hard way, led by angels.

Through Dante, I came to understand the profound truths behind Shakespeare's soliloquies. The bard's eloquent indifference towards death references man's inevitable return to dust as the final act of a play and that life was a drama without substance when loves were lost.

I encourage reaching for the same stars as Keats — courage being the operative word. Life brings enough limitations.

Childhoods of the twenty-first century may be medically safer, but we're more vulnerable to criticism, bombarded as we are, by the media's love affair with actors. The purpose of romantic films is to transport the imagination beyond non-local time to confrontations compressed into a suspended hour. In much the same way, humans can dream a lifetime in a single night.

Sophie had sauntered into the front room of the rectory during my memorial, tail up, chattering like a dolphin, and rubbed against Budge's legs as she read the passage from *Songs of the Portuguese* by Elizabeth Barrett Browning, another poet whose bones had languished long under the golden auspices of a beloved Tuscan romance.

"How do I love thee? Let me count the ways.
I love thee to the depth and breadth and height
My soul can reach, when feeling out of sight
For the ends of being and ideal grace.
I love thee to the level of every day's
Most quiet need, by sun and candle-light.
I love thee freely, as men strive for right.
I love thee purely, as they turn from praise.
I love thee with the passion put to use
In my old griefs, and with my childhood's faith.
I love thee with a love I seemed to lose
With my lost saints. I love thee with the breath,
Smiles, tears, of all my life; and, if God choose,
I shall but love thee better after death."

Challenging life's promises is no less significant than planetary power struggles – where moon turns to sun and Venus aligns with Mars.

Botticelli and I hadn't lived on *borrowed* time; we loved on created time. Our time.

The *Adoration* was the stage curtain connecting parallel theatres. Backstage, our past, present, and future unfolded in a three-act play, except the moon wasn't made of paper, nor were the stars pea-lights against a black screen. And the old cardboard sea with its ominous warning of 'beyond here be dragons,' became a dramatic portent of Dante's *'abandon hope, all ye who enter here.'*

A stage door led to suspended memories of requited love, and there unfolded an origami of misspent life. We rehearsed behind the scenes where we allowed time to catch up in lateral experiences of make-believe. We performed amongst brimstone and angels. Our journey progressed erratically in an improvisation of misplaced years which became a waiting game for Sandro, and ended in a flight of shame for me.

A silent playwright guided us towards the edge of the world, past the painted dragons and into the hell of loneliness. Before we reached paradise we lived thirty more years wandering star-crossed in purgatory, following the trails of the pearls we scattered behind us like breadcrumbs.

It's true that for a while I was a painted face in the crowd across from Sandro – an adoration within *The Adoration*. I am there still, on the left-hand of art, staring through the crowd, looking back at anyone studying the painting from the bench where I'd died.

But don't expect to open a history book and find Sandro Botticelli has veered off-course when he should have been painting *The Birth of Venus* even though a new portrait of me exists in his canon. History stays how it is – perfectly repeating itself like the lyrics of the round, *Life is but a dream.*

Botticelli added me to the *Adoration* as an homage, but he had to change my face to a man's or the church would have destroyed him.

So, later, he placed a painted mask over my face, that of his patron's catamite. A creature who, later, almost destroyed Sandro with jealousy. Look for me with your spy cameras. I am there beneath my tempera skin.

By the time I accepted being adored, the *Thorn Bird's* destructive boar had been redeemed by its Florentine cousin, Il Porcellino.

I realized with a shock I hadn't hated Mary Carson; I felt sorry for her, and that wholly unselfish sympathy extended to me. It had ricocheted back and forth between us, gathering momentum until it had been unbearable. I had discovered the excruciating reality of having zero power to walk myself back from the pit of inconsolable losses that that a fictitious stranger said would come.

As for angels. They're everything awe-inspiring and yet there's much to criticize. Their mysterious ways, so lost on us mortals – jam our expectations of rescue into dark holes full of wishes, ignored like Victorian children, seen and not heard.

What humans need is rarely the same as we bargain the hardest for. And so, angels arrive to tousle our hair like benevolent uncles and deliver lateral lessons of divine morality.

I have learned to process them in different ways: an ordinary man attached to a pair of frothy wings, blindingly brilliant, backed by the sun in a wild moment; or a casual Californian god, blonde to the point of dazzlement, tanned, winged in a white nightgown; or flightless in an ice-cream suit and tie, Gatsby-like; or a transparent beach-boy in a clinging T-shirt – a peripheral vapour. A mirage rippling like a white flag.

They have witnessed the worst of me. I have experienced the best of them.

The ongoing manifestations of Sandro in modern garb were a marvel as well as a reminder. Sandro was more than one man. Renaissance glamour once-removed. retained and enhanced Sandro's sex appeal. It was still his long titian hair which bridged the two looks.

He explored and tasted my century as I had his. He faced the anomalies of cameras, telephones, cars and television. I showed him everything from fountain pens to animatronic dinosaurs and art from the Lascaux caves to Pollock. He ate popcorn and pizza, and drank cola. He discovered a penchant for ice cubes. Who knew umbrellas, fishing line, and balloons would resonate? Flight seemed less crazy than suspending a mobile of paper wings above my bed – an homage to his angelic nature. Loving Botticelli showed me he was, and is, a dreamer who loved to laugh.

The escapade was for me. It was always for me. Botticelli painted a better life for me, but I had to evolve to be with the Sandro of my dreams. Of my past. The old Linton was never going to cut it. The new Linton had to bypass the hell of lacking self-confidence. I had to love myself in order to make the journey to the loving afterlife I had failed to believe in, entering instead, a heaven worth dying for. Did I manage it in one hour or a dreamed lifetime? Sandro says, both.

Somehow, loving Botticelli transcended time as well as his art. Especially his works destroyed by fire and fear. New works created as a result of my influence have been anchored in the reality of 2014 as part of his canon.

Was the auction gold for Sophie and Simkin and Casper and Angelina? It didn't matter. It was for the good. Throwaway sketches of a master artist paid for the care and treatment of blind and homeless cats. Budge became a doctor, and I met the life I believed in most. I didn't have to second guess. Florence revealed its past to me and became the place most comfortable to spend eternity. After all, I was returning home.

Art lives on and artists remain the sketches of who they dreamed they'd be.

Sandro and Orazia found a way to love, and our shadows lengthened as the sun moved.

Like Dante, we left our own treasure map to paradise. Navigation by pearls is surely no less a remarkable way to travel than setting a course by the stars.

Sandro still loves to repeat one of his favorite quotes from Dante, and I never tire of hearing it: *"Remember tonight for it is the beginning of always."*

*"The wisest people
are the most annoyed
at the loss of time."*

~ Dante Alighieri

the epilogue

~ PRESENT TIME ~

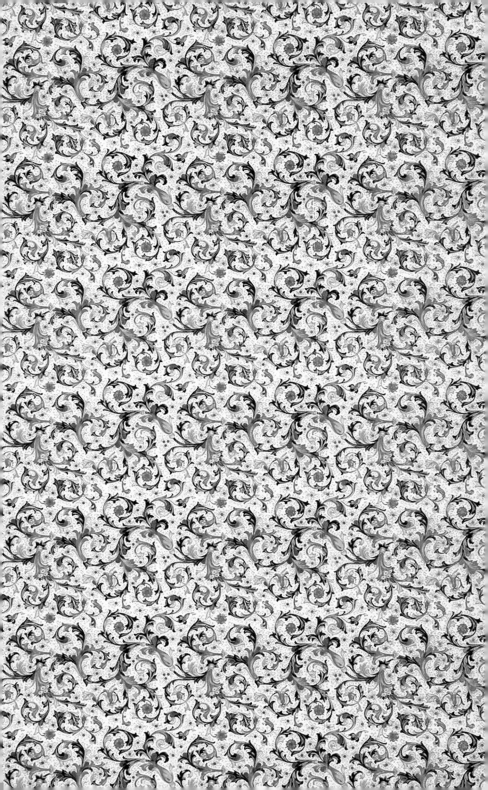

"Tomorrow,
and tomorrow, and tomorrow,
Creeps in this petty pace from day to day,
To the last syllable of recorded time;
And all our yesterdays have lighted fools
The way to dusty death. Out, out, brief candle!
Life's but a walking shadow, a poor player,
That struts and frets his hour upon the stage,
And then is heard no more. It is a tale
Told by an idiot, full of sound and fury,
Signifying nothing."

~ William Shakespeare

class dismissed

The day was warm for January. Sophie crossed the lych-gate to sleep in her favorite spotlight of sunshine atop an oblong shape of fresh grave dirt, making it look like a brown door with a grey fur wreath. Linton's stone marker in St Mary's Cemetery was a cat angel with wings. The inscription read:

QUEENIE
Linton Ross-Howard
January 1, 1949 ~ January 1, 2014
"the best is yet to be"

The firecracker ions swirling between the two angels of St. Mary's made Sophie's fur flare with an unseen force and the surrounding treetops crackle with static. Sophie's tail twitched from the electrical charge, and she silenced it's hum with a paw, drawing it under her chin. She felt the vibrations of friendly footsteps on the frozen ground before she heard them crunch.

"I thought I'd find you here," Budge said. "I rattled your sardine keys old lady. Come on then, it's time for dinner. You can't stay here, you'll freeze."

Sophie allowed Budge to pick her up and be wrapped in her scarf.

All the way from Florence, I heard Sophie call out, *See you tomorrow and tomorrow and tomorrow,* from inside a nest of red wool.

Across the county of Cambridgeshire, a handful of students and alumni paid their respects to my photograph. I watched the brief reception serving Earl Grey tea, petits-four cakes, and miniature sardine-paste sandwiches, followed, most fittingly, in the second floor offices, the *uffizi*, of the Fine Arts Department.

Lange's School of Art ~ Cambridge, March 1, 2015
The Ross-Howard lecture theatre, room 101

"I am delighted to greet this assembly on this special day. My name is Iris. Okay, I'm not going to use my full name. Partly because it's not really me, but also because Iris is enough between friends, and I see many of my aunt's colleagues and students who have become my friends over the past year.

"Today marks the first presentation of the 'Botticelli Scholarship' in honour of its sponsor, my aunt, Linton Ross-Howard, who passed away in Florence a little over a year ago. This award is her tribute to the artist Sandro Botticelli, and to acknowledge her amazing legacy of undiscovered Botticelli documents and artefacts including the unknown portrait *Lady with Two Cats* popularized as *The Cat Lady*. According to one of the documents, these treasures were marked for the Vanity fire, but were singled out and hidden by a sympathetic friend.

"Now, you may think Linton's short-lived retirement was tragic, but my aunt would tell you, you are wrong. She would have considered the circumstances entirely apropos. She always impressed upon me and her students to reach beyond the dry statistics of birth and death, to flesh out an event with the highest interpretation of thought.

"One of her favourite books was Dante's *Divine Comedy*, and she told me that life is essentially an earthly comedy. So, with the deepest respect, I like to think of her passing as a timely exit. Her final commentary of a perfect heaven where she would mingle with her historic heroes and ferret out their lost truths.

"I asked her once, when art began. As usual, her answer was flippant and contained an ultimate truth. She told me art was invented by monkeys with a stick and a patch of wet sand.

"She is not here in body but somewhere traipsing the haunts of Renaissance Florence, or helping to hang old works in an ethereal art gallery of missing paintings, or on a crusade to acknowledge the forgotten unnamed artists, or blissfully sorting the repository of lost documents, destroyed paintings, and piecing together the missing fragments of broken sculptures.

"Most of all, she would be writing the definitive *'Lost History of Art,'* interviewing and debating the finest masters of human possibility because she imagined what most of us fail to remember: that artists are more than the sum of their works.

"Only a handful of artists have been selected by fate to survive the random protocols of posthumous fame.

"They were the men and women shape-shifters who listened to their muses beyond ordinary hearing, glimpsed the horizons of emotionally-charged landscapes with insight, and evoked images which dared to challenge the religious constraints of power and control.

"My aunt refused to see great masters as unstable visionaries for history to preserve under bell jars. 'Saints'

Leonardo, Michelangelo, and her favourite, Botticelli, were real folk who lived down the street.

"She likened art history to a Faberge egg – glamorously decorative on the outside with a dazzling shell that opened like a flower to reveal more than a person could believe possible.

"Today, it is my great honor to award the first Botticelli Scholarship to Miss Sandra Phillips, for her fictional dissertation as observed from the imaginative scrutiny of remote-viewing, titled: *Yesterday in Florence.*

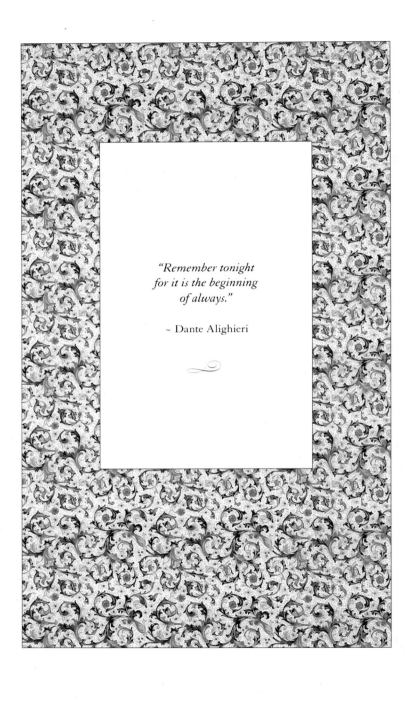

*"Remember tonight
for it is the beginning
of always."*

~ Dante Alighieri

author's bio

Veronica Knox has a Fine Arts Degree from the University of Alberta, where she studied Art History and Painting. In her career as a graphic designer, art teacher, and artist, she has also worked with the brain injured and autistic, developing new theories of hand-to-eye-to-mind connection.

www.veronicaknox.com
www.silentkbooks.com

author's commentary

I have frequently observed that few master painters were able to paint a realistic infant to save their souls.

Sandro Botticelli was no exception. In the case of his 1475 *Adoration,* the baby Jesus has been reduced to a miniature adult, and not too attractive a one.

Any faithful observer of infants would know their heads should be large in proportion to their bodies. Sandro had created a ghastly newborn with a shrunken head, spindly arms, and a sober expression.

I doubt a woman artist would make the same mistake in spite of the accepted convention. But then, women were not considered worthy enough to paint holy figures. Their contributions were limited to hands and feet when an apprentice was insufficiently trained to handle anatomy, but more often relegated to dabble in background scenery.

As for the proportions of the mature body, should Botticelli's seated figures in the *Adoration* ever stand, some would rise to the perilous heights of seven feet tall or more. It is an example of the elongated Mannerist style intruding ahead of its time.

Botticelli's crowd was arranged on various altitudes of sloping ground as if standing on convenient bleachers, so their heads could appear in separate rows, an effect, known sarcastically by art historians as the 'grape-head cluster.' This gave the group the appearance of two-dimensional paper cut-outs from a photo collage.

Adolescent painters were largely mis-trained or self-trained the hard way via erratic learning curves. It was practical for an adolescent art student to be thrown into a production team way beyond their skill. Most of the studio collaborations followed this protocol. Young artists found their own level of expertise by trial and error. They either evolved or became as subservient as the women artists who already worked alongside their male relatives as docile, silent, invisible assistants.

The assembly line of studio production is not dissimilar to a modern factory where individual workers and countless designers are absorbed with separate aspects of the finished product. Renaissance artist's voices are often shouted down by the business of art.

Group murals were often the case of too many cooks spoiling the painting. Art by committee is not the most coherent form of creative expression, but in the case of Botticelli's *Adoration*, the painting was too small to have been created by more than one hand. It is pure Botticelli, but like Linton, I sense a reluctance within his elite crowd of Florentines on a day-trip to Bethlehem.

The artistic brain has always been fooled by the eye. Allegory and colourful costumes distract the discerning observer from awkward body-proportion, deformed anatomy, and perspectives reminiscent of fun-house mirrors.

Incomplete chapters of provenance read as mystery whodunits. The fate of artistic celebrity is a lottery of perverse synchronicity; artists of old misspoke or opened wrong doors as often as we do which is why we can appreciate the masters more when we think of them as human beings, flaws and all, instead of an elite club of selected gods.

It was heresy to sign a work of art, although the most inventive masters found a covert way. The historian's task of settling the who's who of invisible signatures is almost impossible. Few art historians can think like a man from the fifteenth-century. None can be the absolute spokesperson for a Leonardo or a Botticelli. The art of intuition is hardly definitive.

When a hitherto unknown painting materializes, or when multiple artists and their assistants have worked on a large mural, the forensics are even more convoluted. Similarly, the subtle significance of real faces are lost. In the first moments of unveiling within the immediate stirring of public interest, there existed an awareness between artists, their models, and the population in general.

Recognition of familiar faces exposed in the open were obvious. Later, after a few years, their identity receded into the void much the same way old family photographs become a mystery of sepia players lost to memory within a single lifetime.

The faces of friends and apprentices who 'stood in,' or minor players in social and political games, the sisters

and cousins, the babies and the women, lovers and enemies, patrons and relatives, the catamites and strangers,
the jokes and the dares, the rich and the street ruffians,
the famous and the obscure, rubbed elbows and drifted
on. All of them exist forever in the paintings like strangers in amber, but the language of personal symbolism
fades when the word-of-mouth generation dies.

Truth struggles to be present in spite of the rules.
Clients demand, muses command, accountants over-
rule, and plague calls the shots. The best apprentices
styled themselves after their teachers, copying their master's works brushstroke for brushstroke.

Many artists learned on the job from age twelve on,
but Sandro began his apprenticeship at fourteen, spring-
ing from a different guild (that of the goldsmith) which
is why I assume he painted intricate details and missed
the overall plot when it came to large scale murals. He
excelled in more linear works. To me, his *Birth of Venus*
and *The Primavera*, both read like illustrations from a
book of religious illuminations.

Botticelli perfected due diligence in his botanical
research. Every plant, creature, expression, hand gesture, and object was chosen for its representation as a
significant allegorical devise.

At the age of thirty Sandro was not mainstream, he
was building his curriculum vitae at this time, having
worked for sixteen years in the high-profile studios of his
peers. Even though his patrons were political celebrities

(and only the Pope could eclipse the social royalty of the Medici) he was likely too hungry to refuse anyone.

But see what happens? An art history buff will get lost at every crossroad and wax on about more than you ever wanted to know and were never going to ask. I apologise for all of us. You see, we're hooked on art and have combed it from every angle, for every tangle, and now we can even penetrate each layer and pixel with state of the *art* spectrum cameras, but we still don't KNOW. We will never know.

I often imagine what the renaissance artists would make of cubism or the impressionists who were categorically dismissed after their debut. Van Gogh could barely give his works away. It would seem 'art blindness' skips a generation or two before declaring a new breakthrough.

It took the pre-Raphaelites of the nineteenth-century to revive Botticelli who had slipped into relative obscurity even in his own lifetime. Serendipity indeed.

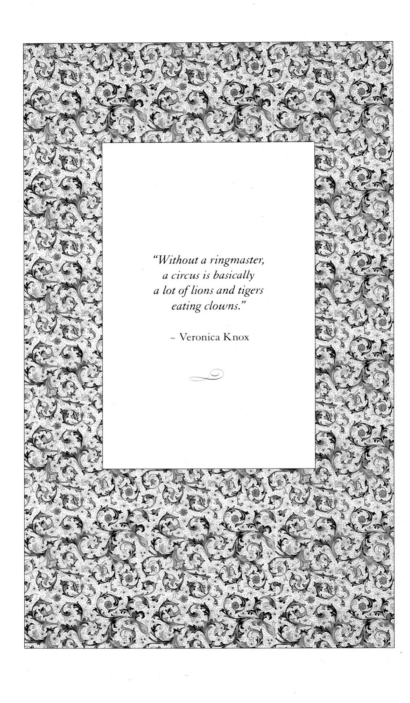

*"Without a ringmaster,
a circus is basically
a lot of lions and tigers
eating clowns."*

~ Veronica Knox

acknowledgments

As an Indie author, I rely on two women wielding very large keys. Indeed, I am indebted to them.

From image to text, the first and final contributor, is my book designer and formatter, Iryna Spica, of *Spicabookdesign*. Somewhere, early in the first draft, I conceive my book covers, and Iryna completes them to ground the manuscript.

For me, it represents an essential element of birthing a novel. I write towards the covers that will eventually manifest into print after hours of painstaking tweaking.

I may be a graphic designer, but I have no way of turning an idea into a digital creation. For these reasons, Iryna and I collaborate over every detail, which over the years has become a finely-tuned visual shorthand of mutual choices.

The finite intricacies of a book's appearance and readability are of prime importance to both of us. Front, back and spine; end papers, interior dynamics, et al. It's in the juxtapositions of visual spaces within the art of typography, and exposition and character arcs, that a professional product emerges.

⌣

In between the visuals of presentation lurks my predator-editor, Linda Clement, who singles out more of my 'darlings' for execution than I would ever have dared.

My words get away with nothing. No comma is left unturned, and though some of mine remain as personal preferences, Linda has cornered the local red pen market in order to herd any wanderings into a coherent story arc.

After months of gruelling cutting, rewriting, and polishing, I feel as if I need to recover from surgery. Does this mean literally? I will have to ask Linda.

Editing is most certainly the ultimate definition of *a means to an end*. But that word 'mean' is a positive one. In the 'mean' time of rewriting, a great editor's challenge is to bypass an author's sensitive skin for signs of weakness without actually killing them along with hundreds of their 'darlings.'

Linda's insight replaces the work of a hundred beta readers. I dread her and love her in equal amounts. She epitomizes the philosophy of it's *cruel to be kind*. No-one is kinder.

Without either of these women, I would only ever own a drawer full of the halves of stories. Those two keys I mentioned open that locked drawer where my final drafts would otherwise languish into dust.

My thanks also go to Giovanna Spagnolo Greco, MA (French) and BA (French, Linguistics, and Education) from the University of Victoria, for editing the Italian phrases.

And so it goes – the precarious nature of controlling a story so it *stays* on the page while giving it the freedom to fly *off* the page.

~ V Knox
June 2014

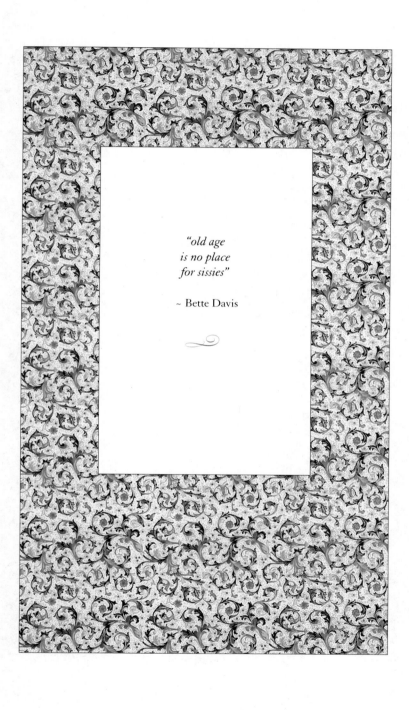

"old age
is no place
for sissies"

~ Bette Davis

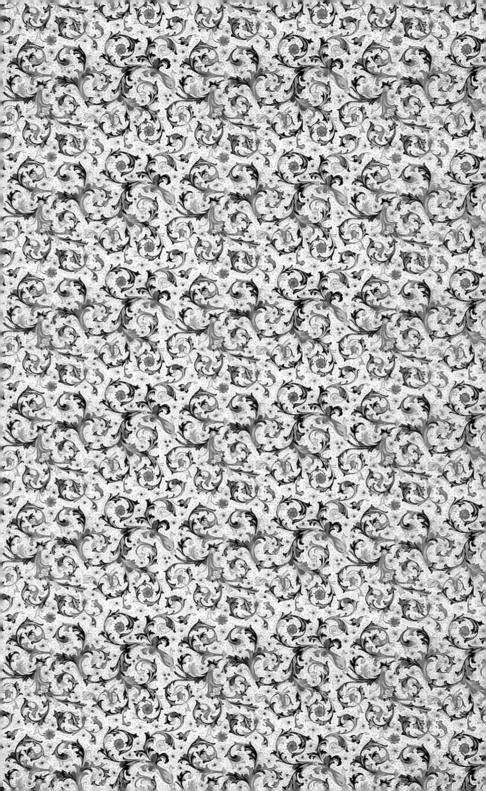